HER DYING KISS

BOOKS BY JENNIFER CHASE

JENNIFER CHASE

HER DYING KISS

bookouture

Published by Bookouture in 2023

An imprint of Storyfire Ltd.
Carmelite House
50 Victoria Embankment
London EC4Y 0DZ

www.bookouture.com

ISBN: 978-1-83790-669-7
eBook ISBN: 978-1-83790-668-0

For all the hardworking military K9 trainers and handlers, and the amazing military working dogs for their selfless and dedicated service

FOREWORD

As a prior Navy Military Working Dog (MWD) trainer, I learned there are indeed three sides to every story: your side, my side, *and my dog's side.* I would like to begin by saying that I regard all other MWD trainers and handlers with the utmost respect, despite any positive or negative experiences I may have had personally with any of the MWD handler brothers and sisters.

I had the pleasure of spending three out of the nine years of my military service at Joint Base San Antonio Lackland, Texas, training MWDs. Most of the time I spent there was in the detection block where we imprinted MWDs to find the scent of explosives and narcotics.

It was a highly competitive environment where each trainer was motivated to outperform his fellow servicemen in exchange for the mutual respect of the other. Failure was never an option with any of the animals we handled. And if there was a dog that was falling behind in his training, he was usually set back with another dog class that was a week or two away from the current class.

The training environment was set up as per trailer of dogs.

Each team of about four or five trainers was responsible for about eighteen dogs on each trailer. The team would go out and literally drive the truck and trailer to pick up the selected dogs, identified by the tattoo on their left ear, from their kennels. Once all the dogs were rounded up, the teams would drive out to their selected training areas. Only a few training areas had central heat and air-conditioning. Most of the dogs were exposed to extreme Texas heat, especially during the summer months.

These extreme conditions would help to test our patience with each other and our dogs. There was constant pressure from the command to push numbers. We had about a six-week deadline to qualify our eighteen-dog trailer in detection. Once a dog was qualified in detection, he would be moved over to the patrol block where he would be trained in obedience and controlled aggression. Based on my personal experience, the detection side of the equation was where most dogs (and humans) faced the most challenges.

There is something about tapping into the search drive of an animal. There is no better feeling than being able to step back and say, "I trained my dog to find that." In my professional opinion, training a dog to search, and to search for a specific item, is one of the most rewarding and challenging feats of any MWD trainer.

One of the many challenges we faced as MWD handlers was communicating the truth of our experience on a daily basis. Each training trial and search problem was recorded and written down by each trainer. However, the behavior result of each dog told the truth of what happened in each training session. If a marker was missed, the dog's behavior would let us know. We would then counter-condition the dog's training to correct any type of issues with a dog's response to odor. This is why it is important to understand the dog's truth in what is happening in any situation. A bomb dog showing a change of behavior while it is in the vicinity of odor is one of those truths. As a result, it was my hope that the work I have put into many of these dogs has served to save the lives of soldiers, marines, airmen, and sailors overseas. Even if just one of the MWDs I trained saved one life, I will be satisfied.

I hope this work of art by Jennifer Chase gives inspiration to many readers through her own hands-on experience. I have had the pleasure of showing her some of the tips and training techniques that may be reflected in her work of fiction. I consider her a great friend and colleague, and I hope we have the opportunity to work together even more in the future.

Very Respectfully,
MA2 A.N.R., 9 year US Navy Veteran

PROLOGUE

There was the gentle ring of two champagne glasses making contact for a perfect toast. The crackling fire warmed the cozy cabin that made for a much-needed romantic getaway. It was everything that cold-case detective Katie Scott could have hoped for as she sipped the sparkling wine with her fiancé, Chad Ferguson, a fire inspector for Pine Valley. Everything was picture-perfect.

The dry bubbles tantalized Katie's tongue as she gazed into the hypnotic flames. Time seemed to stop—at least in her mind. She didn't want this moment to end. It had been so long since they had time to be together away from their stressful jobs and she wasn't going to waste a single moment.

"You're so quiet," said Chad as he moved closer to her on the sofa. "Everything okay?" He nuzzled her neck, gently kissing her.

"I want to remember every detail of this—here and now—with you." She could feel his lips on her neck and the heat of his body next to her as she inhaled the subtle, lingering fragrance of his soap from an earlier shower. She turned her gaze toward him. His intense blue eyes watched her, reminding her of all the times he had been there for her. They were kids when they had first met, then best friends all through school. They had reconnected after she returned home from two tours in the Army as part of a K9 explosives team. Sometimes she felt as if nothing had changed between them since they had first met, but in fact, everything in their lives had changed, except for their unwavering love for one another.

"What's bothering you?" he said.

"Nothing. I just..."

"Don't want this moment to end," he finished her sentence.

"Is that silly?"

"Not at all. Look at everything you've been through over the past year and a half. Those cases. Those killers. But they're behind you now. You deserve a break. Take it, and just be present here and now."

"I know... we both deserve a break."

"And now we can enjoy the solitude and each other." He smiled.

Katie moved closer, wanting only to feel his warmth and heartbeat next to her.

Chad held her tight.

Finally releasing his embrace to look at him, Katie said, "What would I do without you?" Her voice was almost a whisper as she fought back tears—not for sadness but joy.

"Hopefully you'll never have to find out," he said lightly. He kissed her and then rose to refill their glasses.

Katie turned her attention back to the fire, watching the flames lap up the oxygen. What Chad had said was true. Her last cases had been brutal on her psyche, not to mention on her perspective on life. It was fragile. Her experiences had made her feel vulnerable, but as though she didn't want to miss anything. And now, being here with Chad without all the distractions and urgencies of everyday life, she felt free but somehow strangely helpless at the same time. Life could prepare you for the day-to-day stuff of work, but not how to decompress and enjoy all the important moments in between.

"I love you, Katie. And nothing is ever going to change that," he said sitting next to her again.

Katie knew Chad loved her but hearing him say those words now meant more than before. She felt a shift, a kind of change that was coming. They were going to build a married life together. It was probably her imagination, but the feeling was strong. "Love you more..." She leaned into him, connecting her lips with his in a slow passionate kiss.

Several hours later Katie woke with a start, her body tensed, responding to the cold damp air. It was dark—the fire must've gone out in the cabin. She tried to open her eyes wider but her head pounded with a relentless ache, causing her to rub her forehead. Swallowing hard, her mouth dry, she strained to sit up, feeling for Chad's side of the bed. It was empty and the sheets were cool to the touch.

"Chad?" she said.

The cabin remained quiet and dark.

Katie stood up next to the bed, her senses strangely heightened. "Chad?"

She expected to hear him return from the other room, but only silence greeted her. Fumbling beside her, she switched on the bedroom lamp. The room was still. The other side of the bed was made and the pillow was arranged as if someone had recently composed it. Chad's clothes were gone and his overnight bag was missing.

Katie moved slowly across the room and the wooden floor felt cold on the bottom of her feet. The planks creaked beneath her. "Chad?" she said again. Her voice sounded hollow and disconnected.

She moved into the living room, where they had been

sipping champagne earlier in the evening. The couch was neat, pillows in their places at each end. She distinctly remembered they had retreated to the bedroom leaving the sofa in disarray and the glasses on the coffee table. Glancing at the small kitchenette, she saw one champagne flute sitting in the dish rack— not two. Everything looked neat and tidy, as if she was the only occupant.

Where was Chad?

A prickly feeling crept up along her limbs and tickled the back of her neck. It wasn't a pleasant feeling, but one of impending doom as she fought the urge to pass out. Her stomach churned and a sour taste rose in her mouth. She stumbled toward the couch as her vision narrowed. Her heart rate accelerated, making her headache even worse.

As she made her way across the room, using the furniture to steady herself as though fighting a drunken stupor, she managed to fling open the front door. The chilly air instantly blew inside but she couldn't feel it against her face. Her body felt numb, full of nothing but dread.

She stood in a lightweight T-shirt at the cabin threshold, staring into the semi-darkness of the early morning. Her bare feet and legs tingled with goosebumps. The trees looked suddenly like predators waiting to attack, instead of watching over the cabin. The eerie view tilted her further into a state of anxiety. Chad's SUV was still there. Parked in the same place they'd left it when they had arrived.

Her breath stalled.

She ran back inside and grabbed her cell phone to call him. It immediately went to voicemail. There was no sound of a phone ringing anywhere inside the cabin or outside. She tried again and again with the same result. She dropped the phone, it clattered on the wood floor, and she headed back to the open front door.

"Chad?" she said again, almost expecting a different

response. Her voice echoed strangely in the forest. Alone and distant. Pure adrenalin-fueled panic set in like a sword piercing her soul.

Looking down, Katie saw that she had stepped in something sticky. Immediately kneeling, she touched her fingertips to the floor. Turning her hand over, she stared at the crimson substance, rubbing it between her fingers. Blood. Sucking in a breath, she followed the trail of tiny drops, illuminated by the early morning light, outside and along the pathway, where they suddenly vanished in front of Chad's SUV. There were no footprints. Nothing.

Katie stood alone in the cool dawn air as mounting horror and confusion consumed her.

ONE

ONE MONTH LATER

Tuesday 1 1 30 hours

There was a dead body, which was the focus of the synchronized police search. A deceased woman had been found by the utility company during its routine check and maintenance of the meters along the roadway. The body was efficiently wrapped in a large piece of dark brown burlap that had been rolled several times leaving only her head exposed. If not looking closely, you would misinterpret the dumped body for some type of discarded rug.

The victim was a brunette woman with long, perfectly combed hair with the strands resting on the burlap. At first, it seemed she was relaxed and had merely gone to sleep, when in fact, there were pink velvet pieces of fabric covering her eyes, as if shading her view of something.

John Blackburn, Pine Valley Sheriff's Department's forensic supervisor, kneeled down and carefully lifted one of the pieces of velvet, revealing the dark empty socket the eyeball had once occupied. The eye had been cleanly detached. It gave the body a more macabre appearance than the usual fixed-eye stares of the dead.

John's face was deeply sad and his mouth was turned down as he prepared to take a few more photos to document the scene before the medical examiner's office took possession.

He carefully circled the body, taking the appropriate photographs—overall, medium range, then close-up—before collecting any evidence he could find. The young woman looked to be resting as the late afternoon sunshine cast down on her face. Her complexion, pale and ashen, appeared to be scrubbed clean, giving her a waxy doll-like exterior. There were no evident signs of makeup, dirt, or blood on her face.

The south area of Pine Valley was known for several ware-houses that had been empty now for more than six months after a manufacturing company had vacated to a newer and more modern facility in an adjacent town. The front area to the one where the body had been found was overgrown, the weeds a few feet tall and garbage strewn around from where it had fallen out of an overturned, rusted-out dumpster. The dreary gray building looked more like emergency bunkers from a long time ago than a plant that had recently manufactured automotive parts.

Parked along the cracked driveway leading to the loading docks were several police cruisers, county vehicles, and the forensic van. The main area of interest was near one of the loading bays. There were numerous cones and flags around, marking various pieces of evidence for photography documentation. The emergency personnel monitored the area and were conducting grid searches and making sure that no one was in or around the area who wasn't supposed to be there, in addition to searching for more potential evidence. Everyone moved with precision and unity for the common goal of maintaining the crime scene.

"What do you think, John?" asked Detective McGaven. His

towering height made him noticeable from a distance. His badge and gun were attached to his belt. "Is it the same as the other at Lookout Ridge?"

John walked up to the detective and nodded slowly. "We won't know for sure until the body is unrolled and examined under controlled conditions, and I can run some tests... but, the signature appears to be similar if not the same, with the removed eyes."

McGaven scratched his head, still observing the latest victim. His thoughts returned to his partner, Detective Katie Scott, and how he wished she were there examining the crime scene. Her perspective, instincts, and experience over the past year and a half had been more than exemplary—her methods sometimes bordering on unorthodox, but always getting results. He had left several messages for her in hopes that she would open communications and ultimately return to work. His expression was solemn. It was as if a part of him were missing without her. He wanted to go to her house, but respected her need for privacy at this difficult time.

"Wish Katie was here?" said John watching the detective closely.

McGaven looked at the forensic supervisor and nodded. "How'd you know?"

"I feel it too. It seems strange not having her here." He gazed around the area as if he expected to see Katie appear.

"Anything new with this scene?"

John shook his head. "Not that I can see right now. But we'll know more soon."

McGaven was disappointed, but knew that John would do everything he could to find any evidence. The last thing the detective wanted was for these homicides to go cold. He turned away and saw Detective Hamilton speaking with the utility workers. It wasn't his optimum partnership, but he respected the detective and would overlook personality differences to make it work. "Thanks, John," he said as he walked away, moving carefully around the area, looking for possible entrances and exit locations of the killer.

A young blonde woman with short hair was bent over taking a tire impression with a type of dental stone, waiting for it to harden. She looked up when McGaven approached. "Hi, Detective," she said and smiled.

"How's it going, Eva?"

"Good. This is my third impression. Two were consistent with each other and this one is different and definitely older. It's probably not the killer's, but John said we needed to be thorough."

McGaven nodded. "I agree. If this crime scene is connected to the other one at Lookout Ridge, then we need the evidence to tie them together."

"Ten-four," she said and continued her task.

McGaven saw that Hamilton was speaking with the officers first on the scene, so he took the opportunity to check out around the building. Everything was extremely overgrown, looking more as though it had been abandoned for years, not months. The weeds were extremely tall and had folded over due to their height and weight. There was an area where pallets, recyclable materials, and miscellaneous pieces of metal equipment had been stacked in the deserted area.

Still walking carefully, he was trying not to step on something potentially hazardous or possibly evidence-oriented. The farther he walked the quieter it became—the voices around the crime scene seemed to settle to a low hum as he studied the back area. The sun was high and beat down on him making perspiration trickle down his back. He kept walking, but nothing appeared out of the ordinary. He thought about what Katie would do—he had been with her at many crime scenes and knew she would try to get a sense of the area, to look for places where the killer might have been.

The back of the building looked much like the front except more weather-beaten. The gray paint faded in areas and the windows on the second floor were dirty with some broken out. He observed the inconsistencies of the exterior of the building. Even though there wasn't any graffiti to deface the area, the elements had caused rough and weathered places resembling an industrial mosaic appearance.

As he perused the area, he noticed a trail where weeds had been trampled, not by animals, but by something bigger. A person. Stopping in his tracks, he systematically scanned the area. There were no other signs indicating disruption to the weeds, so he cautiously moved forward. He spotted some paper or a piece of garbage rolled up tightly and wedged into the crevice of an exterior vent. It could have been easily missed or even dismissed, but something in McGaven's gut made him take notice. He was going to alert John and Eva in order to have them search and document the area, but his instinct drove him to verify the origins of the paper first after quickly taking a photo of it with his cell phone.

Taking two more steps to meet up with the wall, he retrieved his gloves and slipped them on, and then carefully touched the paper. Leaning in, McGaven noticed that it appeared to be consistent with ordinary computer paper that had something printed on it. It wasn't weathered and the printing was dark and readable. In fact, the paper appeared to be recent.

McGaven gently unrolled the paper. The condition and edges were as if it had been placed recently—there were no folds or fragile areas. As he continued to unroll it, he saw it was an article most likely printed from the internet. To his shock, the title read: *Pine Valley Detectives Solve Three Murders in Coldwater Creek.*

McGaven took a step back—his senses were now heightened as he glanced around, surmising that the killer had placed this article for them to find.

Why?

Was it the killer's calling card? Was he taunting the police?

Was there another article hidden at the previous crime scene at Lookout Ridge they had missed?

The article concerned the last case that he and Katie had worked in a neighboring town. All the details flowed through his mind. It had been tough and dangerous. He carefully replaced the paper where he had found it and hurried to alert John.

TWO

They say love is forever in your heart. They say that love can conquer all, it can mend anything, and it can connect people on many levels. But, it's true that you really don't fully appreciate it until it's gone. You are never prepared for what the journey ahead will be, or if you will survive the loss. Losing a love is a reality you must accept in order to move on.

Tuesday 1345 hours

A large black German shepherd trotted inside the house through the narrow opening of the sliding door from the backyard and took his place on the couch next to Katie. The ex-military explosive detection dog sighed heavily as if he knew and felt his partner's deep despair and wanted to relieve her pain. He inched his long body closer to Katie and nudged her arm with his wet nose. There were so many times that Cisco had comforted her in dire circumstances when they were an Army explosives team for two tours in Afghanistan.

"Hey, Cisco," she said quietly petting the dog. "I know... I know..." Her strained voice faded away.

Katie was still dressed in baggy gray sweatpants and a pale yellow bathrobe. Her dark hair hung loosely around her shoulders. Her eyes were still red from a bout of crying she had had earlier—which had been a daily occurrence for the past weeks. It didn't get any easier with each passing day, not knowing what had happened to Chad. In fact, it became harder and even unbearable at times. She wasn't sure if she would survive the immense loneliness of not knowing where he was or what had actually happened at the cabin.

Working cold cases had educated her to the realities of missing persons, and after a month, it was a probability that they might never find him again—or even if they did, that he would still be alive. She kept her hopes up, buoyed by knowing that Chad was a survivor and he would do everything he could to come home.

Several file folders and yellow notepads were spread on the coffee table in disarray. Katie's investigative notes were written in the margins of the reports. Phone numbers and names of people pertaining to Chad's investigation had been read and reread numerous times. She knew everything by heart. There had been traces of doxylamine, a strong over-the-counter sedative, found on the rim of her champagne flute and inside the champagne bottle that had been left inside the refrigerator, as well as traces in Katie's blood test. Someone had introduced the drug using a tiny needle inserted through the cork. Katie and Chad never noticed the minute hole, but closer inspection from forensics had found it.

But why?

How? When?

There were no fingerprints that weren't accounted for in the cabin, which meant no clue as to how and when the champagne had been tampered with. The blood analysis from the tiny droplets she'd found leading outside was inconclusive. It had been Chad's blood type, O negative, but the tests didn't conclude that the blood came from him specifically. The sample wasn't big enough to give more than the general type. His cell phone had no signal, making it impossible to trace his whereabouts. The fact that it had been turned off made the last known location the cabin—it hadn't been online since. There were no unidentified fingerprints on his SUV. It was dead end after dead end.

Katie had filed a missing person's report with Detective William Ames at the Pine Valley Sheriff's Department. It was the most difficult thing she had ever had to do, giving details of what happened and officially filing the report. She called Ames every day for the first ten days and then every other day after that to find out if there was any more information—*anything.*

Her department worked the case hard, but very little came from it. They dug into Chad's arson cases and the firehouse to find out if there were any strange anomalies, meetings, phone calls, arson investigation cases—anything unusual that might explain the disappearance. Nothing came to light. Even Chad's house was just as he had left it before going away with Katie. It was as if he had vanished into thin air. She had visited the cabin three times to search and go over the evening's activities, but again, it hadn't shed any new light on the case.

Katie glanced down at her paperwork—she wasn't going to let this case become a cold one. How could she? She knew everything about it backward and forward, but she couldn't find anything new—or even figure out the next direction to go in order to search for him.

She had expanded her searches to other jurisdictions as well as nearby cities that he had frequented or had connections. His family had moved away from Pine Valley years ago. His mom and sister were in Florida, upset by the news and desperate for any break in the case, but they still hadn't heard from him. They called Katie almost every day, each time more frantic than the last.

Her cell phone buzzed—another call that had gone to voice-mail, leaving the tenth message and counting for the day. Glancing at the list she saw that Sean McGaven, her partner in the cold-case unit, had called several times and had left five of the messages. Another was from her uncle, Sheriff Scott, and several more from friends including her therapist.

Katie picked up the cell phone, weighing it in her hand. She knew what they wanted and understood their concerns, but she wasn't ready to talk to anyone. She put it down on the table. She needed to get things straight in her own mind. Her thoughts always wandered back to Chad. There had to be something that she had overlooked—something small that would put everything into the proper perspective.

A loud knock sounded at her front door, jolting her out of her thoughts. She didn't move from her comfortable position on the couch and hoped that whoever it was would leave shortly.

Cisco stood up on the couch and barked. The dog wagged his tail as if he knew who it was—a friendly visitor.

At first Katie ignored the annoying rapping.

Then it stopped, to her relief.

Within a minute, she heard a voice from the backyard she instantly recognized.

"Katie?" he said.

Cisco jumped down from his position next to Katie with his tail wagging harder. He trotted to the partially opened sliding door where a man stood leaning toward the opening. He had a military crew cut, was handsome, and had intense dark eyes.

"Hey, Cisco," he said.

Katie didn't immediately rise from the couch. She turned her head toward the door, but looked away.

"Katie, can I come in?" He held up a brown bag and gently shook it. A smile washed across his face. "I have a couple of sandwiches. Turkey with Swiss on sourdough—your favorite."

It wasn't that Katie wasn't glad to see her former Army

sergeant, Nick Haines, but she didn't want to talk to anyone—at least not yet. He had helped her through the most difficult training in her life when she had enlisted in the Army. When she felt like giving up, he always had her back and encouraged her to continue—forceful and direct, but kind and respectful.

Nick had been in a restaurant overseas when it had been a target of a bomb attack where there had been loss of life. Nick in turn had lost his leg in the explosion. It had upturned his life even though he had been honorably discharged. Upon his return, Katie had helped him reunite with his estranged brother who now lived a few towns away from Pine Valley.

Nick and Katie were able to see each other from time to time, which made Katie very happy. He represented a piece of her past that no one else could fully understand—and when she met with him, she felt it gave her some peace from the memories of her past military experiences.

"C'mon, Scotty," said Nick. He had always called her that instead of Katie. "I'm just going to stay out here until you invite me in."

Katie sighed, knowing that he meant what he said. "Fine," she said. "Come in."

He smiled and pushed the sliding door wider so he could enter. His limp was evident but he seemed to move with more ease than the last time Katie had seen him. The physical therapy seemed to be working well and she was happy for him. He moved to the kitchen and set the bag down.

"Do you really have my sandwich?" said Katie trying to force a smile. She tried to sound casual but her efforts weren't successful. Instead, she sounded annoyed.

"Ah, I knew you couldn't resist." Nick opened the bag, retrieving the sandwiches and then pulled two plates from the cupboard. He sat down next to Katie, handing her one of them.

"Darrow's Deli?" she said, realizing that she was starving.

She hadn't been eating on a regular basis since Chad's disappearance.

"Yep."

"Thank you." It was indeed her favorite sandwich and a very thoughtful gesture.

"Now that's taken care of."

Katie gave him that look, which meant don't go there... she was enjoying the company without an interrogation about things she didn't want to answer.

"You've had a month to deal with what's been going on, and this isn't healthy." He gestured to her messy house and the fact she was still in her pajamas. "What are we going to do?" His dark eyes watched her carefully.

"We?"

"Yeah, *we*," he said.

Katie took another bite of the sandwich. "Who put you up to this?"

"No one."

"Really?"

"Well, maybe I talked to the sheriff... and McGaven... and John... and..."

"Alright. I know that I've been in my zone but..."

"Your zone? Is that what you call it?"

"For lack of a better word. Yeah, *my* zone," she said, emphasizing her private space. She liked her small area where she could control what happened.

"Scotty, you need to step back, take a breath, and let us help you." He took her hand and squeezed it for reassurance. "C'mon, you have to see that this isn't healthy."

"I'm not going to quit looking for Chad."

"We're not asking you to, but let the people who love you and care about you help you through this. No matter where it leads."

Katie paused before replying, realizing that Nick was

genuinely trying to help. His face looked strained and it was clear that he was worried about her. "I know," she barely whispered, holding back the tears.

"Scotty, I've never seen you like this. When things were tough, you always rose to the challenge. Always. And you can do this too... but not alone. You have to ask for help."

Katie felt the words stick in her throat and she couldn't respond. She always held everything tightly inside, mistakenly thinking that she could handle all the drama without falling apart.

Cisco moved closer to her, resting his head on her arm.

Nick sensed her pain and moved closer too, hugging her tightly. She laid her head on his shoulder. It felt good to feel the comfort of his arms.

That was all it took for Katie to let go. The tears rushed down her cheeks and she shuddered with gasps of anguish. He let her cry for several minutes in his arms. When she finally stopped, she sat up, wiping her face.

Nick stroked her hair. "Everything is going to be okay. We're going to get to the bottom of this. You have an entire team of people who are here to help—very experienced people. You don't need to carry this burden alone."

She nodded, still trying to catch her breath.

"I may not have detective experience, but I'm here to do whatever you need me to do," he said. "Even if you just don't want to be alone. I can stay in the guest room. Whatever you need."

Katie knew that Nick was an extremely loyal friend and that once she had some news she would be able to talk to him about it. "Thank you, Nick." Her voice was weak and had a shaky quality to it.

"You don't have to thank me—we're family."

She smiled, realizing how much she had missed her Army team—and how much they were indeed family.

He spied the notes and reports on the coffee table. "Okay, what do we have?" he said.

"Take a read and I'll fill you in as well."

"Okay," he said as he began shuffling through the detailed paperwork beginning with the forensic analysis and Katie's account of the evening until she woke up and found Chad gone.

Sifting through the files, they discussed the case. It was the first time in almost a month she felt the heavy burden begin to ease with the help of a friend.

THREE

When you've lost a part of your soul, it can either destroy you or force you to become stronger, no matter what your heart says. You don't have many choices but you must choose one of them. Every day is a challenge—an unrelenting test that will be the most difficult charge you've ever faced in the darkness ahead. You must have the courage and faith to move forward. I've made my choice.

Wednesday 0920 hours

The trail's steep terrain pushed Katie even harder as she ran. She pumped her arms with force and took faster strides. Cisco kept close to her side. She didn't pause for a brief rest; instead, she pushed even harder. It was as if she were chased by a demon that demanded her full attention, when, in fact, it was her own mind that was pushing her.

She took the long way around to get to the Lookout Trail. She had surprised herself that she had accepted her uncle's invitation to meet him. His message had been cryptic. She had also figured that he wanted to talk to her in private, away from their other colleagues, in a more neutral and relaxing environment. There were many times she had confided in her uncle, but since Chad's mysterious disappearance she had kept her feelings close to her chest, not even disclosing her private thoughts to him. After talking with Nick, she'd realized that she wasn't doing herself, and more importantly Chad, any favors by making herself into a recluse.

The air was cool, leaving her breaths short and rapid. There weren't any other hikers or runners in sight as she made her way around the trail, through dense clusters of pine trees, to where the path leveled. Her calves and hamstrings were strained, but she felt she wanted to push even harder. Instead, she reluctantly slowed her pace and waited for her heart rate to return to normal. Leaning her back against a tree for support, she leaned forward to catch her breath.

Cisco padded up to her. He too was panting hard. He did a couple of circles in the nearby area, but didn't want to stray too far from Katie. It was his job not only to protect Katie, but also to comfort her in her time of need.

"Sorry, Cisco, I'll slow the pace down..." she said, winded.

Glancing at her watch, she saw she still had almost a half hour before she was to meet her uncle. She took that time to reflect on everything, not just Chad, but how her life was going in general. She had pushed everything aside for the past month, and had made other things in her life crash down around her. She realized she missed work and the challenges of the cold cases, missed her partner McGaven, training with Cisco, and spending time with her uncle. These areas had come to a standstill and it was time for her to jumpstart them again because she wasn't going to accept that Chad wasn't coming back.

Katie decided to cool down and give her body a gentle rest by walking the rest of the way to Lookout Ridge. It was an area that she seldom hiked, but her uncle had been adamant about meeting there.

As she neared the area, she saw a few remnants of crime-scene tape. It gave her pause. Dread filled her. She now knew why her uncle wanted to meet her at this location. It must have been a crime scene recently. She had been so out of the loop with local news that she didn't have a clue what had been going on over the last month. Now her curiosity was piqued.

Katie was about to search on her cell phone, but the signal was sketchy, wavering in and out.

"Trying to search for the crime?" said a voice behind her.

She turned and saw her uncle coming up from another trail. He was dressed in running clothes, distinguished looking, with cropped gray hair, but still physically fit. "Uncle Wayne," she said. It stunned her that she hadn't realized how much she had missed him until she saw him walking up to her.

"Oh, Katie," he said and hugged her tightly. "I'm sorry for what you're going through. But know that we all want to help and we're going to get to the bottom of this. The press has been hounding us about the firefighter, arson investigator who's gone missing, but we've managed to keep it quiet as we're actively working the case. You know we've been scouring Chad's last cases and talked to everyone at the firehouse to help put together a picture of what happened before his disappearance. With your account of what happened at the cabin too."

Katie felt a lump in her throat and nodded. She fought back the tears as she heard those words. Her world had crashed down when she least anticipated it, and her emotions had been overwhelming her when she least expected it ever since, so she took a few steps away to regroup and get her thoughts together.

"You probably know why I asked you here," he said.

Cisco trotted around them, investigating some low-lying shrubs and tree trunks.

"I'm getting the picture."

"I'm sorry that I didn't just tell you outright, but I wasn't sure if you would come otherwise."

"It's okay." Katie surveyed the area and could see the places where the scene had been searched and most likely where the body had been found. It appeared to have been cleared—the ground was the most level in the forest. The weeds were flattened in between the thick clusters of trees. She took a few steps and carefully navigated her way down a steep area. There was a clearing and it appeared to be a perfect place to leave a body. Something tugged at her. There was a feeling of familiarity to the area and the way that it had been set up. As if she had seen something like it before. "What happened here?" She eyed where the killer might have possibly entered and exited the clearing. It was where a little-used trail came up from below the area of interest, and which led to a place one could park.

Sheriff Scott took a few steps closer to Katie. "I thought you might not have been watching the news. Last week, a first murder victim was found here."

"First?"

"Unfortunately, yes. The second was found yesterday at the old warehouse district."

Katie took everything in. She didn't immediately respond. She began to formulate things slowly as her mind processed. "There's something familiar here, isn't there?" she said. Searching her uncle's face, she continued, "Maybe a copycat?"

The sheriff smiled. "What makes you say that?"

"It just seems familiar, as if I've seen something like this before. Maybe it's because I've seen several bodies left in a wooded area? I know I've seen this before, just don't know where. Maybe I'm just overreaching?" She moved around the area, where she could see evidence had been collected, judging by the indentation of where markers had been located and the extra concentrations of footprints—most likely from John and Eva. "What happened?" Her interest was heightened and she suddenly wanted to know more details.

"You're half right. We don't know for sure, but after the

preliminary examination of the second body there's good linkage."

"Serial killer? What do we know about the victims?" Katie's mind began sorting through all types of scenarios. Had the victims been related somehow, worked together, had the same distinguishing characteristics, or frequented the same type of establishments? The questions started rolling through her mind.

"The two victims aren't officially connected that we know of yet, but they do bear a physical resemblance to one another and how they are missing their eyes and pinky fingers along with the burlap." He hesitated. "We think it might be like the twelve brutal murders from almost twenty years ago. Simon Holden." That name stilted the conversation as his words hung in the air. "I remember it well. I assisted the detectives on the case."

Katie knew who Simon Holden was. She had studied the cases. She had just been a young child when the murders began, but it had been such a notorious case that it had lasted for years. Young women had been out running or walking in a mostly deserted area when they had fallen victim to Holden. She remembered seeing photos of the victims, who had been rolled in a rug and had had their eyes removed. It had been a deliberate, planned, and gruesome spree.

"Uncle Wayne, are you trying to get me to work this case?" Katie watched her uncle, raising her eyebrows in anticipation.

"I think you figured that out after you got here."

"Who's working it now? Gav and Hamilton?"

"Yes. And Hamilton is being stretched thin with his other burglary and forgery cases. That's really his niche."

"I see," she said. She wasn't sure how she felt about diving back into a serious case when Chad was still missing and there weren't any new leads on how to find him. Walking to a large boulder, Katie sat down to let things simmer in her mind.

Cisco made himself comfortable next to her by sitting close, ears perked, staring out at the cleared crime-scene area, alert for anything unusual. His shiny black fur glistened in the morning sunlight while he gently panted.

"I know this is difficult, but... we really need you and Gav working on these cases," he said.

Katie knew that he wasn't trying to push her. But it was important for the victim's families, as well as the town, for them to stop this killer and take him off the streets. She and Gav would be the best team for the job since they had worked similar types of cases. The sharp sense of dread filled her just as it always did whenever they were tracking a killer. "The killer is going to strike again, isn't he?" She kept her focus on the area because she already knew the answer before she even asked it.

"We believe so." His voice was soft but deliberate.

Katie sat quietly for a moment. Many thoughts were swirling through her mind. She didn't take it lightly that the department was stretched thin and that this case might, and most likely would, escalate. With a possible serial killer there was always the threat of more victims. Safety was a prime concern. She contemplated Chad's case and the two murders. To her immense heartbreak, Chad's investigation had been stalled and she was just spinning her wheels at home waiting for any break. She knew that Detective Ames was technically in charge, but she pushed all her strength and resources to investigate everything that they knew. Now Ames was not taking her calls and was abrupt when he told her that they were doing everything they could to find Chad, and she would be the first to know if anything changed.

She wrestled with the decision to go back to work. Her priority was finding Chad, but her job was working for the community, and if women were being targeted, it was her job to stop the killer. Her heart ached with sorrow. After careful consideration, it was clear what she needed to do and she would have to make peace with it.

Her uncle sat down next to her and put his arm around her shoulders. "I'm sorry for putting you on the spot. But the department is now in the hot seat with these cases. The public is demanding justice, women are scared, and we need to catch this killer."

Katie nodded.

"Katie, I want you to be comfortable about this. Your health and well-being is the most important thing to me. I respect your decision, no matter what it is."

They remained quiet for a few minutes—neither spoke but just enjoyed the silence and scenery.

"Okay," she said.

"Okay?"

"Yes, okay," she said and looked at her uncle. It was the best thing she could do under the circumstances. "I'll be fine, but if there's anything new about Chad, then I'll have to follow it."

"Of course. We'll make considerations, even if I have to step in."

Katie turned her attention back to the already worked crime scene. Her mind instantly flipped to the victim, the killer, and how they were going to pick up the trail. As she pondered, she noticed there were pieces of new yellow crime-scene tape near one of the larger pine trees. Judging by the area where the body had most likely been located, she thought it odd that the tape marked an area on the tree trunk. She got to her feet and walked toward the tree for a closer look.

"Katie?" said the sheriff.

She stopped at the tree and inspected the bark area about eye level. There seemed to be a vertical cut that appeared recent. "Was there something here?"

The sheriff smiled and stood up. "Yes."

Katie turned and said, "Was it something from the killer?"

"Most likely."

"What was it?" She watched her uncle's reaction and

thought it strange that his expression turned serious. "Was it something that the killer was warning us about?"

"No. It was a rolled-up news article."

"What kind of article?"

"It was about you and one of your cases last year. Remember the case of the family buried in the basement from that arson case? Chad was the arson investigator on that case."

"What?" She thought about Chad and that particular case. "About me? Chad?" The thought made her uneasy and added another disturbing dimension to the case. "Why didn't you tell me? I would find out when I review the case."

"I know. I guess I was trying to ease you back into the investigations."

"This is a major development, don't you think?" Katie tried not to sound flippant about it. "Should I be worried?"

"I've already taken the necessary steps and have had various officers watch your house around the clock."

"Why didn't you tell me?" The thought made her uncomfortable, bordering on annoyed, because she could take care of herself—she had a security system and Cisco.

"It has been difficult since you were not taking any of our calls. I've been respecting your privacy."

Katie realized that her behavior and reclusiveness had made it difficult for everyone in her life to get near her. Her heart ached, not only for the situation surrounding Chad, but for those who cared about her and were still here. "I'm so sorry." She held back tears, trying to regain her composure. "I'm so sorry for pushing you away—pushing everyone away."

"It's okay," he said and hugged her. "We all knew it was best to let you figure things out first and reach out to us when you were ready."

Katie sighed. She was going to have to pull her emotions together. She needed to get caught up on the cases if they were going to find the killer before there was another victim.

FOUR

After Katie returned home from meeting with her uncle to shower and get ready for work, she made her way to the Pine Valley Sheriff's Department, which was about twenty minutes away. She observed one patrol car across the street from her home.

Before focusing on going back to work, she made a quick phone call to Detective Ames. Pressing the extension, she waited.

"Detective Ames," he said.

"Hi, Detective, it's Katie."

"What can I do for you?" he said without any voice inflection.

"I'm checking in to find out if anything has changed or if you're following a new lead."

"Katie, you will be the first to know. I promise. Concentrate on your cases or yourself right now." He tried to sound respectful, but it was clear that he was losing patience.

"I want to stay on top of it."

"Katie, we've got this. Okay?"

She stayed silent, not quite sure what to say.

"I'm sorry. I'll call you if there's any news." He ended the call.

As she drove to work, she tried to push Chad from her mind, as her thoughts became a loop of the killer's actions and the behavioral evidence left behind at the crime scene as she wrestled with the little bit of information she had learned from her uncle.

Pulling into the police department parking lot, Katie parked next to McGaven's black truck. Cutting the engine, she sat, gathering her thoughts. It seemed that she hadn't been to work in such a long time that she needed to catch her breath and ready herself to dive into two active homicide investigations—a little different than her previous cold cases.

Katie took a moment and slowed her breathing, which in turn decelerated her rapid pulse. No matter what she did her thoughts were never far from Chad—his smiling face. She thought about their last night together and the conversation they had had about the date on which they wanted to get married. It almost brought her to tears.

Opening the door, she stepped out and hurried to the back entrance to the police administrative building. Once inside, she headed down the hallway and stopped at a door with no identification. Swiping her card, the door buzzed and popped open.

Katie stepped inside. The familiar quiet as she walked through the area and soft buzz of the ventilation system greeted her. It amazed her how quickly her routine came rushing back to her. She walked past several office doors that were closed, turned left, and headed down the hallway to her and McGaven's cold-case office. Due to the space limitations in the detective division, the cold-case unit was in the forensic department, making it easier for the detectives to be near forensics along with case files.

She heard two voices talking and immediately recognized them. Pausing at the partially open door to a large examination room, Katie pushed it open and saw John and McGaven discussing one of the cases.

Katie couldn't help but smile. It was one of her favorite parts of the investigation, working with her partner and the forensic supervisor.

McGaven turned to see Katie. "Can we help you?" he said with a deadpan expression.

Katie's smile grew. "Well, I'm not so sure if you can," she said.

"Get over here," said McGaven as he hugged his partner. "I'm so glad you're back."

"It's not the same without you," said John.

Katie felt a little emotionally overwhelmed, but she kept her feelings controlled. "It's nice to be back."

"I was just talking to John about the evidence, but if you want to familiarize yourself with the case first before we dig into the science stuff, let's go." McGaven gestured to the back storage, which had been turned into their main base of operations for their cases. It was a place big enough to lay out everything they had so far on the cases as well as their own notes on large whiteboards.

"I'll be here when you're ready," said John taking a few extra seconds to look at Katie before going back to work.

Katie wanted to get a firm grasp on the cases before diving into the evidence, so she followed McGaven and entered their homicide command center. She was surprised at the amount of information already displayed. The main wall had photographs from the two crime scenes. Lists of potential suspects, persons of interest, and background information on Simon Holden were neatly presented.

"These crime scenes are definitely reminiscent of those Simon Holden cases."

"Strangulation?"

"Yes. It's as if..." She didn't finish her thought. Then she said, "The placement and locations seem very intricate."

She quickly scanned the information and took a moment to take in all the evidence. Theories began to unfold in her mind as to the killer's profile—his identity, behavioral patterns, and signature. Both women had been strangled and stripped nude before being placed in their final positions.

Katie continued, "Doesn't it seem strange that these cases are so similar?"

McGaven took a moment, nodding his head. "I agree. Are you thinking it's a copycat?"

"We can't rule anything out yet." She studied the recent crime scenes a bit further.

McGaven waited patiently as his partner assimilated everything they knew up to date. He sat down at the large table and began some computer searches. It was his usual task when they worked cases together. It allowed for Katie to begin to create a profile of the killer and to look for other avenues as he scoured for more information. They had established a solid protocol that worked efficiently for them and had helped them to solve all of their cases so far.

Katie stood looking at the photos of the first crime scene at Lookout Trail. The woman was of average build, brunette with long hair, which had been carefully positioned and combed. She had been wrapped in burlap with only her head showing— placed specifically in the clearing Katie had just seen. The woman's eyes were covered with fabric. It was eerie and gave a bit of an otherworldly vibe, as if she had been dropped on earth by aliens. The towering trees made for a forested protection like a giant umbrella. One of the things that came to Katie's mind was Sleeping Beauty.

What was the killer conveying?

Why did he remove the eyes and then cover the sockets with fabric?

What did it signify to him?

Usually when killers cover victims' faces, it means that there is some type of familiarity to them. They knew the victims personally or even intimately. But this killer took their eyes, ensuring that his victims could never see again, but was almost gentle in covering the gaping holes. This suggested to Katie that the killer had thought about it and had prepared his execution of his signature very carefully. It was something extremely important to him and she was going to unravel the mystery of why.

Katie read the autopsy report highlights. It stated that the left pinky finger had been removed and the digit wasn't left at the crime scene, indicating that perhaps the killer took it as a trophy along with the eyeballs.

What did the pinky have to do with the eyes?

Katie lingered at the photos of the woman's hand missing a pinky. It wasn't done with precision, in contrast to the eyes, but rather it appeared to be hacked off post-mortem with some type of sharp knife, she guessed.

"Are you looking at the missing pinky?" asked McGaven as if he read her thoughts.

"I've seen other fingers removed from murder victims, but why the pinky?" She turned around and looked at her partner. "Have you searched any other cases with victims missing pinkies?"

"Yep. Nothing so far. At least in Sequoia County."

"Try doing a larger search."

"On it."

Katie read the general list for victim number one. Her name was Gina Hartfield, twenty-seven years old, single, assistant to a real estate developer, Sampson & Crawford. She lived alone and had had a heart condition called congenital anomalous coronary artery. She had received treatment but still took medications. She appeared to be very active, running almost every day, which was how she had become a target of the killer.

Katie began to run ideas through her mind of what the killer was hoping to accomplish, either through his own fantasies or through what he wanted the police and public to think. It was an action to instill fear but there was a theatrical element to the crime scenes. But why? What drove him?

"What do we know about Simon Holden?" she said.

"Just that thirteen years ago he was tried and convicted of twelve murders with the same MO as our current homicides." He frowned. "How could this be? He's in jail for life under twenty-four-hour supervision. There's been no indication that he's had visitors recently." McGaven shuffled through some files on the table.

Katie knew by her gut instinct that there had to be some connection. These crimes wouldn't just resurface without having anything to do with Holden.

"What's going through that mind of yours?" said McGaven.

"I'm thinking about Holden. What are the odds that these types of murders would show up now?"

"I see where you're going with this. You think copycat or someone close to him?"

"Maybe," she said slowly. "I'm thinking it has to do with him, maybe not directly but indirectly. I don't know how, but these cases are too similar to dismiss it." Katie kept reading about the cases and the articles highlighting the court proceedings. It seemed that Holden liked attention and he behaved with many theatrics—outbursts in the courtroom, changing attorneys several times, and having his lawyers ask outrageous questions, to law enforcement specifically. But he had always claimed his innocence—that he hadn't killed those women.

"I've been reading about Holden. It makes for an interesting read, that's for sure."

"What about the pinky angle?" she said. "Was there ever a reasonable explanation for removing it?"

"I don't know about reasonable. But nothing I could decipher... and yes, Holden has all his digits."

Katie smiled. "You know me so well. That was my next question." She thought for a moment. "What about the pinky?"

"What about it?" he said.

"Does that digit make it easier or more difficult to use your hand properly?" She continued to study the victims, trying to connect something—behavioral evidence left by the killer—something that wasn't easily seen.

"Hey, check this out," said McGaven. He keyed up more websites. "This would be a great trivia question."

Katie faced her partner. "What do you mean?"

"Well, it says in several sources from doctors and physical therapists that when you lose a pinky finger it makes your hand fifty percent weaker."

"The pinky?" Katie was surprised. "Not one of the other fingers, like the index?" She looked at her own hand.

"Nope. It goes on to explain that your pinky is needed to work with the other fingers to grip objects and that strength dwindles significantly without it." McGaven skimmed a few more articles.

"So..." began Katie. "The killer takes the pinky of his victims as a way to indicate that he's taking some of their strength?"

"Maybe a type of fetish? A trophy?"

"He takes their eyes so that they can't see... and their finger removal makes them weaker..." The visual made her extremely distraught. The heinous nature inflicted upon the victims made her more queasy than usual. She tried to shake it off.

McGaven looked at Katie. "You okay, Katie?"

"I'm fine. It's just... I may be reaching, but why wasn't any of this talked about during the Holden case?"

"It could have been mentioned during the trial. I'm having Denise get a trial transcript to see if there's anything that might help us," he said.

"Great idea. See, you had everything under control." She was actually quite impressed by everything that had been posted.

"Not quite."

"What do you mean?" said Katie.

"*Now* we have everything under control with you here." He smiled. "I'm really glad you're back."

"Thanks, Gav," she said. "It's good to get back to work." She averted her gaze and stared at the murder board.

Her partner stood up and approached her. "Katie, I hope you know that I will help you night or day if you need it. I'm here to back you up on anything for Chad's investigation. You know that, right?"

Katie knew it, but having McGaven standing in front of her telling her so made her emotions spike. She swallowed hard—she had to constantly keep her feelings in check, and it was becoming tougher. "I do. Thanks, Gav." Katie turned her attention back to the board and the two crime scenes. "Can we get the files for Holden's crime scenes? Specifically the crime-scene photos."

"Working on it."

She turned to her partner. "Who was the lead detective?"

McGaven flipped through notes and stopped. "Detective Raymond Torrez. He retired six years ago and unfortunately died four years later of a heart attack."

Katie was disappointed. "My uncle mentioned that he helped on the cases with support."

The door burst open.

"We have another one," said John.

"Another body?" said McGaven.

"Yep. All hands on deck."

"Where?"

"Wellington Park—next to the preparatory school," he said and left to get ready to roll to the scene.

McGaven looked at Katie. "Looks like you're going to hit the ground running."

Katie grabbed a small notebook. "Let's just hope this time we can catch the killer before he strikes again."

FIVE

McGaven drove as Katie surveyed the area, trying to ascertain why the killer wanted to dump a body at this particular location. It was a residential area, a neighborhood not far from the park with a prep school next door. The trees and foliage were moderate, but not dense, making it possible that someone could have seen the killer. The school was out on break, so there weren't any students or teachers currently around. Did that mean something important to the killer? Why here? A school?

"This is it," said McGaven as he found an available space to park along the partially gravel road.

Katie stepped out of the car and quickly scanned the area. It was cool but there was still a little sun. She took a deep breath, feeling the brisk air fill her lungs and relax her. She considered the climate. Depending upon how long the body had been out in these conditions, it was probably still somewhat preserved. The sun had dipped late in the day and was now behind some tall pine and oak trees, with just some strips of light penetrating through.

A stocky deputy with dark hair approached the detectives. His nametag said Halleron.

"What do you have?" said McGaven.

"Dispatch received a call from the construction company, D.W. Contractors, that they found a body. They were picking up extra material from the park reconstruction when they found it. Female. Looked to be late twenties or early thirties. Wrapped in some type of material or burlap."

"Thank you," said McGaven.

"Let me know if you need anything else." The deputy hurried away to assist in keeping the area secure.

"Let's go."

Katie saw that the park was small—something that would suffice for a small older neighborhood. There were only four picnic tables and two barbecue pits, with a small playground with bars, slide, and four swings. To one side, there were construction items for building a retaining wall that consisted of four-by-four planks and concrete blocks and bricks. She looked across to where the hillside seemed to be eroding and the construction company had been working to shore up the area. They had left their remaining supplies neatly stacked on the side of the park that shared the property line for the school.

As the detectives arrived, they saw the crime scene, which had been cordoned off around the construction area and the playground.

Katie immediately thought the area was too small. "Can we get the search area expanded? Two to three times bigger."

Two of the deputies hurried to accommodate the request.

McGaven looked at his partner. He didn't question her, but clearly wondered why she had requested the change of the area of interest.

John and Eva were preparing to document the scene and gather evidence when Katie and McGaven were finished with their walk-through.

Two employees from D.W. Contractors were waiting anxiously, stretching their necks trying to see the investigation unfolding, as deputies were taking their statements.

Katie stopped.

McGaven mirrored his partner and hung back a little bit to let her take everything in before moving forward.

It was late in the afternoon and it seemed strange that the body had only been discovered at this time instead of earlier in the day. Surely, someone who had been walking by or enjoying the park would have discovered the body earlier.

Katie glanced around and then looked down. She didn't notice any tire impressions nearby, which meant that the killer had either lured the victim or had carried her to the dump site. "No tire tracks," she said to her partner and moved closer to the scene.

She moved forward slowly and deliberately, trying to visualize how the killer had approached. There were grassy sections, but most of the walking area was loose gravel or mulch. The area had been raked recently, probably by the construction workers when they were cleaning up. There were no footprints. It seemed strange and out of the ordinary. One of the first things she noticed was that two six-foot pieces of lumber were strategically placed. One was laid perpendicular to the body while the other was horizontal. It made a makeshift "L" shape.

She stopped to study the lumber for a moment.

Perfectly placed between them was the body that had been rolled up in burlap. The rest of the cement blocks and lumber were still neatly stacked a few feet away. A heavy blue tarp had been secured on half of the supplies. Again, there were no footprints.

Katie turned toward McGaven. "See if there are any footprints leading to the body from the other surrounding areas." She pulled on her gloves.

He nodded and took off in a clockwise search around the park and school regions.

After Katie had scanned the construction supplies and was satisfied nothing looked out of the ordinary, she turned her attention to the body. It looked similar—if not almost identical—to the other two bodies that she had seen in the photographs. A woman in her twenties or thirties with long dark hair that had been meticulously combed and which lay at the top of the burlap. The wrapping covered the body and only a portion of her neck along with her head were showing.

Katie kneeled next to her, studying her. There were no identifying marks on her face, only dark discolored marks on her upper neck. The victim's face had been washed clean. There were no visible traces of makeup, dirt, or other substances.

Whenever Katie approached a homicide victim at a crime scene, she almost always avoided looking at their faces because of the eyes. The eyes were always telling. Sometimes they appeared to be staring right at her, following her as she moved around the area. And sometimes, they gave the impression that they were accusing her, as if they were telling her to find their killer. The most common were the eyes that stared out in space and had nothing behind them. It was clear that the person was gone and had succumbed to their horrible fate.

As Katie examined the pink velvet coverings over the eyes, it made her nervous and unsettled, not knowing what to expect. She slowly moved her gloved index finger and cautiously moved one of the pieces of fabric, uncovering the dark, gaping hole where the eyeball had been.

Katie stared at the empty orifice for a moment, trying to decipher the killer's language of why. What made him go the extra mile to remove the eyes after strangling the victim?

She stood up straight, giving the area a slow three-hundred-sixty-degree turn. She saw the park and playground, the looming aged trees, and the driveway leading into the school.

Walking over to the school side, she noticed that several bushes and undergrowth had been disturbed. It wasn't clear if it had been done recently or days ago. The road itself that led into the school was paved and had been well taken care of—no cracks or potholes.

McGaven jogged up.

"Anything?" she said.

"Nothing looks disturbed. No footprints or drag marks. But John and Eva will scour the areas and document them anyway."

"I may have found where the killer entered."

McGaven looked to the school side. "From the road leading into the school?"

She nodded. "I think so. There's no other possibility."

"The deputies are canvassing the area, including the school. There should be security and maintenance—making someone who might have heard or seen something." He watched his partner closely. "You okay?"

"I'm fine."

"You seem to be wrestling with something."

"This scene seems strange—where it's situated and how the killer dumped the body." She looked at the body again. "It's like it's halfway completed. Like the killer decided to keep it simple."

McGaven nodded but didn't add anything to her observations.

"Detectives," said one of the deputies as he jogged up. "We found something."

Katie and McGaven followed the officer through the playground and into a small clearing. It was difficult to see at first what he was talking about, but behind a bush and sitting on a large slate rock there was a small wallet that would be normally kept inside a pocket when out jogging. A driver's license was placed by itself about a foot away from the wallet and revealed the victim was Brianna Garcia. She was twenty-five and lived less than a mile away. This was definitely something different from the previous scenes.

John approached the detectives. "You ready for us?"

McGaven eyed his partner.

"Yes, please document all the surrounding areas as well. I want to get an overview of the area."

John smiled. "I have a surprise for you. We have a drone that we can use to take photos above the area—around the trees, that is."

"That's great. Thank you, John," she said. Katie suddenly felt overwhelmed, which was unusual, but in her unique circumstances was probably normal. She hadn't thought about Chad at all for a little while, but the second that she did everything seemed to come collapsing down around her and she felt immediately insecure about what she was doing.

McGaven noticed his partner's sudden change in behavior. "We got a message from Dr. Dean at the morgue," he said, looking at his watch. "He wants to see us."

"Sounds good," said Katie, trying to push through her emotions.

"We're going to be here a while," said John. "Let's meet up at 0800 tomorrow back at the lab?"

"Sure," she said. "See you then."

Katie caught up with McGaven as they returned to the car. He was looking at his cell phone. "Looks like Denise sent me some photos from the files she found from Holden's crime scenes... and oh wow... take a look at this." He showed the phone to Katie.

Katie scrolled through the photos from the first victim through the third and she almost gasped. The photos from twenty years ago showed nearly the exact crime scenes as the ones from this year. The first was posed at the hiking area, the second was at an industrial building near the cargo bays, and the third was at a playground. The bodies were also wrapped in a type of burlap, and the victims were all young women in their twenties.

"What do you think?" said McGaven.

Katie was almost speechless. "I knew there was something strange and reminiscent of a staged crime scene, but this... is absolutely uncanny." She kept scrolling as McGaven looked over her shoulder. She stopped on the fourth victim. "Look at this." Her stomach dropped as she realized that there would most likely be another victim.

"I need to call the watch commander and have all units notified," said McGaven. He took back his phone and made the call. "This is Detective McGaven... We've received some information regarding the current homicides and all units need to be alerted that..."

Katie was still reeling from the last photo as her partner called in the alert. The crime-scene photo from years ago showed a woman rolled up in burlap material next to an apartment complex. But that wasn't the most disturbing aspect of the photograph. There wasn't just one—there were two bodies.

SIX

Katie remained quiet during the entire ride to the morgue. Her thoughts were on the potential discovery of a recreation of a fourth crime scene from Holden's long list of victims and she hoped that their current cases weren't going to come to that. But at the same time, her mind couldn't shake the recurring memory of Chad and the last evening they'd shared together at the cabin —it stayed relentlessly in her mind. She relived that night constantly, trying desperately to remember anything that would answer the question of what happened to him. The memories were on the border of becoming obsessive.

McGaven cut the engine and didn't move. He seemed hesitant and it was clear he had something weighing heavy on his mind. "Katie, I know you're getting sick of hearing this... but..."

Katie watched her partner. He seldom looked this serious, so she waited to see what he had to say.

"Are you okay? I mean really okay?"

"Gav, I'm fine. Not great, but I'm handling it."

"Anything new in the investigation?"

She sighed. "No, not yet."

"I can see you're struggling. I'm not saying that you aren't doing your job—far from it—but I can see the grief and sadness in you. I've never seen you like this since I've known you."

Katie took a moment before she answered because she wasn't sure if she could stop from breaking down. "I'm not going to lie. This has been the worst thing I've ever experienced in my life—besides losing my parents." She paused to keep her voice even. "It's not like most losses or tragedies we all experience at some point in our lives... It's the not knowing and the question of why that's eating away at me."

"You know that we're all here for you. Anything you need."

Katie touched Gav's arm. "I know. Thank you. I just have to process everything first my own way."

"Okay. I understand."

Katie smiled. "I know you do."

"Let's go talk to the doc," he said.

Katie followed her partner into the morgue. When they entered it seemed to make everything more intense. Both detectives hated being there but it was an important part of their job. The unnatural coolness of the atmosphere. The disinfectant smells. The stark stainless steel all around, the specialized tables holding bodies that had been dissected, poked, and prodded. All made their visits that much more uncomfortable. Even the tile floor that made Katie's boots louder as she walked into the exam area.

Dr. Jeffrey Dean approached the detectives. It wasn't usually difficult to spot him because of his unorthodox way of dressing in a colorful Hawaiian shirt with vibrant reds and blues, and loose khakis. This time he was wearing running shoes instead of his usual braided sandals, along with a white smock with a few blood spatters on the sleeves.

"Detectives," said the medical examiner. "It's nice to see you both." He looked at Katie as if he wanted to say something else but decided against it.

Katie had to admit that Dr. Dean was one of the most well-adjusted medical examiners and was normally in a good mood whenever she had worked with him. There were some difficult and unusual cases but Dr. Dean was always patient when explaining details of the autopsies to the detectives, even with his heavy workload and lack of a full staff.

"Dr. Dean, we received your message that you had some time," she said.

"We won't take up much of it," said McGaven.

"Don't give it another thought. There's always time for homicide cases."

Dr. Dean directed the detectives down the hallway and into a small examination room. It was unusual; they were generally invited into the main exam room where there was plenty of room to move around. Katie was curious, but was more interested in the findings from the first two victims.

They entered the small room where two autopsy tables stood side by side. The quarters were cramped, forcing Katie and McGaven to stay closer to the bodies than they wanted. The first two victims weren't covered but lying waiting for examination. Katie couldn't help but notice that their left pinky fingers were missing. She already knew, but seeing it firsthand made her realize that the killer was definitely sending a strong message—it might be his way of affirming his fantasy but Katie knew that it meant so much more.

"Okay," began Dr. Dean as he picked up two file folders. "First victim, Gina Hartfield, twenty-seven, relatively good health, no substances in her system either legal or illegal, except a prescription for a heart condition that most likely occurred when she was a teen."

"Was she sexually assaulted?" said Katie.

"No indication."

"I read your report but I like to hear it from you. Cause of death?"

"Asphyxiation. Manner of death, homicide."

"Manually, or with some type of rope or material?" said Katie.

"It appears that it was manually. You can see where the fingers pressed inward against the trachea."

Katie moved closer to Gina and examined the woman's face. Her hair was long and appeared to be clean. Her skin, now bluish, was perfect, almost flawless, but her neck showed the signs that she had been manually strangled. There were dark bruised areas where hands and fingers had squeezed the throat. "Was she bathed?"

"There's some indication that she had been washed, but John will have the tests back and be able to answer your question with more accuracy."

Katie looked at the left hand with the missing digit.

"It was removed post-mortem," said the examiner as if he knew what she was going to ask next.

"It's not a clean cut."

"No, it looks more like it was removed with a regular kitchen knife and not something more precise—like a scalpel or saw."

"So it would be difficult to tell what type of implement was used," said McGaven.

The medical examiner shook his head. "It's like a needle in a haystack, I'm afraid. If you find a particular knife, then we can have something to compare it to the wound."

Katie felt her enthusiasm begin to fade. She thought about the clock ticking down and the potential of finding two victims dumped at one crime scene. She felt her chest tighten but kept her focus on the bodies in front of her. She moved to the next table, where another young woman lay. She realized that the second victim resembled the first—not in a twin sense but they looked as if they could be related, like a cousin.

Was the killer targeting specific-looking women?

"Victim two, Jenna Day, thirty-one, good health, just had some dental work done so there were some mild painkillers in her system," said Dr. Dean as he read the notes in the file. "Her injuries, strangulation, and pinky removal almost identical to the first victim. Also no signs of sexual assault."

Katie listened as her mind collected everything she had heard into a list. She knew that the real question everyone wanted to ask was right in front of them.

The room was quiet, extra cool, making Katie shiver slightly. "What about the eyes?" The eyes of the victims were now a dark abyss. It was a stark reminder that the killer had an agenda and would do anything to keep it until they could stop him.

"Interesting," said Dr. Dean.

Katie and McGaven looked at him. He had never said that before.

"What do you mean?" said Katie.

Moving to Gina, he indicated with his index finger. "See here," he said.

Katie and McGaven leaned forward.

"There are no gouging marks or pressure points to show that the killer had any difficulty removing the eyeball. There are careful cuts of the sensory fibers, and the ligaments holding the eye in place."

Katie paused. "So the killer had trouble removing the pinky but used skill to remove the eyeball?"

"That about sums it up."

Katie looked at McGaven, who was still studying the bodies.

"I don't want to take up more of your time, Dr. Dean, but if we have any questions..."

"Of course, Detective Scott. I look forward to it. And I know you're going to catch the killer." The doctor smiled at both detectives. "I have an unusually heavy workload." He gave a partial wave and left the room.

It was one of the shortest visits to the medical examiner's office that the detectives had ever had, but it spoke volumes with regard to the victims' injuries and what appeared to be the link between the two homicides.

After Katie and McGaven left the morgue, they walked back to the car in silence, which was another first after viewing bodies.

McGaven stopped Katie before she got into the car. "What do you think?" he said.

"I know it's not one hundred percent proven yet, but there's a definite link with the strangulation, the staging of the bodies, and the missing eyes and pinkies. We will know for sure when we hear back on the third victim, Brianna Garcia."

"I agree."

"We have to stop him," she said.

"We need to study those transcripts from Holden's trial and crime scenes," he said. "Denise just emailed us the information. Fun reading tonight."

"Looking forward to it," said Katie. It was going to be something that kept her mind occupied. "After talking to John tomorrow, we have to start a more comprehensive list of people to talk to, besides family, in order to find some connection and a victimology timeline."

"It's going to be a long day tomorrow. Go home and get some rest."

"I will," she said. "But there's one person we need to talk to right away."

"Who?"

"Simon Holden."

"You sure?"

"Yes. We need to set up a visit with him and the sheriff needs to know."

"I'm on it."

SEVEN

Wednesday 2105 hours

Katie drove home with purpose. She always felt the most useful when she was working a cold case or a current homicide. The evidence coming to light and the urgency involved made her feel more alive and needed. The challenge of her work gave her life meaning, to solve cold cases, protect the public, and put dangerous people behind bars.

Her cell phone rang. She hit her hands-free function, not looking at the ID and assuming it was McGaven with more thoughts about the case.

"Scott."

"Scotty, it's Nick."

Katie's train of thought came to a screeching halt. There was an awkward momentary silence.

Chad.

"Did you find out anything?" she said, trying to keep her voice steady.

"A few things, but I think it's best we meet. I went by your house and saw you weren't home, but there was a patrol car just down the street. Are you still working a case?"

"Just left the office."

"Can you meet me at Cork and Barrel?"

Katie took a moment to think as she glanced at the clock. It was about nine. Her uncle had sent a text earlier that he had spent some time with Cisco and she didn't need to worry. It was usual for him to do that when there was an intense homicide case taking long hours. "I can be there in fifteen minutes."

"See you then." He ended the call.

Katie's heart skipped a beat and her hands slightly trembled. Nick sounded serious but he was difficult to read at times. It could be just an update and there was nothing to find—or it could be something he found out that could be the break in the case she needed.

Katie increased her speed as fast as she dared and made it to the bar in less than ten minutes. As she stepped from her Jeep, she quickly scanned the parking lot and noted that there were about a dozen cars parked.

She took a deep breath, let her hair out of the ponytail, and walked to the entrance. She didn't want to look too much like a cop so she opted for more of a casual appearance. A couple burst through the door and the guy managed to get a kiss from his companion before they went to their car. The display struck Katie and reminded her of Chad. It both amazed and saddened her that small things could conjure up memories of him.

Pushing on, Katie opened the door and stepped inside. It was dimly lit. There were three people at the bar and the rest were at various tables. The noise was at a low to medium level of conversation. The jukebox was playing an old song from Roy Orbison about losing a loved one.

The tall good-looking bartender was laughing with one of the patrons and noticed her enter. His eyes followed her as she walked across the room. She didn't know if he stared because she was a woman walking into the bar or if she gave off the impression that she was a cop. Either way, it didn't matter.

Katie quickly found Nick sitting at a corner table drinking a bottle of beer with his back against the wall patiently watching her approach. She had known where he would be waiting, in the same position as so many other times she had a drink or meal with him. He was always hyperaware of what was going on in a public place and knew what each person was doing at any given time. That was the curse of having been a military police officer.

She moved to the table and couldn't help but slightly smile at the Army sergeant waiting for her, not saying anything yet. His dark eyes, shaved head, and slight beard stubble were unmistakable. It gave him a mysterious charisma. He kept a stoic expression but his expressive eyes gave away that there was so much more to him. He had a mix of sorrow and concern for her.

Katie pulled up a chair and sat down.

"You made it here in ten minutes instead of fifteen," he said.

"What can I say? I didn't take into consideration that there wasn't as much traffic at this hour."

Nick made eye contact with the waitress, indicating to bring another beer. He then leaned forward and lightly took Katie's arm, squeezing it gently before he let go. "If I didn't know you better, I'd say you look like a detective with the usual business going on and not someone whose heart was breaking."

Katie sighed. She wasn't surprised that Nick could read her well. "I'm keeping it together," she said. She was focused on wanting to know what he had found out, but afraid of what she might discover.

The waitress set a bottle of imported beer along with a fresh frosty glass on the table.

"Thank you," said Katie to the server. She opted to drink from the bottle instead of pouring the beer into a glass. The chilled bottle felt good in her hand, helping her steady her nervousness. The cold beverage calmed her and was refreshing.

Nick watched her closely as if gauging how he was going to tell her what he had learned.

"Okay, I don't like tense silence. What have you found out?" she said, keeping his eye contact. Her breath became shallow, almost stopping completely as she waited, gripping the beer bottle a little bit tighter.

Nick reached for his iPad and pulled it from a leather cover. "I was able to get store footage."

"Footage?" she said.

"I spoke with Chad's co-workers at the firehouse and found out from Derek that he had remembered an appointment Chad had with someone at Dayton Electronics." He accessed photos for Katie to see.

"Dayton Electronics?" She looked at the pictures of the business building and parking lot. She didn't recall Chad mentioning anything to her about it, but that wasn't unusual. Details of his investigations weren't usually a topic of conversations.

"Apparently, someone called him two days before your getaway to tell him they had information regarding one of his arson investigations. The Walton house located on the east side of Pine Valley. It burned down under suspicious circumstances over a month ago."

"Who wanted to talk to him?"

"That's where things get strange. I went there to try to find out who it was, but no one had a clue what I was talking about. The employees and manager were nice and seemed helpful, but something wasn't right."

Katie listened carefully, trusting Nick's instincts. If he said something wasn't right, it probably wasn't. "They still haven't dumped Chad's cell phone to see who he spoke with the last couple of days before the cabin. I'll call in the morning and see if they can get an order from a judge." She took a long drink of the beer in hopes it would somehow dull the pain she felt.

"With their help at the store, I was able to download this security video of Chad entering and exiting the business. But no one really remembered him."

Katie watched the video. Chad exited his SUV and walked to the entrance of the building. Before he entered, something must've caught his attention because he looked to his left and paused. She watched him, his walk, his demeanor, etched in her mind. Seeing him after more than a month made her heart ache.

"Okay, now watch him leave."

Katie almost couldn't bear to watch him again, but couldn't tear her eyes away from the video. As Chad left the business, almost twenty minutes later, he stopped again, looking toward the same area as he did when entering. It seemed strange to her that no one remembered him. Within a moment, he walked back to his vehicle, got inside, and drove out of the parking lot.

"See how he kept looking at this area?" said Nick pointing to the section of the parking lot. "Now, check out the full frame of the footage." He moved to another angle of the video. It clearly showed a dark truck in both frames.

"Is that the same truck?" said Katie.

"I think so. But there's no identifying features, no license plate visible, and you can't identify who's inside. Take a look at this closer." Nick enlarged the areas when Chad was looking in that direction.

Katie leaned closer and watched the footage several times. "There was definitely someone in the truck—slight movement—but it's unclear if it was a man or woman. I think Chad could see them though. Maybe he thought he had seen the person or truck before?" The new information intrigued her, but at the same time she became frightened for a variety of reasons. "What do you think?"

"After seeing this, I made a decision."

"What do you mean?" she said, feeling a slight buzz from the beer because she hadn't eaten in a while. Her nerves at least had leveled off and she began to relax.

"Well, I know there's an intense missing person's investigation from the Pine Valley Sheriff's Department, but this footage took place in Sacramento. I'm sure they have access to it."

"And?"

"So I decided to reach out to Sacramento PD."

It gave Katie pause due to the fact that she had started her police career as a patrol officer for Sacramento Police Department before she enlisted in the Army. Memories of being on patrol came rushing back. It seemed such a long time ago, but it wasn't erased from her memory. She waited to hear what Nick had to say.

"I tried a couple of times to call the detective division, but no one returned my call. Finally, a Detective Daniels called me back. He said that he had reached out to a Detective Ames at Pine Valley Sheriff's Department to find out more information and to check on who I was."

"Wait. Evan Daniels?" she said.

"Yeah. He said that he knew you." Nick watched Katie's reaction, which seemed mixed with both surprise and uncertainty. "You know him?"

"Yes."

"And? Did you work with him at SPD?"

"Well, yes and no."

"What does that mean?"

More emotions came flooding back. She hadn't thought about Evan Daniels since the last time she saw him. "Yes, he was a patrol sergeant when I worked at SPD, but he was also a K9 trainer."

"Okay." His eyes searched her face for some type of answer.

"He took a leave of absence from the police department to be a military working dog trainer as a contractor. It was a six-month deployment. I'm not sure of all the details as to why and how, but he left for that tour shortly before I went into the Army."

Nick listened intently. "So what's the connection? He was a military contractor and you were in the Army."

"Right. But he trained the dogs for all military branches during his assignment."

Nick leaned back. "I remember you went to a training facility for two weeks during your seventeen-week course with Cisco."

Katie finished her beer. She nodded slowly, trying to decide which one of those memories she should disclose to Nick. That period in the Army had been a stressful time, when she'd been trying to get her life straight. Chad hadn't been in her life for a while and she'd thought he was gone forever and moved on. They had parted ways and Katie hadn't thought that Chad would ever return to Pine Valley.

"I'm getting the feeling that there's a story here," he said, not hiding his slight amusement. "Did you spend time with him?"

She couldn't divert the truth even though she was a bit embarrassed. "Yes."

"Did you train with him?"

"Yes." Katie felt like she was being interrogated, but she wasn't prepared to share personal details—at least at this point.

"Okay, that's why Detective Daniels seemed a bit extra interested in what you are doing now."

"Meaning?"

"Well, interest and attraction among men and women isn't completely lost on me, you know." He smiled.

"I won't deny we had an attraction and we spent time together, but..."

"But what? That's your business." He downed the rest of his beer. "If you need or want to talk about it—you know you can trust me. Otherwise, it's none of my business."

It was clear that Nick was trying to make Katie feel comfortable and make light of the relationship. "I appreciate that." She changed the subject back to Chad. "What did he say?"

"He viewed the video. And we talked about Chad's days before his disappearance. Since he was in Sacramento, Detective Daniels said he was looking into it and the other locations that Chad was supposed to have visited leading up to..." Nick didn't finish the sentence.

It sounded encouraging to Katie and it was something new added to the case. "Okay... we're building the days before Chad's disappearance. It was more than I had, but I was so obsessed and focused with the cabin that I didn't pursue his whereabouts prior to the cabin." She could barely get the words out. Everything about the case still, even after more than a month, felt surreal to her. "Can you forward the surveillance footage to John? Maybe he can enhance it or find more clues?"

Leaning forward, Nick took Katie's hand again. "Of course. We're going to locate more evidence in finding out where Chad is. Daniels said he will keep me in the loop and he's sending everything we've found so far to Detective Ames. I will help you as long as you need it."

Katie squeezed his hand with both of hers. "I don't know how to thank you." She tried to keep her voice from cracking under the emotional strain.

"Scotty, there's no need to thank me. I've got time. Actually, I've been thinking about getting a PI license to keep me busy since my discharge." He quickly glanced around the room, still keeping a mental inventory of the people and actions in the bar. "We've been through a lot and have seen hell—literally—together. I've always got your back."

After Katie got home, she felt guilty for thinking about the time she had spent with Evan. It felt as if she had been cheating on

Chad, but the truth was that it was during a time when she had been single and trying to figure out her life and what she wanted to do. So much had happened since her two tours and that time, it seemed like it was from another lifetime. Now it was coming back into her life.

She took some time to unwind, cleaning up dishes, putting some laundry away, and playing with Cisco before getting ready for bed. Walking outside for a moment, she felt the cool air brush past her face. Cisco jumped up and down, wanting to play. He always seemed to have a last burst of energy before bedtime and his wolf eyes urged her to throw the ball. She chucked it several times, much to his joy. Making sure that she took in slow, even breaths, she felt her muscles relax before going back inside.

Katie skimmed through some of the Holden transcripts and looked at photos of the crime scenes again. She studied the locations of the scenes and the placement of the bodies. She looked at the current scenes to see if it was possible that it was the work of a copycat killer—or even a killer who was being coached. She contemplated these ideas for a bit before she became weary and ready for bed.

Her mind wouldn't let her thoughts of Evan stray from her awareness, giving her a momentary pause from worrying about Chad.

She remembered everything about the intense military working dog training. She also remembered every detail about Evan. And now he was part of the missing person's investigation. She wasn't sure what she thought about that new update or how it would, or wouldn't, affect the case.

Before she drifted off to sleep, her thoughts fell back to one of the best two weeks she had spent during her time in the Army.

.   .   .

Katie had just completed the arduous training with numerous military working dogs after a long week. The earsplitting sound of nearly one hundred dogs barking at the kennel was forever ingrained in her mind. Exhausted and nursing sore muscles, she was looking forward to a break and some sleep. She had been pushed to the limit, learning how to read the dog's body language, how to mark their correct behavior responding to training with cues, while trying to elevate her own skills and excel as a military dog handler. It was a lot to handle. She had Evan Daniels to thank for it. He pushed her hard, made her accountable when she was struggling, exhausted, and wanted to make excuses, but he always made sure she was also given credit for when she began to improve and then excelled.

One particular time she remembered vividly. It was an unusually long day of training dogs in obedience and bomb search. The dogs were all going to various military branches for their assignments.

The day was extra hot and miserable, but the fast pace and the diversity of dogs—German shepherd, Belgian Malinois, and some Labradors—kept Katie focused and challenged.

As Katie moved through the training area, she was fully aware of Evan's directions. "Read his behavior" and "Don't stop." And "Allow the dog to search and find it without your guidance." His words resonated through her mind even when he remained silent, watching her closely.

The intense heat of the day accompanied by the moderate breeze made Katie slow her pace. From the time she rose in the morning to the time she went to bed, the temperature remained almost the same. It caused her body to conserve energy, making it difficult at times to push through her training.

Katie had been working with a beautiful sable German shepherd, named Nitro. She sent him into a location where he was to find explosives. It was an area filled with obstacles and pieces of equipment, both low on the ground and standing tall. There were *plenty of diversions. She followed the dog as he changed his demeanor, honing his scent, tail downward, stiffening his body, ears forward and alert, and then funneling the explosive odor through his nose to lead him to the exact location of the training aid. Ultimately, tapping his nose in the area and giving his sit alert, staring diligently at the location waiting for Katie to mark his behavior and reward him with his toy.*

At the end of working, all she wanted to do was sleep. The next day she had a day off and looked forward to it. Instead, Evan had waited until Katie was alone and casually approached her. He asked her if she would like to go have a drink. She did. It was clear that the two of them had an attraction for one another, but they had always made sure everything had been professional— even at Sacramento PD. That included the short period of time when he was her patrol sergeant. It had never seemed like a good time before—until that particular day after dog training. Katie had enjoyed the company as they laughed and talked about their experiences at Sacramento PD.

After a few drinks, Katie and Evan went for a walk and continued to unwind. The sun had already set, but the sky was still an intense orange red. It was still extremely warm, but it made Katie relax and begin to feel more comfortable. She didn't want the day to end. She looked at Evan and they made eye contact for several seconds. That was when he slowly closed the gap between them, pulled her close, and gently kissed her lips.

EIGHT

After a mostly restless night, Katie arrived at the Pine Valley Sheriff's Department. She exited her Jeep and headed to the building with Simon Holden the serial killer on her mind. Her thoughts were also filled with so many emotions that she felt like she was on a rogue teeter-totter, but she knew she had to stay focused on the cases.

Once inside the forensic division, Katie hurried to their cold-case office to leave her belongings, then followed the voices she could hear to the main examination room. McGaven was already there along with John and Eva.

"Right on time," said her partner.

"Then why do you always beat me here?" she said.

"It's a gift."

A few more pleasantries were exchanged before the crew got to work.

"We're still running tests from victim three, Brianna Garcia, but I have some information for you both from Gina Hartfield and Jenna Day," said John.

Katie watched John move to another computer with a large screen. Eva stayed quiet, working on another computer.

McGaven moved closer to his partner, eagerly watching the monitor in front of John.

"Unfortunately, the bodies themselves didn't have any type of evidence. They both had been washed clean. However, we did detect traces of the soap used that hadn't been completely scrubbed and washed away. It was a combination of borax, baking soda, and a bar soap consisting of glycerin, coconut oil, and lye."

"That sounds more like laundry soap," said Katie.

"Very astute. That's exactly what it is."

"Would it be homemade or store bought?" said McGaven.

"I've run a database search for the basic soaps and laundry detergents that are common in most stores. I couldn't find the exact combination, but... most commercial soaps seemed to have the same types of ingredients but not exactly like this one. I can't swear in court for one hundred percent sure, more like eighty percent, but this combination seems to be homemade."

"So our killer makes homemade soaps and uses it on his victims? Seems extravagant," she said.

"Maybe that's what the killer uses on himself?" said McGaven. "Like he is allergic to chemicals or keeps a more natural approach to his life."

"Good point," she said. "It gives us something personal about him."

"There were no substances found in their systems, except Gina Hartfield for the medication apixaban, brand name Eliquis."

"What's that for?" she said.

"It's a blood thinner that's commonly used for anything related to the heart in which doctors want to prevent any type of clotting."

"To prevent stroke or heart attack?" said McGaven.

"Generally, yes. According to Gina's records, she had her heart condition from a very young age and obviously she was prescribed this medication for it."

John forwarded to two photographs, side by side, of both women's necks with the strangulation impressions. The images were magnified. "I wanted to show you this."

Katie leaned in and studied the images. They both looked the same, except one of them was more pronounced than the other. "They look almost identical."

John nodded. "I had to double-check to make sure I had the correct photos. There's little doubt that these strangulation marks were made by the same person. They're almost exactly the same."

Katie stepped back to think about what it meant for the killer to be able to replicate the same actions to kill each woman. It showed an organized mind but being able to duplicate the action, in the same places, with the same pressure, in the same way was statistically impossible. The killer was also very strong. No two things ever happen in the *exact* same way, but this was uncanny.

"What are you thinking?" said McGaven as he watched his partner process the evidence in her mind.

"It's just that this seems extraordinary—highly skilled." Turning to face her partner, she said, "I didn't notice this same accuracy in the strangulations on Simon Holden's victims, did you?"

McGaven shook his head. "No, I didn't."

"So we have a killer who's mimicking Holden's MO but they have their own signatures?"

"Well, if you think the strangulation is almost identical, you're going to like the amputated pinky and eye removal," said John. He clicked on one of the files. Immediately two photos appeared, again side by side, showing the women's missing pinky finger.

"What the...?" said Katie. She studied the magnified images, which showed the skin tearing and removal of the bone and digit. The tears and flaps of skin looked eerily similar. "John, how is this possible? There are so many variables. The position the killer took when applying the cutting device, when he removed the finger, pressure, technique... How can they look so similar?"

"I just show you the evidence and facts. How and why is up to you guys," said John.

Katie glanced around the room, trying to grasp what all this meant to the victims and the killer, and Holden. It was something that she had never encountered before. Similar victims. Similar manner and cause of death. But not like this. She was missing something about these cases.

"Now the eyes," continued John. "There's nothing we can contribute here, but they were meticulously severed and cut with something very sharp—most likely a scalpel."

"And both were extracted the same way?" she said.

"Yep."

"Is there any forensic evidence?"

"Once we get something to compare—like the cutting devices."

"What about the burlap?"

"We're still searching. But I'm afraid it's not any type of specialty. You can purchase bulk burlap at a wide range of places. We've combed over the natural material looking for anything that might connect the killer to the victims, but nothing so far."

Katie sighed. She then realized that the killer seemed to favor natural types of items like the soap and the burlap. It was definitely an aspect that would be added to the profile.

"I've saved the best for last," said John.

"I knew it," said McGaven.

"You know at the crime scenes we found these articles

about the previous cases you two have investigated?" said John. He rose from his chair and went to a large backlit table. Carefully opened and unrolled were the two articles.

"Anything unusual about them?" said Katie.

"Not at first, but when we put them under different light sources, we got something."

Katie's interest was definitely piqued. She quickly read the headlines, which had to do with their last two cases.

John changed the light source and showed there was something on one of the corners.

Katie and McGaven leaned in closer.

"Is that... a fingerprint?" she said.

"Not a fingerprint but a partial palm print. It's definitely in rough shape, but it's still an identifying print that we can compare when you get a suspect."

"I see."

"I'm sorry that I couldn't be of more help, but we're still running some tests and I'll update you when we get anything new," said John. He looked at Katie. It was clear by his tense expression he was also concerned about her.

"Actually, there's a lot of behavioral evidence here that I will be adding to the profile." Katie tried to sound optimistic. She was more than ready to question some friends and family about the victims.

"Got something!" said Eva. She had been working diligently on the other side of the room. Sitting on a stool, she had been focused on various images on the screen in front of her.

John, along with a curious Katie and McGaven, moved closer to Eva's screen.

"I finally got you," she said with intensity, talking to the screen.

"What?" said Katie.

"Eva has been working with this new identification software that IT Electronic gave us to try out and review," said John. "I thought it would be perfect to have a go at cleaning up the security footage of Chad."

As soon as he said Chad, it was like an electrical shock ran through Katie's body. She had been able to compartmentalize her serial cases and Chad. And just for a short period of time, her mind hadn't been thinking of him in an endless loop.

"Wow, look at that," said McGaven.

Katie stared at the screen where it showed the profile of a man in his forties to fifties. It was clear that he was watching Chad. He had a digital camera in his hand and appeared to have been taking photos. The unidentified man had slightly wavy hair, an aquiline nose, beard stubble, and was wearing a dark button-up shirt.

"I know it's not a perfect image, but it's still something to go on," said Eva. She finally looked at John and the detectives. "I'm still trying to clear up the type of truck, but it's been frustrating. I'm going to run what we have for facial identification and see if anything pops."

"Thank you, Eva," said Katie. She finally felt like they were making progress on what happened to Chad and why, but she needed to get a break in the serial cases. It was difficult to concentrate with the new lead. Katie wanted to call Detective Ames immediately and push Chad's case.

NINE

Katie parked in front of the building for Sampson & Crawford Real Estate Developers. She thought the building was rather run-down for a company that developed real estate for sale and investment. There were few modern touches or identifying aspects—it looked almost like a warehouse than a business. Paint was peeling on the sides, two of the windows were cracked, and there was no landscaping, making it seem that it had been long abandoned.

McGaven craned his neck checking the place out. "The building is kind of old and shabby, don't you think?"

"I was thinking the same thing," she said looking at her notes. "It's the correct address and there's the sign." The sign, brightly painted in teal and brown, appeared to be fairly new and in contrast made the building look even more outdated.

"What do you think?" he said.

"Well, we can sit here and discuss it... or we can go inside and check it out," she said and smiled.

"Ah yes," he said. "Katie's back with her sarcasm still intact."

Katie couldn't help but chuckle. She had missed McGaven's sense of humor.

The detectives exited the car and took a moment to scan the area.

Katie felt exposed for some reason as she searched for video cameras, but there weren't any visible. It still didn't mean that they weren't being watched—security videos could be disguised as something else. She looked at the corners of the building and under the eaves—nothing stood out except for the fact that termites had eaten areas of the wood, making ragged holes.

Before entering the building, Katie and Gav decided to walk around the back because there were no cars parked out front. The paving was cracked, with various potholes marring the sloping driveway. Once around the building, there was a parking lot with several vehicles.

"I guess employees have to park in the back," she said as she walked past the cars and looked down in a large ditch. The property had a gradual grade and the years of deterioration and weather had created the deep gully.

Katie thought about how Gina Hartfield had driven to work every day and parked here. She remembered how her body had looked wrapped in burlap, her eyes missing, and her carefully combed hair left displayed for anyone to see. She would never know that she'd become a crime statistic or the victim of a serial killer based on how she looked. A deep sense of loss flowed through Katie like a wave of despair. She pushed past her feelings knowing that her own grief was forcing these emotions to envelop her mind and body.

"What's up?" said McGaven interrupting her thought process.

"I'm not sure." Katie scanned the ditch as she kept her breathing normal. She noticed that it was the catch-all for blowing outdoor debris, garbage, and a myriad of other items. She saw what appeared to be the remains of a dead animal—most likely a squirrel, another rodent, or even a feral cat. There was also what appeared to be some material in navy blue and beige fuzzy yarn, most likely a scarf of some kind, which was probably something that had blown there from the last storm.

McGaven stood next to his partner looking down. He too seemed curious about what the ravine had caught in its trap. "Ready?"

"Yep. Let's go see what they can tell us about Gina Hartfield."

The detectives retraced their steps to the main entrance at the front of the building.

Katie pulled open the glass door and they entered through a long tiled hallway. Their footsteps echoed down the walls. The narrow passageway led to an opening where there was a receptionist desk. A middle-aged woman with short dark hair was typing on a computer keyboard and didn't seem to notice or hear the detectives arrive. Katie and McGaven stood at the desk for a moment.

"Excuse me," said Katie. "Detectives Scott and McGaven to see Jeff Braxton."

The woman looked up, took her glasses off, and studied the detectives for a moment. It was usual for most to eye their badges and guns before responding. "Of course," she said. "I'll go get him." She then rose and disappeared around the corner.

Katie could hear soft voices in the building, but nothing that indicated if they were discussing their visit or if it was just work talk.

The receptionist returned and said, "You can meet him in the conference room. It's just around the corner and the first door on the left." She went back to her desk.

Katie looked at McGaven with a questioning look. He seemed to mirror her expression as he followed her.

The work areas were open-plan. Several tables were lined up in the middle of the large room where people could easily meet. It seemed like an interesting setup for a real estate development company. It would be better suited to a more creative environment than a financial one. There were several employees busily working at their desks who didn't pay the detectives any attention.

Katie saw professional photographs along the wall—some were standard pictures of buildings while others were taken from airplanes or drones with aerial views. At the end of the display were two large doors. She slowly pushed one open.

A heavyset man sat at the end of a long conference table. He had a large stack of files he was sorting through. His eyeglasses were perched on his head, his tie was loosened, and a large steaming cup of coffee sat next to him. It appeared that he was in for a long day of paperwork.

"Mr. Braxton?" said Katie.

The detectives stood at the opposite end of the conference table patiently waiting.

The manager looked up and stared at Katie. He immediately stood up. "Detectives," he said. "I've never met a police detective before." His tone clearly sounded as if he was impressed by their presence.

"Thank you for taking time to see us this morning," said McGaven.

Braxton's expression turned gloomy as his voice lowered. "I still can't believe that Gina is gone."

Katie studied the manager. His reaction seemed genuine. She had witnessed many people's grief on hearing of someone who had died or been murdered, learning over the years that the body language and grief varied from person to person. "We're following up with people Gina knew, wanting to get a sense of what kind of person she was and what she did during the week before her death."

"I see," he said, taking a deep breath. "Gina was such a breath of fresh air. Always upbeat and happy. You can ask anyone here, she would make herself available to help when needed."

"She sounds like she was a great person," she said.

"She was..." Braxton's voice trailed off as if he remembered something about her.

"Mr. Braxton, can you remember or recall anything she might have said about someone bothering her—or something new she was planning? Anything out of the ordinary?" Katie watched the manager, trying to get a sense of his relationship to her—friend, boss, or someone wanting more?

Shaking his head, he said, "No. Everything seemed like it always was. She never let me know about anything out of the ordinary. You might want to ask Cecelia, the one with short blonde hair, before you leave. I know they were close."

"Thank you. We will."

"How long had she worked here as an administrative assistant?" said McGaven.

"Three years. In fact, I was preparing my annual employee reviews. She was due for a raise. But now..."

"We know that she was single. Did you ever see anyone visiting her—a boyfriend or anyone?"

"No. I don't recall her having anyone visit her here at the office."

"Did she have any other problems? Like money or family issues that you knew of or heard about?" she said.

"No. She was a great employee."

"Did you notice anything changing in her work performance?"

"I don't think so," he said slowly.

"Did anyone ever visit her?" she asked again.

"I'm not sure. Like I say, you would have to ask one of her co-workers."

Katie set one of her business cards on the table. "Thank you, Mr. Braxton. If you think of anything or remember something, please reach out to us."

"Yes, of course," he said. "Detectives?"

Katie and McGaven turned to face the manager.

"Please catch the person that did this," he said. His eyes looked glassy as if he would cry. "Please catch them," he repeated.

"We're doing everything we can and following every lead," said McGaven.

Katie exited the conference room. As she turned to the left to find Gina's co-worker Cecelia, she saw an area near the coffee station that had photographs of Gina Hartfield along with flowers and cards decorating the zone with respect and remembrance. Katie walked up to the photos, studying them. She was almost always smiling her big beautiful smile and her eyes seemed to sparkle. Her long dark hair was most often pulled back in a ponytail. Leaning closer, Katie studied the photographs, trying to decipher who the other people were. Most of the images were just of Gina with various backgrounds —ski slopes, gym, beaches, and wooded areas.

Katie took out her cell phone and quickly snapped a couple of shots of the photo wall. She wanted to have it as reference. She turned to see McGaven talking with an attractive blonde woman, who was obviously Cecelia. Her face was drawn and sorrowful and she struggled to get words out. Her hands moved erratically as she spoke. It was clear that this co-worker was devastated and scared by Gina's death.

Katie decided to leave McGaven interviewing Cecelia and went to leave the office building, glancing back once more. The young woman hung her head, shoulders forward, as she recounted something McGaven had asked her. She gestured to the photo of her friend and wiped her tears. It was difficult to watch the friends and loved ones of murder victims, so Katie left and went outside.

She wanted to have another look around. Something was tugging at her intuition. As she stepped outside, the cool air blew through her jacket as if telling her that she needed to see something. Following the weather-beaten drive around to the back of the building, she stood once again at the ravine, not exactly knowing why. She took a few photos on her cell phone, documenting the area. Maybe it would jog her memory at a later time.

As Katie headed back, she slowed her pace, studying the back of the building. There was a back entrance that didn't have any identifying signs or numbers. She assumed that the employees entered and exited from that location.

Nothing seemed ominous, but Katie wondered if someone had been watching Gina. It was certainly a possibility, and would make sense, since the victims were taken without anyone seeing or hearing the incident. The killer could easily have been in one of the many parked cars or have taken up a location in the wooded area on either side of the parking lot. Several scenarios filed through her mind as she tried to figure out how the killer chose Gina as his first victim. With the planning and staging of the crime scenes, it was obvious that the killer had watched his victims, learning their schedules, deciding where to strike, and waiting for the right moment.

Katie walked back to where she had parked just as McGaven exited the building. He had his small notebook in hand, jotting down what he had learned.

"Anything?" she said.

"Nothing that stands out, but Cecelia did say that Gina had met someone at the gym."

"Did she say anything more? Like his name or what he looks like?"

"No. She said Gina didn't want to jinx it because she had

just met the guy," he said. "Unfortunately, she's new to the area and doesn't have any family."

Katie sighed. "Not much to go on."

McGaven read his notes. "She did say it was the All Fitness Gym on Third Street."

"It's a start." Katie opened the car door still thinking about the photographs and the ravine. "Let's go check it out."

TEN

Katie pulled the unmarked police sedan into an available parking space in front of the All Fitness Gym. It was an updated building, freshly painted with splashy colors of yellow, pink, and dark blue. It was an absolute contrast in appearance from the real estate developer's site.

The detectives watched men and women enter and exit the facility. There were large picture windows across the front and you could view patrons on various workout machines through the glass.

"Let's go and see what they have to say," said Katie.

The detectives left their vehicle and entered the building. They were immediately greeted by upbeat music and the hum of the machines.

Several workout customers gave Katie and McGaven a look but were content to go back to their routines. Most people gave McGaven a look because of his height—he appeared to be someone to take notice of.

A perky blonde decked out in pink and white workout attire was at the front desk. "Hi, how are you today?" she said.

"Hi," said McGaven and flashed his sincere smile. "We're detectives McGaven and Scott from the sheriff's department. Can we speak with the manager?"

"Oh, detectives? How exciting. What shall I tell him is the reason for your visit?" she replied with an eager expression.

"We just have some routine questions about a case we're working on," he said.

"Oooh, a case. Is it a murder case?"

"Yes, but we really need to speak with the manager. Is he available?"

"Of course. I'll go let him know you're here." The receptionist gave McGaven another look and winked at him before she disappeared to another area of the gym.

Katie smiled. "Should Denise be jealous?"

"Funny. I can see your sense of humor is also coming back."

"Maybe you should think about joining a gym?"

"Not my kind of scene. I prefer free weights at the department and running outside."

"I agree," she said looking around. "But it is quite social here."

A tall dark-haired man, lean, muscular, accompanied by the receptionist walked toward the detectives. He smiled broadly as he approached.

"Detectives," the man said, shaking their hands. "I'm Willis Anderson, the manager, but my friends call me Wiley." He looked directly at Katie. "And I don't think I've ever seen such a pretty detective before."

McGaven stepped closer to him. "Is there a place we can talk?"

"Yes, of course. Please follow me."

Katie and McGaven followed the manager as they passed through various rooms, each with different machines, and classes going on. It was a bustling place for lunchtime and Katie wondered how many people had jobs to go back to.

Wiley opened a door at the far side of one of the cycling rooms, which led to several private offices down a long hallway.

The detectives followed him into a medium-size office with comfortable leather chairs. The walls were covered by amazing blown-up photographs of skydiving, skiing, and mountain climbing.

"Are these all you?" said McGaven studying each one.

"Yep. And loved every minute of it." He sat down behind the desk and gestured to the detectives. "Please, have a seat."

Katie made herself comfortable and kept her focus on Wiley Anderson, ignoring the distractions of the adrenalin-filled, high-action photos and the rows of hydration bottles filled with some type of protein drink. "Mr. Anderson, we are investigating a murder case and would appreciate it if you would not share any of the information that you may now learn."

Wiley's face took on a wide-eyed expression and he leaned forward, resting his elbows on the desk. "Of course. What can I do to help?"

Katie searched her cell phone photos and stopped on a picture of Gina Hartfield. "Do you recognize her?"

The manager looked at the photo for a moment. He shook his head. "I'm sorry I don't seem to recall her. You have to realize that we have eight hundred clients—I can't remember them all."

"Can you check your computer to see if Gina Hartfield was a member of this gym?" she said.

"Of course." Wiley opened his laptop and typed in her name. He waited a moment and read the results. "It seems that she had a special coupon for a free month to try out our facility."

"How long ago was that?" said McGaven.

"It was... three weeks ago. She still has another six days on her pass."

"I see. Is there anything else you might have about her visits? The times of day she was here. Classes she took. If she had a trainer?"

"It looks like she signed up for yoga and cycling in the evenings along with weight training. And... oh, she did meet with one of our trainers, Butch Turner."

"Is he here today?"

"Let me see, I haven't seen him but..." The manager keyed up the employee list. "Yes, he's scheduled to be here in about ten minutes for a client."

Katie thought about the gym and how many people passed in and out. It would be easy for someone to watch other patrons without being noticed. "Mr. Anderson?"

"Wiley," he said and smiled.

"Wiley. Could you search for two other names from your memberships?"

"Of course."

McGaven looked to his partner as if to say I'm on the same page.

"Jenna Day and Brianna Garcia."

Wiley pecked away at the computer. "Okay, yes. Jenna Day is a member and Brianna Garcia was a member, but hasn't paid her dues in four months." He looked at the detectives.

Katie felt quietly ecstatic that she had found a connection between the women—more than their appearances, that was. It was the first break in the case and their victimologies. At least a place to start.

Wiley pushed a key and the printer hummed. "I've printed everything out for you." He rose from his chair and grabbed the papers, handing them to Katie.

"Thank you," she said scanning the documents.

"Is there anything that you can recall about anyone having an issue with another patron?" said McGaven.

"What do you mean? Like a complaint or fight?"

"Anything that stands out in the past month or so."

Wiley thought a moment and shook his head. "The only thing I can think of... there was a patron who had some issues with their billing and credit card, but that was a couple of months ago."

Katie stood up. "Thank you, Wiley. This has been really helpful." She left a card on his desk.

"I hope it will point you in the right direction," he said shaking the detective's hands. "Please follow me and I'll introduce you to Butch Turner."

The entire gym had quieted down by now and there were less people using the equipment than when the detectives had first passed through the workout areas. On their way back Katie casually scanned the rooms, looking briefly at each patron, trying to ascertain if the killer had been there and wondering if they had been a member, a staff employee, or someone who had a free pass.

Butch Turner wasn't easy to miss. He was a stocky, muscle-bound man in his early forties. His black T-shirt appeared to be a couple of sizes too small, which accentuated his thick muscles. He had jet-black wavy hair that seemed to glisten in the light with hair gel. Bent over a bench press, he was helping a young man with the repetitions of weights.

"Excuse me," said Katie. "Mr. Turner?"

The trainer looked up. "Yes?"

"May we speak with you for a moment?"

"I'm in the middle of a session. Can it wait?"

"That's okay, Butch. I'll be fine for a few," said the patron.

Butch sighed like he was being inconvenienced. "Fine." He

glanced at the detectives' guns and badges before he walked out the front door and moved closer to the side parking lot. He then turned to Katie and McGaven. "What's up?"

Katie said, "We're Detectives Scott and McGaven from the sheriff's department."

"I already cracked that code," he said pointing at their badges. "I don't have long. Let's get to the point."

McGaven stepped in. "We're investigating the murder of Gina Hartfield."

The personal trainer's eyes grew wide with disbelief.

"And we're tracing where she had gone in the last week before she was killed," said Katie.

"Oh no, Gina? Nice girl. Really enthusiastic. I wish all my clients were as nice and hardworking. What do you want to know?" His tone had softened some and he wasn't as hostile.

"Can you tell us anything unusual that might have happened?" said McGaven.

"Unusual?"

"Like if anyone was bothering her or if she seemed to be acting out of her normal character at her sessions," said Katie.

"No, not at all. Like I said, I wish all my clients were like her."

"One more thing," she said. "Where were you on Monday and Tuesday evenings?"

He paused a moment. "Home," he said flatly.

"Did anyone see you? Did you leave for any reason?"

"No. I was home."

Katie watched his reaction carefully. The big man seemed to clench his fists often and he now seemed nervous about something, which could be related to the fact that he'd just found out one of his clients had been murdered. His eyes looked away from them often. "If you remember anything, please give us a call," she said handing him a card.

Taking the card, he said, "Yes, for sure. I hope you find out who killed her." He lowered his head and walked back inside the gym.

McGaven took a couple of steps toward the car and then turned. "What do you think?"

"I'm not sure. The manager and Butch seemed genuine, but I can't help but think that there's something either they're not telling us, or something we're not seeing."

McGaven smiled. "It's your curious mind. It makes everyone seem guilty of something."

"Well, aren't we all guilty of *something*?"

ELEVEN

Thursday 1410 hours

Katie finished her turkey sandwich still watching the apartment building of Bobby Cox—the boyfriend of Jenna Day whose body had been found at the vacated warehouse area. They had run down his ID and background. He had avoided their phone calls, and they had decided to wait outside his home for a while before knocking on his door. His actions appeared suspicious and the detectives wanted to find out if he had something to hide.

The photos of the crime scene were rooted deep in Katie's mind. The images of both Gina Hartfield and Jenna Day rolled in burlap, eyes gouged out, and throat crushed made for an endless loop of recollections for her. There were still so many questions that she needed to have answered. The feeling of being overwhelmed began to surface again.

McGaven was searching for any background information on Gina or Jenna. He scoured material and files, looking for anything that might help them or bring new information to light.

Katie watched the complex. She had memorized the boyfriend's face from his driver's license photo, so that if he walked out they would immediately recognize him.

"Think he's just sitting in his apartment?" said McGaven. He had already finished his sandwich and was gulping the last of his soda.

"Yep."

"He didn't answer his phone."

"Of course not, especially not if he had something to hide."

"It's not clear if he and Jenna had any problems, but the boyfriend is always a good place to start," he said, still digging for information. "You don't think that he could have killed three women to throw suspicion off his intended victim?"

"Haven't you been a cop long enough to know that we don't always know what people are capable of? It's possible, but not likely. Still, we need to make sure he's not a person of interest."

"You're right. I've seen things that I will never be able to unsee and never understand why someone would do that to another human being." He scanned through more pages. "It looks like Bobby Cox hasn't been in trouble. He doesn't have a gun registered. And he's currently laid off from Brighton's Tire Center. Does that spell trouble?"

"Depends. When was he laid off?"

"It looks like a month ago." He looked at further information. "And, he did work for the automotive manufacturing place at the old warehouse—only six weeks but still that could mean something since Jenna was found there."

"Well... it's about time to have a chat. Maybe he'll be able to shine a light on Jenna's last week."

"You know, both Gina's and Jenna's families didn't know anything about what they were doing or if they had any problems. Do you think this Bobby will be any different?"

As the detectives searched for family members, it became clear that the victims had another thing in common: they were all relatively new to the area and had similar lifestyles and little family nearby.

Katie opened the car door, tired of waiting. "Let's go ask him."

McGaven joined his partner as they moved to the building.

Katie slowed her pace, watching every area before they arrived. Something told her that they needed to be alert. They were looking for apartment number twelve, which was on the second floor.

They ascended the outside staircase until they reached the apartment. The windows were dirty and the front door had deep scuff grooves low down, as if someone had been kicking at it. There was no mat or anything else personal at the entrance.

Katie waited a moment and listened. No sound. But she had a hunch that Bobby was in there. She knocked. Taking a breath, she waited on the left side of the door as McGaven took his place on the right.

There was a sudden crash from inside.

Katie pounded on the door. "Bobby Cox! Open up! Sheriff's department!" She pulled her gun.

McGaven followed suit. "I'll take the front," he said.

Katie nodded and ran down the back staircase. Her heart was pumping hard as she skipped every other stair. The back staircase was narrower and steeper than the front. By the looks of it, people rarely used it.

There was another crash below that sounded like trash cans toppling over. Katie ran faster.

Just as she reached the bottom of the stairs, she saw a man getting to his feet after falling.

"Bobby Cox! Stop!" she yelled.

But the young blond man got his balance and bolted.

Katie was annoyed, hated having to chase guys down.

They were behind the apartment complex and it was narrow with overgrown shrubs poking at her legs as she ran. It was an area that didn't seem to get much sunlight, so there was the unmistakable moldy odor that seemed to permeate everything.

Bobby Cox was running as fast as he could until he tripped over a garden hose, instantly falling to the ground. He flailed his arms as he face-planted in the dirt.

Katie took the opportunity and jumped him. "Stay down. Put your hands behind your back."

"Why? I didn't do anything."

"Do it now!"

The man slowly put his hands behind as Katie swiftly hand-cuffed him. "What were you thinking?" she said, looking up at the window he apparently jumped from. "I'm surprised you didn't break your legs—or worse." She stood up and caught her breath.

McGaven met her. "Looks like you have everything under control." He looked down at Bobby and shook his head. "Why did you run?"

"I didn't know you were really cops," said the man straining to turn his head to look at them.

"Not very smart."

"I see that now."

"Do you know why we're here?" said Katie.

"It's about Jenna, right?" He squeezed his eyes shut. "Oh, Jenna. I'm so sorry," he said, obviously holding back tears.

McGaven bent down and helped Jenna's boyfriend up. "C'mon, you're going to take a little ride with us." He called in to dispatch for a patrol officer to transport Bobby to the department.

"For what?"

"Well, for obstructing and running from us. You're wanted for questioning in the murder of Jenna Day."

Bobby Cox hung his head as he was led out from behind the apartments to the street.

. . .

Katie stood in the middle of Bobby's living room. She couldn't believe that anyone lived in such a mess. It was more disorganized and cluttered than filthy and unclean, but everything seemed to be out of place.

"What do you think?" said McGaven at the doorway.

"I'm not sure, but this isn't the mind of an organized serial killer."

McGaven took a couple of steps inside the room, pulling on his plastic gloves.

Katie scanned the room. She realized that the probable reason everything was such a mess was because it seemed like Bobby had been looking for something. "It looks like someone, maybe Bobby, flipped this place."

"I agree."

"What was he looking for?" said Katie.

"Maybe it wasn't Bobby and that's why he took off on us the way he did." McGaven stood at the window leaning out where the boyfriend jumped from. "That's a jump I wouldn't have attempted."

"He must be desperate or scared of something to make that jump," she said.

Katie started at one side of the living room while McGaven began on the other, which meant they would end up meeting each other.

The couch was intact but the back cushions had been moved and weren't settled back to where they should have been. She pulled them forward and peered behind but there was nothing. Books and magazines were scattered on the floor. An ashtray had been flipped upside-down and the ashes were scattered leaving an unusual darkened squashed area on the beige carpet. It appeared that someone had stood there and then moved back and forth.

Katie scanned the room. There was something that was important to Bobby, or perhaps someone else, that had been in the apartment to warrant this type of search. Looking through tossed items, on bookshelves, behind furniture, inside drawers, she continued to look for something that raised some suspicion.

"Anything?" said McGaven.

"No," she said, disappointed.

Looking at his partner, he said, "You think that there's anything here related to Jenna or the murders?"

"At this point, I'm not sure of anything. But... I want to be thorough." She hesitated before she continued. "There's been something bothering me and I can't quite put my finger on it. There's something that doesn't quite add up."

"About Bobby Cox?"

"About the crime scenes."

"The staging?"

"That's part of it, but like I said before, it feels like someone has taken a page out of the serial killer handbook."

"That's curious," he said.

"I'm not explaining it correctly. Everything we have seen from the crime scenes and the bodies so far seemed to be what the killer is trying to make us see." Katie spied the hallway where there were two linen cupboards, doors slightly ajar. She couldn't see inside, so she walked over to them to look at them more closely.

"Interesting perspective." McGaven watched his partner walk to the hallway.

She opened the linen and extra storage closet. At first, she saw only towels and sheets. Pulling out the linens, she saw there were some things jammed in the back. Her hands reached against something scratchy. She stopped and peered in.

"What's up?" said McGaven, straining to see over her shoulder.

"I'm not sure but it looks like..." Katie pulled out a rolled-up piece of burlap. It wasn't exactly like that used to cover and roll up the bodies, but still, this piece had clearly been hidden.

"Is it?"

Katie pulled it out into the light. "It's not the same. It's lighter weight. Let's document and bag it for evidence. Maybe there's something that connects to the crime scene? But why would it be in Bobby Cox's linen closet? Maybe it's old or part of something else?"

"Still, he's got some serious questions to answer."

Katie and McGaven stood outside interview room three at the Pine Valley Sheriff's Department. Bobby Cox was held inside.

Katie paced back and forth with her notebook and an evidence bag that held the burlap. She contemplated the best way to approach Jenna's boyfriend. Go in hard? Be sympathetic and play to his sensitive side with Jenna? Or gauge how he responded to her questions and then go from there?

"You ready?" said McGaven. He gave her the look he always had before a suspect interrogation. His eyes were wide and he had a slight smirk. It was a time when they would either get a break and a new direction in a case, or get nothing and go back to square one.

"As ready as I'll ever be. You sure you don't want to take lead on this?"

"It's all yours. I'll follow you." He gave her a smile before entering the room.

Katie sometimes liked to stay standing during an interview. It gave her a sense of control over the person she was questioning when she was higher than they were and could move around the room. McGaven would either sit close to the subject or stay in the background—depending upon what the situation called for.

Bobby sat with his head down—he didn't look at the detectives when they entered. He wasn't in handcuffs but his hands and forearms were on the table with his fingers lightly intertwined.

Katie made an immediate impression as she tossed the evidence bag holding the burlap on the table. It landed slightly in front of Bobby—only then did he raise his head and look at Katie. His eyes grew wide and he blinked several times in confusion.

"Mr. Cox, do you understand why you're here?" she began.

He nodded.

"Can you please answer the question?"

"Yes. You want to ask me about Jenna."

Katie moved from one end of the table to the other, making it hard for Bobby to stay focused on her. Often such tactics would keep the person from being able to form a story instead of telling the truth. "How did you meet Jenna?"

"We've known each other for a while—about seven years. We met at school, UC Davis. But we didn't finish."

"Why is that?"

He shrugged. "Ran out of money."

Katie paused. "Were you serious?"

"I thought so."

"Did you want to get married?"

"I thought about it."

"Didn't Jenna want to get married?"

"She wasn't sure."

"Why is that?"

Bobby struggled with answering the question. "Her parents were the problem. Their marriage was horrible and there was abuse that Jenna witnessed. It made her uneasy about marriage."

"Was there physical abuse with her parents?"

"Yes."

"Was there physical abuse in the relationship between you and Jenna?" Katie watched him carefully.

"No." He shook his head adamantly. "No. Never. I loved her."

"Were you still dating or involved when she was murdered?"

"Yes."

Katie stayed still and leaned on the table in front of him, giving him no other place to look. "Did Jenna have any problems? Any issues with someone else?"

"No!" he said, standing up. "I've been trying to figure this out. It doesn't make sense. Nothing makes sense..."

McGaven took a step forward. "Sit down."

Bobby took his seat once again. This time he ran his hands nervously through his hair, looking down at the table.

"Jenna's body ended up at the south warehouse district."

"So?"

"Didn't you use to work there when it was occupied by the automotive group?"

"Yeah, so?"

"So you would be familiar with the location and know that it would be a while before anyone would find Jenna's body." Katie stood up straight and moved around.

This time McGaven pushed the other empty chair up next to Bobby and sat down. He didn't say a word—just watched Bobby closely.

"Are you saying that I killed Jenna?" His voice went up an octave and he could barely look at Katie. "I told you I loved her."

"Sometimes people do strange things for love... including killing someone so no one else can have them."

"I didn't kill Jenna..."

Katie pushed the evidence bag closer to Bobby.

"What's this?" he asked.

"We found it in your linen closet in the hallway."

"What? I've never seen this before."

"You sure about that? It was there behind your towels," she said.

Bobby sat up straight, staring right at Katie. "I'm telling you, I've never seen that before."

Katie set down an empty notepad and pen. "I'm going to need you to write down everything you know about Jenna. Last time you saw her. Last time you were out at the south warehouse district. And where you were when she was found murdered."

"Okay. Then can I go?"

She nodded. "For now. But I need for you to write everything down."

Katie and McGaven left the interview room.

Once out in the hallway, Katie turned to her partner. "I believe him that he had never seen the burlap."

"What makes you say that?"

"He didn't even know what it was. But that doesn't mean he might not know something. There's definitely something he's hiding."

"I agree."

"He'll be in there for the next half hour or so finishing up his account of everything. So in the meantime, let's get some eyes on him for the next couple of days."

"On it," said McGaven, already making arrangements.

TWELVE

Friday 0645 hours

Since the fourth crime scene in Simon Holden's crime spree had left two bodies at an apartment complex, patrols in the vicinity of apartment buildings in Pine Valley had been established. Katie quickly read the deputy reports. She realized that it was a huge undertaking and it would be lucky if anyone were to see anything. It made her suck in a breath, feeling tension rise in her body as she tried to figure out what else they could do to get ahead of the killer. By her calculation, they had forty-eight hours.

While they still waited for the confirmation to see Holden, Katie spent more than thirty minutes writing out basic information about the killer and victims on the whiteboard. Bits and pieces of the criminal personality began to take form.

Killer:

Same types of women, twenties, long dark hair, same general features.

Strangulation—precise and closely similar between victims (highly skilled).

Copying the same crime scenes of incarcerated serial killer Simon Holden.

Removing eyes and pinky fingers (taking away sight and strength).

Cleaning the victims with natural soaps. Meaning? Getting ready for a viewing or something else—funeral?

Copycat? Connected to Holden?

Forensics:

Homemade soap to clean bodies and comb hair.

Potential palm print (distorted, ragged) on one of rolled-up news articles about cases Katie and McGaven worked. Why previous cases? Is it a challenge for them to solve these cases?

Velvet pieces of material.

Clean cuts to remove eyeballs.

Ragged cut to remove pinky fingers

Burlap material wrapping the victims (again, natural material).

Victims:

Victim 1 **Gina Hartfield**, *body left in woods at Lookout Ridge, single, twenty-seven, worked as assistant for real estate developer. Membership at All Fitness Gym. Father lives outside the area. No other immediate family.*

Victim 2 **Jenna Day**, *body left in front of abandoned warehouse, twenty-eight, relationship with Bobby Cox, worked as health care assistant. Membership at All Fitness Gym. Two sisters and mom and dad in Southern California. No other immediate family.*

Victim 3 **Brianna Garcia**, *body left in a small neighborhood park, twenty-seven, single, worked as a delivery driver for local stores. Membership at All Fitness Gym. Aunt and uncle, brother outside the state. No other immediate family.*

Katie stood at the murder board trying to make sense of the behavioral evidence as well as the criminal profile. It was quiet in the forensic division—the only sound that kept her company was her own thoughts. There was no one around and it was even too early for McGaven. The silence gave her some peace.

Why these women?

Were they carefully selected?

Did the killer stalk them first? Finding out their routines and schedules?

Katie arranged the crime-scene photos in an order that made sense to her. She put them in chronological order, entering the crime scene by first having photos shot from far away and then gradually those taken nearer, until finally close-ups of the victim's faces. She wanted to see how the killer possibly saw the crime scene and his own handiwork. She was certain everything had been planned, shown in the details and skill left at the crime scene. She surmised that the killer had spent considerable time admiring the victims without them looking at him. She imagined that the killer had covered their eyes as the last thing he did before leaving, just as Simon Holden had to his victims.

She studied the pictures of the areas around the body, trying to deduce why the killer had chosen each particular location. They were similar but not the exact same locations to the body dumps that Holden had made all those years ago—partly due to the changing environment of the area after years of construction. She turned over and over in her mind the fact that the first victim, Gina Hartfield, had been left deep in the woods on a trail. The victim at the second crime scene, Jenna Day, had been left in front of a large empty warehouse. That of the third crime scene, Brianna Garcia, had been left in a small neighborhood park.

What was the killer trying to say?

What was the killer's motive?

On top of the worktable lay the transcripts for Simon Holden's trial stacked in tall neat piles. In large manila envelopes were the crime-scene photos for each victim.

Katie had a theory regarding the older serial victims and the obvious copycat relevance, but she wanted to see if there was anything else that might help them. She took the set of crime-scene photos of the first victim and laid them out on the table. She did the same with the second and third victims. Studying them carefully, she realized that the clues had been staring at her. Even though she and Gav had discussed the crime scenes before, now she actually stared at them.

"How can it be this easy...? There has to be something else," she said, taking one of the photos from each of Holden's crime scenes and tacking it up on the murder board against the current crime scenes. "How could we have not seen this?"

"Seen what?" said McGaven from the doorway.

It always amazed Katie that he could sneak up on her without a sound. "This," she said pointing. "I've been so preoccupied with the killer's signature and motive that I didn't see this."

McGaven slowly entered the room, scanning the photographs that Katie had added to the board. "They are almost *exactly* the same. Just as I said about Brianna's crime scene."

Katie and McGaven stared at the pictures, blown up larger than viewing on the cell phone, of the three current crime scenes and the first three crime scenes of Simon Holden. They were eerily similar. The first one was in the forest between pine trees, the second was in front of an abandoned industrial building, and the third was in a local park. It was eerie. The only difference was the almost two decades.

The detectives remained quiet a little bit longer, digesting what they were seeing. The similarities could mean that their cases were the work of Holden, or a copycat.

"Copycat?" said McGaven.

"It might seem that way, but I'm not so sure."

"Why?"

"It's Holden."

"What? It can't be. He's in prison. And unless he has escaped and we don't know about it, he's still there."

"I know this sounds crazy, but hear me out." She approached the board with the first crime scene. "See," she said. "Look at how everything is so precise. There's been special care to replicate the almost twenty-year-old murder scene. Someone took great care to stage the scenes just like Holden's. It was skilled. Remember what I said about the strangulation marks—*skilled*. Who would do that except for Holden?"

"And wouldn't that be a copycat?"

"Yes and no."

"Okay," he said and waited to hear her out. "Walk me through your theory."

"First, someone would have had to have seen the police crime-scene photos in order to get this exact duplicate of the area. And, to my knowledge they don't print or post these for the public. Even if someone were there, they still wouldn't be able to make this match so accurate."

"Maybe they took a photo? Maybe someone working around the crime scenes then gave out information?"

"It's possible, of course, but there would be no way it would have the details of the bodies, because they were rolled in burlap."

McGaven nodded. "I see your point. So now what?"

"Well, the first thing that comes to mind..." she said. "After reading some of the trial's transcripts, I know that Holden was known for his theatrics. He loved the spotlight and would get it any way he could. Every night, the news ran articles on something new that he had done in the courtroom. He had to keep the attention on him. What better way than to begin his killing spree all over again?"

"Isn't that a bit extreme even for a narcissistic psychopathic serial killer?"

"This guy is unrelenting and tenacious. I wouldn't put it past him. But..."

"There's something else that's on your mind," he said.

"I just think that, for whatever reason, Holden's back," she said. "I'm not sure how, but I am sure about the why. To be special and in the spotlight again."

"But Holden can't be the serial killer."

Katie slowly nodded. "Agreed. I'm not saying that he isn't involved, but things don't add up with him. And why recreate these crime scenes? Why now?"

"I'm going to check out everything about the locations where the bodies were found to see if there's any connection to

Holden," said McGaven as he sat down at the table to open his laptop. "Owners, businesses, neighbors, I'm on it."

"Great."

Katie thought about what McGaven said. It made sense, but at the same time, it was going to take quite a bit of research to find anything. She had the impression that Holden excelled at not having made mistakes, even though he had finally been convicted of twelve murders. The crime-scene photos were a major factor, but there were also several eyewitness accounts of him leaving one of the crime scenes. Juries unfortunately sometimes voted more on emotions rather than a list of facts.

A knock at their door interrupted the detectives.

"Hi," said Sheriff Scott as he stood at the doorway.

"What brings you down here?" said Katie. She was glad to see him but knew that he had only come in person because he must have something to tell them that was too important to say on a call.

The sheriff looked at the murder board, studying the photos and Katie's new list. "That brings back some memories."

"We're trying to retrace Simon Holden's crime spree," she said.

"Well, I've been on the phone with the warden at Mansfield State Prison."

"And?"

"And, he has given you both access to Simon Holden for an interview. Remember, this is a courtesy and it will also depend upon if Holden wants to talk to you. And he's in solitary."

Katie was eager to talk to the infamous serial killer.

"And Katie," the sheriff stressed, "you need to be careful and hyper-vigilant. Just because he's in prison doesn't mean he's not dangerous. He'll try to get inside your head. I watched more than half of his trial and he was clever, crafty, and intelligent."

"If he was that intelligent he wouldn't have been convicted," she said.

"Katie, I'm not joking around. Make your visit count and keep him from getting into your head. Is that understood?" He eyed both detectives. "That's an order."

"Of course. We'll be careful."

"Don't worry, Sheriff, I'll make sure Katie stays in line and goes by the book. We both will," said McGaven.

The sheriff turned to McGaven. "Thanks for the confidence. Be vigilant and report back to me."

"We will," said Katie.

"Get going," he said. "You have an hour to get there." He left.

"Wow," said McGaven. "We're going to meet with an infamous serial killer."

"Hopefully we'll find some answers we need, or at least a new direction to take in this investigation."

THIRTEEN

Friday 1255 hours

"Nothing unusual. In fact, everything reads normal. Middle-class family. Lived in a middle-class California city of Pleasan-ton. Mom was a nurse and Dad was an electrical engineer. No reports of abuse," said McGaven as he read over some history for Simon Holden. "Never in trouble, or reported problems with the police. I don't think he ever received a parking ticket."

"Serial killers don't necessarily come from severely abusive and broken families," said Katie. She kept her eyes on the road, not wanting to miss the cutoff heading to the prison. She was surprised by the fact she was nervous as she went over in her mind how she would question the killer.

"True." He read on. "Holden attended UC Berkeley and received a major in engineering and a master's in chemistry. Looks like he was going for his PhD and he suddenly retracted his thesis to the board." He scanned for more information.

"That thesis would make for an interesting read."

"No doubt," he said. "I just don't see anything that raises a warning flag."

Katie followed the signs and exited the freeway. "Don't forget about the trial transcripts. He's unpredictable and only wants you to believe what he wants you to know."

"And the sheriff made it perfectly clear that we need to be vigilant."

Katie nodded.

McGaven studied his partner for a moment before returning to the background information about Holden. "So Holden has spent the past almost eight years in prison and it looks like all of his appeals were exhausted six months ago."

"Six months? So it's taken him... what? The last five and a half months to come up with a plan to bring back these serial cases?"

McGaven didn't immediately respond. "Do you really think that he's behind all this?"

"I do. There's too much for someone else to be able to duplicate. It's where the investigation is taking us right now..."

"Maybe they had spoken to Holden a while back?"

"It's possible... but I don't think so," she said.

"Well hopefully we're going to find out."

Katie turned the sedan into the main entrance of the prison and they drove to the gate.

Katie and McGaven had to relinquish their weapons and secure them in lockers before they were allowed to continue through several checkpoints inside the prison. Each had a highly fortified heavy metal door that took two prison guards to unlock and lock again before the detectives could move forward.

The detectives were reported as special guests. The warden had given them access to a meeting room where Simon Holden would be waiting for them. They were instructed where to go, passing through more security areas as they forged deeper into the prison's depths. They were not allowed to bring anything into the room: no pen, no notebook, no personal items such as jewelry, watches, or even spare change. Nothing could be taken into the room that could pose any type of a security risk.

Just because he's in prison doesn't mean he's not dangerous. He'll try to get inside your head.

All these thoughts were swirling through Katie's mind, making her more and more uneasy. She had investigated, arrested, and interrogated killers before, but there was something different about this particular one due to the graphic nature of the crime and the number of victims.

Just as they reached the meeting area, Katie and McGaven were stopped by one of the correctional officers.

"Detective Scott. Detective McGaven?" the serious stocky guard said to them—giving a nod to each detective as a formal greeting.

"Yes," said Katie. "Is there a problem?"

"I've been informed that you, Detective Scott, are the only one allowed to speak with prisoner Holden."

"Why?" she said.

"The prisoner has changed his mind and said he would only speak with you."

"Wait a minute," said McGaven.

"It's okay, Gav. I'll be fine."

"I don't—"

"I'll be fine. We didn't come all the way out here to turn around without talking to him." She turned to the guard. "Can we get a list of all the visitors that prisoner Holden has had?"

"Of course."

"I really don't think—"

"Gav," she insisted. "I'll be fine. Get all the information you can about him. There will be a guard."

Another guard escorted McGaven away, leaving her at the meeting room door.

Katie was ready. She thought it would be a benefit if only

she interviewed him. It had been her experience that a male prisoner liked to talk to a woman, if only so he could brag, shock, or come clean about something.

The correctional officer walked to a heavy metal door and inserted two keys to unlock it. "I'll be right here if you need anything." He opened the door.

"Thank you," she said.

Katie took a breath, stood tall, and entered the room with all the confidence she could muster.

The space was larger than she had anticipated with an over-sized meeting table set in the middle. She assumed it was designated for more than just the inmate and one attorney. There was a guard in the far left corner standing at attention; he didn't acknowledge Katie, but it was clear that he was watching for any false move from the prisoner.

The door shut behind Katie and she heard the two locks engage. Now, she was trapped with a serial killer and there was no turning back. There was one empty chair facing Holden across the table. She walked to it and slowly pulled it away from the table. The metal scraped across the floor, almost making her shudder. Normally she would stay standing when questioning a suspect, but in this instance, she wanted to be up close, making it personal.

Sitting across from her with his wrists shackled to the table through heavy metal loops sat a man. His eyes never moved from Katie as she made herself comfortable—at least, as much as she could be under the circumstances.

Katie had seen photographs of Holden, but they were more than fifteen years old. He was then in his late thirties, thick brown hair, clean-shaven, with menacing dark eyes. The man who sat in front of her was older—much older-looking than the photos available. He had shaved his head and was now sporting a grayish mustache and goatee. There were now dark tattoos coming up from his chest area near the sides of his neck, but it was unclear what they were and what they represented.

"Mr. Holden," began Katie. She was aware of her voice and tone and kept herself in control as a professional police detective.

"Simon. I prefer to be called Simon." His tone was flat and precise in diction.

"Very well, Simon. I'm Detective Scott."

"I know who you are, Katie."

"Detective Scott," she said.

He smiled, showing his surprisingly white teeth. "Of course, Detective Scott." There was an eerie quality of how he addressed her.

Katie glanced at the stoic guard who hadn't changed his position or focus. "Do you know why I'm here?"

He shrugged. "I can only speculate that you want to know something about the murders that are running rampant around town. Am I correct?"

"Yes, you're correct." It unnerved her that a convicted killer knew what was going on in the news.

"Then ask away."

"Three women have been murdered."

"So sorry." His eyes and expression were emotionless.

"And they were murdered, posed, and the crime scene staged to look like your crime scenes. What do you know about that?"

"What do you think I know?" He kept intense eye contact with her.

"That's why I'm here, Simon."

He smiled but never took his eyes away from her. "I don't think I know anything about your murders. And if you've read the trial transcripts, you know that I'm innocent." He raised his hands slightly to indicate he was incarcerated. The handcuffs rattled on the table.

Katie returned his smile. So that's how it was going to be—verbal ping-pong. She wasn't going to let the killer get the upper hand. "Well, Simon. That's where you and I have our differences."

He seemed to be intrigued by her statement as his eyebrows rose slightly.

"You see, I think you're lying."

"Really?"

"I think you lied all the way through your trial."

"Interesting, Detective Scott," he said. "That's not really the right approach to ask me about your murders, is it?"

"I've got your attention."

"Touché."

"I think that you had someone continue your work—your obsession—your fantasy."

"I like the way you think, Detective, but again, not the best way to ask me about your murders." He leaned back, clearly pleased with his answer.

Katie had to carefully state what she wanted to in a way that wasn't pleading or desperate. "Let's cut through all the crap. Do you know anyone who would want to continue your killing spree? Or, did you train someone before you were arrested?"

Holden's expression turned from a smile to a frown.

"You trained someone before you were arrested and waited until all your appeals were exhausted. Then you had given strict instructions that after all that... your trainee, your minion, wait, better yet, your *accomplice* was supposed to keep your murders going. Am I getting warmer, Simon?"

"I see you've had time to think about this... I applaud you."

"So is that a yes?"

"Hardly. I'm giving you credit for a fantastic theory. Even if it's purely fictional."

Katie knew that she had hit a nerve with him. He had

underestimated her. "Just the fact that you think it's a fantastic theory says quite a bit."

"You think that I didn't do my homework before your visit today?"

"Are you saying that you researched me and my cases?" She knew that she was getting somewhere. Even if he didn't come right out and say it, he implied that he did know something about her. Her mind flipped to the rolled-up articles about the cases she and McGaven had worked on left at the crime scenes. It was the only difference, an added clue that was at the current scenes and not Holden's.

There was a lingering silence as they sized each other up.

"Alright," he said as his eyes narrowed. "I've received information about you and your cases."

"That's impossible, I thought," she said with some sarcasm.

"Just about everyone in here gets some kind of perks or information about the outside."

"So are you saying that someone is impersonating you—a copycat? Because when we catch them—and we will—they will get all the glory of their kills. And you? Well, you won't."

"I see what you're doing, Detective. I know you're good, in fact, you're really good at what you do. But I'm better."

"That little touch at the crime scenes was good, not that good," she said.

"What do you mean?"

"Oh, Simon. You know what I mean. Trying to bait me? I'm sure you knew that I would come here to try to talk to you. Try to get some answers, right?" She watched him closely. Now he didn't seem like a crafty serial killer, but an aging man who wanted to repeat his day in the limelight.

"What's the big deal? There's nothing wrong with reading about you and your partner's cases."

Got him.

It was all that Katie needed to confirm that Holden was

indeed involved in some way in the current murders because no one knew about the articles besides police personnel. She didn't know how they were going to catch him, but they were going to do everything they could.

"Thank you, Mr. Holden," she said as she rose to leave.

"Where are you going?"

"I'm done here. Thank you for your time." Katie walked to the door and knocked twice.

"So you are okay with not knowing where Chad is?" he said.

Katie's blood ran cold. Sounds became muffled. Her stomach dropped as her body tingled in that way just before a panic attack. She couldn't let Holden see that he had rattled her. How could he know about Chad? He had saved this bit of information for this exact moment.

"Come back and visit any time. We can chat about Chad," he said.

The door opened and Katie quickly slipped through. She could hear Holden laughing until the door closed again.

Katie and McGaven had exited the prison, retrieved their guns and belongings, and headed to the car before she spoke.

Once inside the police sedan, McGaven turned to his partner. "You okay? You look like you've seen a ghost."

"It went fine until..." She couldn't finish her sentence. She was angry, deeply sad, and felt as if the wind had been knocked out of her.

"Until what?" he said.

"Until Holden asked if I was okay with not knowing what happened to Chad."

McGaven was taken back for a moment. "How would he know about Chad?"

She turned to her partner. "Because he's somehow behind

this—all of this. He waited for the right moment to say something about Chad." She took a breath, dialing back her emotions. The meeting with Holden was like a hit to the gut.

"What are you saying? Holden had Chad kidnapped?"

"Obviously I can't prove it, but after talking to him, I know there's something more. It's a gut feeling. We're just going to have to prove it—by finding Chad."

"Katie, you realize what you're saying?"

"I know *exactly* what I'm saying. It's all a part of his comeback plans."

"Take a breath," he said. "Start from the beginning."

Katie reached into her inside pocket and retrieved her cell phone. "I'll do better. I didn't leave this with our other stuff, but I recorded our meeting from my hidden cell phone. Listen for yourself."

"Katie, Katie. You little sneak." He took the phone as she started the car. "I don't know if I should be upset with you—or totally impressed."

"You'll understand what I'm talking about when you hear him." She backed the car up and proceeded to the exit.

McGaven pulled his small notebook from his pocket. "I have some news of my own. I got the list of everyone employed at the prison from his incarceration. And, the names of all the visitors that Simon Holden has had the entire time he's been in prison."

Katie smiled. "I'm going to like this, aren't I?"

FOURTEEN

McGaven walked to the whiteboard and picked up a pen. "Okay," he said and began writing a list of names. "Terrance Lane, Harry Winslow, and, drumroll please, Butch Turner."

"What? Butch Turner, the personal trainer?"

"The one and only."

"Why?"

"It seems that his uncle, Randall Turner, was friends with Holden's dad, David Holden."

"So why would he visit Holden?"

"Don't know, but we need to find out."

"Okay, slow down. Who is Terrance Lane?"

"He's a businessman of good standing in the community. He's been on boards and is involved in charity work. He has investments in the Pine Valley area and has many friends, including well-known politicians."

Katie thought about it and wondered what that man had to do with a serial killer in prison.

"I know what you're thinking. Why a guy like that? Right?

But listen, it seems from a couple of the guards that Terrance Lane had some heated conversations with Holden, which makes me believe it's possible that information was being passed to Holden."

"So smart, Gav. I have to agree with you."

"And a couple of the visits Lane had his bodyguard, Sean Hyde, with him. So that means he must know something too."

"It could just mean that Lane wanted someone to be a witness of what's said. Or he's concerned about his safety. We need to dig a bit deeper—but at a distance—and quietly. We don't want to let anyone on his crew know that we're looking into him."

"Harry Winslow?" she said.

"He is just a guy who happens to own several buildings around Pine Valley, including the All Fitness Gym. Looks like a bar he owns is under some type of investigation—drugs being sold. I'll talk to narcotics about it. One of the guys on the task force is a friend and we came up through the academy together."

"Okay..." Katie's mind catapulted between each prison visitor. "Why would these men want to visit Holden? Terrance Lane could be part of some philanthropist group, doing good works, against the death penalty and such. Maybe he wanted some publicity."

"I'll have Denise search for anything about Lane to see what he has been doing the past seven years."

"And for ownership of the buildings and properties where the bodies were found."

"Good idea. She's also checking the employees for us."

"This is a strange serial web," she said studying the board. "Somehow we have to find the links between the crime scenes, Holden, and these men."

"Don't forget whoever is killing these women is just as ruthless as Holden. And... for some reason the person pulling the strings has hooked us into the web with those news articles."

That made Katie even more nervous about these investigations. "Gav," she said. "I want you and Denise to be extra careful—I mean it. Remember it wasn't too long ago that everyone connected to one of our investigations was being targeted. Maybe you should stay with Denise and her daughter Lizzie."

McGaven took a breath as he paced back and forth. "You're right."

"Maybe patrol?"

"I'll see, but our patrol right now is stretched to the limit looking at potential dump sites. And we have two deputies out with sickness and surgery."

"Hey, guys, I have something for you," said John at the doorway.

Katie and McGaven followed the forensic supervisor to the examination room.

"I don't mean to interrupt you, but I thought you wanted to see this. Everything with Brianna's crime scene and body is almost identical to Gina's and Jenna's. But Eva has something new and interesting for you."

Eva sat on a stool in front of a computer screen. "We've managed to pull another palm print from Brianna Garcia's wallet, which had been left on that rock." She clicked through and showed the prints side by side. "I was only able to obtain four points, but it still looks the same as the one taken from the news article. Not identical but a start." She smiled at the detectives.

"That's great," said McGaven.

"Great work, Eva," said Katie as she studied the screen images. "Are palm prints just like fingerprints for identification?"

"Yes, with the arches, loops, and whorls," said Eva. "But,

there is an added identification referred to as columns. Most people are born with three major creases on their palms. Each line, though, is a different thickness, prominence, and length. But it's still unique for every person."

"Can you run any type of comparison through a database?" said McGaven.

"Collecting palm prints are still at its infancy, but they are making some headway," said John. "They're still at the beginning of collecting them for study through CASIA Palmprint Image Database. As far as for law enforcement, it's still a ways yet."

"But you can compare from another palm print from a suspect?" said McGaven.

"Absolutely. With only four and five points for comparison, I'm not sure if it would hold up in court, though."

"But for investigative purposes, it's a good start."

"Definitely," said John. "With that being said..." He walked back to his computer screen. "We've been able to identify the tire impressions from both Gina's and Jenna's crime scenes, at least the similarities to individualize the treads."

"Are they the same?" said Katie. Her heart almost skipped a beat in anticipation.

"If you mean are they made from the same make and model of vehicle? Yes. They were made from a late-model Ford F-150 truck. Most likely late-2018 model or later, which are the most common for these types of vehicles."

"That's great news. We now know that the bodies were transported by a truck."

"But it is one of the most common trucks on the road today," said McGaven. "And being in the mountains in rural areas, there are going to be a lot of them."

"I may have some good news," said John. "We're still tracking down the type of tires and potentially the year. However, there was an anomaly in one of the treads."

"What sort of anomaly?"

"There was some irregular wearing of the tread, and it left a visible and identifiable mark."

"That's great," she said. "Now, again, we have to have something to compare it to." She watched John's expression seem to cloud. "What are you not telling us?"

"I don't want to make things worse," he said.

"What do you mean?" Katie felt her stomach drop and her breath stilted.

"Well, we've managed to clean up the photo of the truck parked out in front of Dayton Electronics."

Katie could barely breathe as her limbs felt tingly and weird as if she could pick up anything at the moment until she heard what John had to say. She noticed McGaven begin to shift his weight back and forth.

"We were able to identify the make and model of the truck. It's a late model, 2019 to present, of a Ford F-150."

Katie stepped back in shock.

"That is a common type of truck, don't forget," said McGaven. He tried to ease his partner's concern.

"True," she barely said. "But it confirms my biggest fear about these cases."

"What's that?"

"It could mean that this entire serial investigation is a whole lot bigger than we previously thought."

FIFTEEN

Katie had just arrived at her home when she got the call about the Pine Acres Apartments from the watch commander requesting her presence. She dropped off her things and took Cisco with her as she raced to the complex that had over forty residences.

As Katie drove, a myriad of thoughts harassed her mind. The watch commander hadn't given any details for her. McGaven had also been requested. She wondered if he would beat her there since he was closer.

Her main concern was that the killer had struck again and they hadn't been able to stop him. But the commander hadn't said anything about homicides. What was going on? Katie's instinct brought to her attention that the killer, or Holden himself, had changed their strategies. The call must have had to do with the cases, so she pressed on and hurried as fast as safety would allow.

Cisco whined from the back seat, which was usual when Katie's senses were heightened and something big about a current case was pending. The dog was in tune with Katie, just as he had been during her Afghanistan tours.

"It's okay, Cisco," she said, trying to reassure the dog when really she was the one needing that support. It was during these times that Katie's mind wrapped right back to Chad and where he could be at that exact moment. If he was trapped and couldn't get out—there would be no one to hear his pleas.

Katie turned onto Pine Acres Road and immediately slowed her Jeep before the Pine Acres Apartments. There were three sheriff's deputy cruisers already parked, along with McGaven's truck. She could see the deputies standing at the main entrance just behind a rock wall. From her vantage, she could see that it was an open area next to the apartment complex that had been landscaped like a park, with grass, plants, a fountain, and picnic tables. It made Katie hold her breath for a moment.

Could it mean?

Dread filled Katie. They were too late. It was the worst thing she dealt with as a police detective.

She quickly pulled in behind McGaven's truck. She didn't see her partner and assumed that he was at the scene already, assessing the situation and waiting for her. Katie exited her SUV, leaving Cisco behind.

Katie was immediately struck by the heavier than normal aroma of pine. It usually comforted her, but tonight it almost made her sick to her stomach. She hurried up a walkway as the small pebbles crunched underneath her feet. Entering the apartment's open-space area, she spotted McGaven talking to a patrol deputy. She recognized the police officer as Deputy Brent Dasher. He was a nice cop who was always very helpful to the detectives at the crime scenes.

"Hey," said McGaven.

"What's up?" said Katie looking around but not seeing anything. "Why were we called here?"

"You need to see this," he said.

"I received a call that someone had dumped a couple of rugs at these apartments," said Deputy Dasher.

"A couple?" she said as her heart pounded in anticipation.

"This way," said the deputy.

The detectives followed the officer to the far side of the building.

Katie was slightly confused. No one had said anything about bodies or the killer. They walked toward the side area, passing expertly tended flowerbeds that ran alongside the building. The soil was dark and rich in color and the bushes were neatly trimmed along the top into a perfect geometrical design.

The area revealed two perfectly rolled-up pieces of burlap material lined up next to each other. The difference from the other crime scenes was that there weren't any bodies. It was as though it was just an eerie reminder of the other dumping areas.

"There's no bodies?" said Katie relieved.

"Nope. We did a perimeter search and found nothing," said the deputy.

Katie looked to McGaven. "What do you think? Is the killer toying with us?"

"I would say so."

"And I find it interesting this happened after my chat with Holden," she said. "Thank you, Deputy Dasher. Can you and the other deputies canvass the area for any eyewitnesses who might have seen who did this?"

He nodded and left to join the other deputies.

Katie pulled on gloves and leaned down to the wrapped burlap. "What is he trying to prove? Is this the killer, or maybe someone else who heard about the murders?" She studied the material. It appeared to be the same as that used in the murders.

"Let's get John and Eva out here," McGaven said, already calling John from speed dial.

Katie nodded. "Maybe we might get lucky and find some physical evidence."

She stood up and began scrutinizing the building area looking for video cameras, but there didn't seem to be any. "No cameras?"

McGaven ended his cell phone call. "Not on this side. They are only at the main entrance and down the apartment hallways."

"I see..." Katie followed the building around to where there would be cameras and noticed that the lenses were covered with something. "Did you see this?" she said.

McGaven was immediately at her side looking at the cameras. "No. John needs to document whatever is here."

"Detective," said Deputy Dasher.

McGaven walked to the officer as Katie decided to investigate further.

She followed the building structure, but nothing seemed to be out of place. Everything was tidy and there was no trash or discarded items. Trying to retrace how the killer, or other person, accessed the property without being seen wouldn't be difficult due to the heavily forested area behind it. It wasn't the largest apartment complex and had many ways to approach without being seen. Someone could approach from another property and sneak up behind the building. No one in the front or most of the apartments would see them.

Why this apartment complex?

Is it a warning?

Katie continued around the building and found a maintenance area. She paused, looking to see if anyone was around, but it was vacant. There weren't any residents wandering about, but maybe they didn't know what was going on.

Katie was just about to turn back and join McGaven when she noticed that a maintenance door had been left slightly ajar. It hadn't been latched all the way, as if someone hadn't wanted to be locked out. She stood at the door and turned to see that the cameras weren't facing in that direction. It could be where the killer or copycat entered the area carrying the rugs. It would make sense, so Katie decided to investigate.

Still wearing her gloves, she put her hand on the doorknob and slowly pulled the door to her. It opened effortlessly without any noise. Peering inside, she saw an area where extra maintenance and gardening supplies were kept. It was also a place where the electricity breakers and sprinkler controls were located. There was the distinct smell of potting soil and cleaning solutions. Still curious, Katie entered. Surprisingly, it was larger than it looked from the outside and ran along the length of the building. She followed the trail through the maintenance labyrinth. There were motion lights above illuminating the way but they were dim and seemed to need to warm up a bit in order to provide adequate lighting.

The outdoor and chemical smell became stronger, making Katie breathe more shallowly to prevent the unpleasant odors from overpowering her. There was a weird sound farther in that made her think of some creature hiding in the darkness. Perhaps it was rodents making their homes in the dark, dank surroundings.

The squeaking noise almost hypnotized her and she wanted to find out what it was. Then it changed to more of a clanging sound—as if something was gently blowing in the wind against something metal.

Katie kept moving forward. She absently glanced behind her and no one was there. Half expecting to see McGaven searching for her, she dismissed a lingering paranoid sense that she wasn't alone. She kept moving, wanting to get to where the noise was originating from.

She approached a place where some old outdoor grills and tables were stored. She quickly examined them and realized they must have been stored for quite some time. There was heavy dust and cobwebs on them from months if not years of being stored.

Katie moved around them and saw a smaller wooden door that must have been boarded up. Now the narrow board with numerous nails that had barred it had been removed and was lying on the floor.

She stopped.

Listening.

The metal jangling noise had stopped. She felt cooler air blowing by her legs. It was coming from the gap between the door and frame.

She moved forward and put her right hand on the door, feeling a draft through the crack. Without moving her palm or making a sound, she could sense a slight vibration and pressure. Her pulse pounded in her ears. A sensation of detecting someone else on the other side of the door made her arms tingle and goosebumps prickle up the back of her neck.

Taking two quick breaths, she heaved the door wide open. Light and a rush of air flooded inside and momentarily obscured Katie's view. There was a figure in the dwindling light, but she couldn't identify them or even know if they were one of the police officers or apartment residents. As Katie struggled to focus, the figure rushed at her, shoving her hard, and then retreated.

Katie lost her balance, falling backward. She missed the larger pieces of equipment and dropped to the ground landing on her back. Taking a moment to regain her senses and balance, she climbed to her feet, readied her weapon, and took off after the assailant. As soon as she was outside the old wooden entrance, she was met with silence and knew the area was vacant.

She ran toward a privacy fence, glancing along it and locating a gate. Quickly moving through the area, she was met again with a vacant zone. There was no one around. She looked in every direction. It wasn't clear where the person who pushed her went.

Breathless and frustrated, Katie decided to retreat as she holstered her weapon. As she walked back to the main front area, she found it livelier than before. John and Eva had arrived. There was another patrol cruiser. The deputies were canvassing the area and apartments.

McGaven spotted her and quickly approached. "Where did you go?"

"Checked out the maintenance area."

"Why are you so dirty?" he said.

"Someone was hiding at the far door, which hadn't been used in quite a while. I think it was how the person was able to bring in those two rolled burlap rugs without being seen."

"You ran into the killer?"

"I don't know who it was except it was a man and he was able to escape without a trace—again." She watched some of the people now meandering around trying to get a look at what the police were doing. "Whoever it was knew exactly how to move around here without being seen."

"John," said McGaven as he passed by. "We need another area searched and possibly fingerprints taken."

"You got it," he said.

"I'll show you," said Katie.

John and Eva followed her to the maintenance area.

Katie could barely keep her wits about her. Her heart pounded like a jackhammer in her chest. She had been in physical contact with someone who most likely was the killer.

SIXTEEN

Love has a way of sneaking up and grabbing hold of you when you least expect it. Love is something that can come in many forms—from friendships, lovers, and family. And when you do something that changes you in some way by shifting perspective into that new direction, it's a new love, and then you couldn't imagine doing anything else. It changes you forever. It's in your soul. It's a love that is so strong because when you're not involved in that special activity—you feel lost without it until you embrace it once again. Training with dogs, forming an unshakable bond, and performing a duty together that is unlike any other type of work. That is a form of true love.

Saturday 0640 hours

Katie couldn't sleep so she had decided to get up early and go for a run. It was better than tossing and turning with her thoughts always falling back to Chad. She and Cisco made their way to Lookout Ridge, where Gina Hartfield's body had been dumped and discovered.

The run early in the morning helped to clear her head so she could think logically about the crime scenes. McGaven had wanted to join her but had to take Denise's daughter Lizzy to soccer practice. Katie would update him later if she found anything or had new theories they could explore.

She stood on the ridge looking down at the area that had been Gina's final resting place. It was difficult for Katie to not be personally invested when there's a murder victim, a family mourning, and a killer to catch. How could you not have a personal stake?

Cisco trotted up after fully investigating a group of bushes and a very large pine tree. His jet-black fur made him appear like a wolf, especially with his amber eyes surveying the area.

Katie decided to move down the incline and walk the scene again. With the vivid photos of the crime scene and the one from twenty years ago firmly anchored in her mind, she moved closer to the spot with Cisco at her heels.

The sun hadn't broken out from the cloud cover of the early morning. The air was still crisp, making Katie zip up her navy hoodie. She knew it wasn't as cold as she felt, but recently she noticed that her body temperature seemed to fluctuate when she became stressed—usually colder as her blood pressure took a dip.

Dismissing her chills, Katie stood at the exact location where Gina's body had lain wrapped in burlap. The natural fabric had to mean something important to the killer—or at least some type of convenience. Maybe it was used as a way to somehow preserve the body? Like a mummy? Or for a funeral? Why?

Katie stood still, feeling the coolness of the air, and listening to the forest. It was her way of calming her body and mind to really focus on the scene. She wanted to know where the killer entered, how long he stayed to pose the scene, and how he exited. Timing was important. And how much time the killer spent in each phase was significant.

Katie walked to the obvious area on the far side of the crime scene. It was a little-used path, more of a walk-through and animal trail. It progressed in a crisscross pattern that eventually led to a gravel parking area surrounded by large boulders so cars wouldn't veer into a ditch.

The access was somewhat easy to navigate, but there wasn't any indication of footprints. It was the same at the other scenes. Katie contemplated this dilemma.

How was the killer getting in and out of the crime scenes without leaving footprints or drag marks behind?

Katie went through the trail to the parking area, but nothing stood out to her. Retracing her steps, she returned to the scene. As she stood at the top of the path, she noticed that the area appeared to be cleared on each end. It wasn't like a piece of machinery had done the job, but rather, something much softer.

She thought that she should run Cisco around the area to see if he targeted anything that had been missed by forensics as well as herself.

"Cisco," she said, catching his attention. Once the dog sat and waited for a command. "*Such.*" She told him to search the area.

It was all Cisco needed to hear. He took off around the perimeter of the main crime-scene area—first with his nose down, then at head level trying to catch a scent. The jet-black dog made an almost perfect perimeter search then funneled his direction. He lingered at the far side.

The sun began to break through the overcast coverage and highlighted the area. It was light streaming through the trees, but it was clearer for Katie to see. On either end of the mostly level area, as odd as it appeared, it looked like someone had swept the dirt and pine needles with a type of broom. Cisco remained in the vicinity checking out the area but not indicating anything specific.

Katie took a closer look. There were some fresh footprints that were similar to the police-issue boot, but around it the soil was loose without needles, leaves, or dead foliage. It wasn't natural. It had been wiped smooth of footprints or drag marks.

Katie took about twenty minutes slowly searching the area for any indication of what had swept the area. Just as she was about to give up—definitely feeling like she was looking for a needle in a haystack—that's when she saw it. There were two long strands of a stiff, natural-colored grass lying five feet away from where the body had been located. The hearty strands didn't match anything around the forest area or nearby. She immediately took her cell phone and photographed it in the place where she found it and the surrounding area.

Katie decided that she would take it and have John analyze it for its origin. It reminded her of a garden broom, the type that would be perfect to sweep away footprints without it being noticeable. It was a longshot, but it would explain why they hadn't been able to find any identifying footprints or scuffle or drag marks.

Taking one last good look around, Katie didn't see anything that would prove to be a new clue so she headed back to where she had parked her Jeep.

Taking her run down to a nice steady jog, she tried to enjoy being out in nature. It was truly a gift of the incredibly beautiful place she lived.

Cisco ran ahead of her and started barking.

"Cisco, *hier*," she said, calling him back to her, not concerned about what the dog was barking at. If she had to guess, it would most likely be a squirrel or something close to it.

Katie hurried up the path until she reached the parking lot where her Jeep was parked. It was there she saw a man next to a large tan SUV bending down petting Cisco.

"Hey," she said. "Please don't pet..." She didn't finish her sentence when she saw the guy stand up. A handsome man with a dark crew cut, slight stubble, with a muscular fit physique enhanced by his casual running attire smiled broadly at her. Cisco was enjoying the attention.

"Katie," he said smiling. "Look at you. Still as gorgeous as ever."

"How?" She stared at Evan Daniels in disbelief. Her heart stuttered a bit. Her previous supervisor and military working dog trainer for two weeks was now a detective at Sacramento Police Department.

"Cisco, I think for the first time your mom is speechless." He laughed.

Katie walked to Evan trying to hide her surprise. "How did you know I was here?"

"I'm a detective now, remember?" he said. "I spoke with Detective McGaven and he told me that you would be out here at the first crime scene checking things out."

"Why are you here?" said Katie, not knowing what else to say.

"Well, nice to see you too." He chuckled. "I'm off this weekend and I took a couple of days of personal time next week to help out with Chad's case."

Katie tensed as she thought of Chad and what they had found out so far. "Do you have anything new?"

"Some things that might help with more video footage of what we already have, but I wanted to check out places here—where he was last. I already spoke with his supervisor and a couple of the guys at the firehouse. But I wanted to keep digging. If that's okay with you?"

"Of course," she managed to say. She felt an overwhelming level of emotions and memories parade through her body.

A dog barked from the inside of Evan's SUV. It was a low, deep woof.

"Who's that?" she said.

"That is Mac. My sable German shepherd."

"Did you bring him back?" Katie saw the dog stick his wet nose through the crack of the back seat window.

"Yep, fell in love with this guy. He technically flunked out of military school for his dislike of gunfire, but he's as solid as they come and has been with me ever since."

"That's great," said Katie. She didn't quite know what to say and had trouble meeting Evan's gaze. "Explosive or drug trained?"

"He's protection and explosives."

"Like Cisco." She nodded and thought about all of her extensive training for explosives detection and how helpful Evan had been to her in that time. More memories flooded back.

"Katie," he said. "I'm so sorry that you're having to deal with this about Chad."

She nodded and didn't trust herself to not cry.

"I will help in any way I can."

"Thank you. McGaven and I are in the middle of a serial case, so it's been difficult to stay focused on Chad..."

"I can't imagine. McGaven briefly brought me up to speed on that. And I spoke with Sheriff Scott as well. I didn't want to muscle my way into the investigation and out of my jurisdiction without an invitation."

"Good thinking. You don't want to cross the sheriff," she said. Katie couldn't help but smile.

Evan walked to the back passenger door of his SUV. "Want to meet Mac?"

"Absolutely." She turned to Cisco. "Cisco, *platz*." The dog obediently downed and waited next to her vehicle.

Evan opened the back door and a beautiful sable German shepherd jumped out. He ordered the dog to heel at his side and then sit, waiting for the next command.

"Wow, he's beautiful."

"Come say hi."

Katie walked up to the shepherd. "Hi, Mac," she said petting him. "Do you know how handsome you are?"

Evan laughed. "I think he might."

"Where are you staying?" she asked.

"Just outside Pine Valley at the Hotel Suites. They allow dogs and there's plenty of room on the property for Mac to get some exercise."

"That's great," said Katie. She knew the location.

"So," he said. "Did you find anything new?"

"Maybe," she said, holding up the remnant of the natural broom. "I'm going to drop it off at the forensic lab on my way home."

"What's your schedule today?" He kept his eyes locked on hers.

"Surveillance. We have a couple of persons of interest to check out while a deputy watches the third one." She referred to the suspects on the murder board.

"I wanted to check out Chad's house with you. Would you be okay with that?"

It stung Katie for a moment and the thought of being inside Chad's house again made her sad. "Are you looking for something specific?"

"I'm sure you've already looked through his house, but I wanted to see if there's anything indicating a person he's talked to or where he went. Just being thorough."

"Okay." She pulled her cell phone from her pocket to text instructions. "Pick me up at my house in about an hour? It'll give me plenty of time before I meet up with McGaven."

"Sure." He gave her his cell number.

Katie sent her home address to him. She turned to leave.

"Katie?" he said.

She turned to face Evan. Concern washed across his face.

"It's great to see you—I'm so sorry it's under these circumstances."

"It's nice to see you too."

Katie opened the back door of her Jeep and let Cisco inside. She got behind the wheel, starting the engine, and then slowly pulled out of the parking lot. She watched Evan in her rearview mirror working with Mac—it brought back memories and a spark. His body language and instructor skills were just as she had remembered, demonstrated in his incredible ability to read dogs, get their attention, and praise their behaviors. It was flawless. It created a bond that couldn't be broken.

She finally turned her attention back to the road and drove back to her house.

SEVENTEEN

Katie rode quietly with Evan as he drove to Chad's house at 1188 Spreckles Lane. Her thoughts were a combination of grief, loss, uncertainty, her past with Evan, and the serial cases she was currently coping with at the moment.

"Nice area," said Evan. It was clear that he didn't know what to say under the circumstances.

They pulled into the narrow cobblestone driveway.

Katie's heart nearly skipped a beat when she saw Chad's Jeep parked, but realized that it had been towed back to his house for storage—at least for now. So many memories flooded her mind of times she had spent with Chad at his new home. He had been updating and working on it for months—and was proud of what he had accomplished. He planned on selling it when they decided where they were going to live after getting married.

"Ready?" said Evan. His dark eyes watched her.

"Yes."

They both got out of the SUV as Mac let out a few whines before they walked to the front door.

Katie had the key in her hand and she felt her nerves become volatile. As she raised the key and inserted it into the lock, her hand trembled.

The door opened. The inside was stuffy and warmer than it should be. Everything was just as it was the last time she had visited. It struck a chord with her the heaviness and vulnerability she now carried everywhere with her. She expected Chad to come out of the kitchen with something funny to say about his day at the firehouse.

"Katie? You okay?"

She was still standing at the threshold and hadn't entered the house yet. "Yes, I'm fine." It had become her standard response whenever anyone asked how she was doing. She couldn't stop to think about how she was really feeling because it would derail her and she wouldn't see things objectively.

Katie entered the living room as Evan closed the door.

"What do you want to look for?" she said.

"I read the missing person's report and I read your account of the evening leading up to his disappearance," he said. It was clear that he was trying to be aware to the sensitive and personal nature.

Katie scanned the living room out of habit so she wouldn't have to look Evan in the eye, but as she did, she noticed something out of place. The training manuals for the fire investigation that Chad always kept on the bookshelf were now on the coffee table.

"Katie?" he said in a gentle voice.

She turned to face him.

"Please forgive me if I say anything that might upset you."

"You haven't said anything that would be construed as that, except proper questions for this case," she said trying to stay stoic and relaxed when inside her heart was breaking. She did appreciate his concern.

"Just now, I got the sense you noticed something."

"You're right," she said, remembering how detail-oriented he was. "Chad kept his training manuals on the bookshelf and now they're on the coffee table."

"When was the last time you were here?"

"Just after his disappearance. I stayed here for a while thinking he might come home. I know how stupid that sounds... They are basically shutting me out of the investigation. I'm too close. I can see that, but I'm also the last person to have seen him. It's just stupid of me..." Her thoughts and growing frustration jumped to the meeting with Holden and what he said to her as she left the meeting room.

So you are okay with not knowing where Chad is?

"Katie, it's not stupid. You are an amazingly strong woman and I don't know how you can keep yourself together."

Katie didn't want to have a heart-to-heart with Evan. They didn't have time for her to talk out her feelings—and anyway, that wasn't who she was. She moved to the coffee table and picked up one of the books. She randomly thumbed through it, not thinking clearly that she should have been more careful in handling items—but forensics had already been through it previously. There were yellow highlights, small sticky pieces of paper with notes, and dog-eared corners. Chad had been studying intensively for the test that he had to take for fire investigation.

"Anything?" said Evan.

"No. Just his notes for studying for the fire investigator exam." She kept turning the pages but there were just the same types of notes. Then she came across a page that had a vertical fold instead of a small creased top corner. "This seems strange."

"What?" Evan moved closer.

"It may be nothing, but... when Chad would study or read

any kind of new material he had a specific way of doing that."
She flipped the pages back. "He would always highlight and
mark certain pages with the corner crease."

"Dog-eared."

"Exactly, but here..." She flipped back to the vertical crease.

"Maybe it somehow got creased by the way he put the book
down or..."

Katie shook her head. "I don't think so. It seems very
precise. Neat."

"What are you trying to say?"

She looked at the coffee table and back to the bookshelf. "I
think someone moved these books and made this crease."

"So you're saying that after Chad's disappearance, someone
came into his house and moved his study books?"

"Yes."

"Okay, but why?"

"I don't know."

"Let's just say the person who came into his house and
moved his books was the same person who kidnapped him... the
big question is why?"

Katie took a moment as she looked around at this house, and
not seeing anything else out of place, she opened the text book
to the folded page. "Oh," she said.

"What?"

"This page is a chapter that talks about explosive evidence
from a fire with specific fire patterns that result from incendiary
devices and explosives."

Evan read the same page. "And these types of examples
have to do with commercial and industrial fires. Does any of this
mean anything to you?"

"I'm not sure."

"What's the matter?"

"It's just that my gut is telling me that this has to do with the
serial cases we're working on."

"There hasn't been any fires or explosions, right?"

"No, but it's like this is telling me of something that's going to happen. There's nothing trivial about this killer or Chad's disappearance. It seems that the killer is carefully planting evidence for us to find. I can't dismiss this." She turned to Evan. "I haven't told you that I spoke with the serial killer Simon Holden."

"When?"

"Yesterday. And he wouldn't talk to Gav and me—just me. When I was leaving he said, 'So you are okay with not knowing where Chad is?'"

"How would he know?"

"Exactly. How would he know anything about Chad unless he's being fed information of what's been going on?"

"Visitors?"

"Or officers inside the prison—or even staff like medical or kitchen personnel."

"That's a lot of ifs and maybes."

"You're right. But I want to follow every lead." She took her phone and snapped a few photos of the training manual, the folded page and the coffee table before making sure there were no more folded pages in the other manuals.

"What was his last investigation?"

"It was a suspicious house fire—the Walton house over on the east side of Pine Valley. I don't really know anything about it."

Evan looked around the rooms and examined anything that might indicate what Chad was working on. "Here's a phone number for Dayton Electronics, but there's no way to tell when he wrote it down."

"Let me see." Katie knew that Chad had a system for his notes and kept a small notepad on the end of the kitchen counter. He would jot stuff down when he thought about it. The store's number was after his notation of an employee meeting at the firehouse, which was two days before their trip. "This had to have been written the day before we went to the cabin. I can tell by the previous note."

"Okay. That would make sense since the video cameras show him there at that time. He wrote it down and then put it into his phone with driving instructions?"

Katie felt uncomfortable being in Chad's house without him. It was as if he had died and they were going through his belongings. She moved through the house and scrutinized it to see if anything else was out of place. Since it was a small house, it didn't take long. And it was a good thing that Chad was relatively neat and organized.

Once Katie had finished, she lingered at the front door. She couldn't take the atmosphere anymore, so she went outside to wait for Evan. Taking several deep breaths, she steadied her nerves and pulse.

The door opened five minutes later and Evan stepped out. "That's all I needed. We did learn a few things that might prove helpful. Don't you think?"

Katie secured the door and made sure it was locked. "Maybe. I need to get back to meet up with McGaven for our surveillance."

"No problem," he said reaching out to Katie and gently taking her arm. "I was told that you have been holding on to everything tightly."

"I'm fine, Evan," she said and pulled away, even though she felt a slight attraction. She knew that McGaven or possibly her uncle had told him about her keeping everything close and not initially asking for help. They meant well, but she didn't appreciate her personal business being told to someone outside her immediate circle of colleagues and friends.

"You're not."

"What?"

"You've been through a terrible... traumatic experience. You need time to process everything and a time to move forward. You have great people ready and willing to help. And I'm here too."

There was a sting of realism that plagued Katie. She knew everything that the people closest to her were saying was the truth. But she still wanted to keep everything inside—otherwise she would fall apart. If that happened, she didn't know if she would be made whole again. She couldn't speak, so she just nodded at him.

"It's okay. Just know I'm here too," he said.

They walked back to Evan's SUV. He opened the door for her.

"Thank you, Evan." She meant it, appreciating his support.

Evan sat back into the driver's seat. "We're going to find him."

Katie watched Evan as he clenched his jaw as he backed out of the driveway. She knew that he was intent on finding Chad as well. His tenacity for working cases was well known at Sacramento Police Department. He wanted to be the best at what he did—and he wanted everyone around him to succeed as well.

Katie kept quiet about her theories and thoughts of what happened to Chad. Too many things were coming out, but not one thing pointed them in the right direction.

Who had entered Chad's house?

Why had they marked Chad's fire investigator's explosive chapter?

More importantly, why had Simon Holden referenced Chad's disappearance?

EIGHTEEN

Saturday 1400 hours

Katie was relieved when she finally got home—her body and mind were overloaded with the aftermath of emotions. The visit to Chad's house was too real and painful, and she wanted to take her mind off his disappearance for a couple of hours. Seeing Evan again had raised some feelings, which made her feel even more sensitive and confused. She took care of Cisco, had a quick shower, and got ready for the assignment of watching Terrance Lane. McGaven and Katie had decided to observe their main suspects through their high profiles and good standing in the community.

McGaven had managed to find a way for them to enter a gala charity for underprivileged children that Lane would be attending. It was a way where they could observe him close up and try and learn more background about him from some of the guests.

Katie didn't like surveillance or undercover work as much as some police officers, but this situation was a welcome distraction that she desperately needed. She opted out of wearing a dress just in case she needed to investigate anything—wearing a skirt could be tricky during investigations and she couldn't hide her backup gun as easily. They would be entering the kitchen area as expeditors from the caterers and wouldn't be put through the metal detector as rigorously as the guests were.

Katie opted to wear a dressy pantsuit and silk blouse. It would make her look more like a civilian than a police officer. She fixed her hair and wore some makeup. She secured her backup gun in an ankle holster. Before she knew it, she heard a knock at the door.

Cisco happily barked and circled the living room until Katie opened the door to McGaven. He was decked out in a nice suit and tie as opposed to his boring detective suits.

"You look great," she said, trying to sound optimistic.

"And you, looking beautiful. I wouldn't know you were a cop if I didn't know you. You clean up nicely."

"Thank you... I think." She smiled.

"You ready?"

"Yep." She grabbed her small purse and said goodbye to Cisco.

They drove to the convention center downtown. It was packed with town cars, limos, and expensive sports cars.

"Wow," said McGaven trying to find a parking garage they could get to.

"This dinner is a big deal." Katie wasn't looking forward to going inside. With such a big crowd it would be difficult to sort out who they wanted to speak to—while keeping an eye on Lane.

McGaven found a nearby parking garage and ascended to the third level before finding a parking place. "I guess I didn't do my research well enough."

"At least we have a back way into this event that shouldn't

raise suspicions." Katie tried to sound optimistic but now she wondered if this was such a good idea.

"I hope that Deputy Tamblin is having good luck tailing Butch Turner," he said. "He jumped at the overtime."

"That's great." She thought about where the beefy trainer would go or if he was the type to just sit at home. Soon they would find out.

After securing McGaven's truck, the detectives made their way to the elevator. The doors opened and then dropped them in the busy area of traffic and pedestrians.

It didn't take as long as Katie had expected to reach the hotel. There were signs indicating where the caterers were to enter. They reached the back entrance. Caterers and other workers were coming and going with special supplies of large silver serving dishes, decorations, and huge containers of fresh flowers—some looked exotic and unusual. The detectives blended into the group and no one gave them a second look. Everyone moved with purpose and energy. It took an extensive amount of planning and the timing was imperative for this type of event.

McGaven flashed their hotel passes as they moved through the large kitchen, part galley and part open. Then they moved quickly to get away from the crowd. Katie casually watched the faces and didn't notice anything unusual. She didn't think she would, but being aware of the surroundings was a habit. She wondered if the killer might be somewhere near—waiting, watching, or taking orders from someone else. It made her shudder to think about.

Katie felt her body tense as her breathing became shallow. She was confused as to why she was experiencing such symptoms. They were going into a large gathering to hopefully find out more information about the man who had visited Simon Holden in prison. And why? The last thing that Holden said to her was eerier the more she thought about it—and it stayed with

her. It was definitely more than just a comment to provoke her—
it was said to instill fear and uncertainty. She wasn't going to let
that killer derail her ability and skills to solve the serial case.

"You okay?" said McGaven as he stood close to her. "You
feeling okay?"

"I'm fine. Just a little tired. Nothing I can't handle."

"You look a bit pale."

She spied the lady's powder room. "I'll be right back." Katie
didn't wait for her partner to reply, but quickly made her way
through a couple of groups keeping her ears alert to anything
said about Terrance Lane.

The restroom lounge consisted of several areas where you
could sit down and rest or apply makeup. The bathroom stalls
themselves were down a long hallway. The sinks were bright
white porcelain and their fixtures and faucets were gold. The
walls had paper with tiny flecks of gold in the design, and all the
seating areas had overstuffed white linen pillows scattered on
them.

Katie made her way to a sink that was the farthest away. She
watched her reflection and stared at her pale complexion. The
lighting was a perfect soft hue that made her skin appear flawless. Studying her makeup, she realized to her surprise it had
been applied well.

Moving her hand underneath the faucet, the slight flow
activated. The cool water felt good against her palms and wrists.
She sparingly dabbed her face to try to bring the blood back to
her cheeks. Within minutes her complexion looked healthy and
refreshed.

Two women in their late thirties or early forties bustled into
the room, each wearing a tight black cocktail dress. It was clear
that they had been drinking a cocktail or two. They spoke a
little too loudly and swayed slightly when they began to touch
up their makeup.

"Did he finally ask?" said the tall redhead to her friend.

Putting on more lipstick, the brunette said, "Yes and no."

"What do you mean?"

"Yes, he asked, but it wasn't him. It was one of his security guys."

Katie kept running the water, but was alert to their conversation.

"Is that his game?"

"Well, we play all kinds of games," the shorter woman said playfully.

"Where is he going to take you now?"

"Not sure. We might fly or take his yacht. Whatever my big Terry wants to do." She gave a mischievous smile.

Katie thought she might be referring to Terrance Lane.

"He is the biggest donor, right?"

"Of course, but it's all for show. He wants everyone to love him before he makes his big speech to run for the Senate."

"How does his wife feel about that?" She giggled.

"Who cares?" She showed her friend the stunning diamond earrings she wore. "As long as I still get gifts and fabulous vacations, I don't care."

Katie dried her hands as she took a careful visual of the women so that she could identify them if needed. She left the women's lounge and looked for McGaven.

She spotted her partner near a buffet table casually eating and surrounded by a small crowd of people. It wasn't difficult to find him because his height meant he towered over most others. He appeared to be involved in the conversation. Katie wasn't sure if she should join in. Instead, she took the opportunity to move around the room and check out what was going on.

The charity event was lovely. The food was presented meticulously as a team of waitstaff made sure everything was available for guests. The room was filled with white-covered tables with arrangements of tropical flowers in the center. Guests were allowed to mingle and sit down to eat in a leisurely atmosphere. Most people were dressed high-end casual. A string quartet played at the edge of the room, adding an intimate element to the surroundings.

Katie heard loud voices and laughter. Turning to see where the commotion was coming from, she recognized Terrance Lane. He had quite the entourage hanging on his every word. There was a solemn man in the background who seemed to have an earpiece, which was obviously his personal bodyguard.

Lane was tall and appeared to be in good shape. He wore slacks and a cashmere sweater but seemed to make sure that he always had his best side toward his audience.

Katie wasn't sure if she liked the man—it was as if he was playing a role for everyone to see, but she suspected there was something more. Perhaps it was her imagination, but she thought she saw him glance in her direction.

"Hey," said McGaven, appearing beside her holding a glass.

Katie eyed the glass.

"Don't worry, it's sparkling water. I got thirsty after those incredible crab cakes."

Katie laughed. McGaven had a way of making situations lighter than they actually were. He was her compass and her balance in any situation. She didn't know what she would do without her partner—and hoped that she never had to experience it. "I guess I missed those crab cakes."

"So good," he said while casually scanning the room. "So, anything interesting?" His gaze stopped on Terrance and the crowd around him.

"I think I found his mistress. Or maybe just one of them."

"Point me," he said trying to act like any other guest. He leaned into Katie and then laughed as if they shared a private moment.

Katie took his arm and moved her body forty-five degrees so that he could see the two women from the ladies' lounge. "Red-head, brunette in black cocktail dresses."

"Aw, yes." He took a sip of water. "Do you think we will find out why Lane would visit a serial killer?"

Katie smiled as a group passed by them. "Not yet. Maybe it's more about the criminal justice system and reform than Holden himself. It's difficult to tell."

"Good point. I'm going to move around the room and see what I can learn," said McGaven as he casually leaned into Katie, giving her a kiss on the cheek for appearance.

"Don't eat too much," she said. She watched as McGaven effortlessly merged himself into the crowd. She sometimes forgot that he was a very social person who loved to meet new people. This surveillance gig was perfect for him.

Katie decided to check out some of the displays. There was one that had incredible black-and-white photographs of children. Some were happy and inspiring photos of kids playing outside at a park or in school while others were showing poverty, despair, and even trafficking. The photo presentations were placed carefully to make the biggest impact as guests took the time to look at it. After all, the charity was all about helping children.

Katie continued to an area where there was another display. It was about Terrance Lane, and included his businesses, investments, and charities. She was sure it wasn't all of them, but it gave an overview of the man—basically what he wanted everyone to see. It intrigued her, so she took a moment to read what had been exhibited. She didn't want to use her cell phone to photograph anything so she would have to rely on her memory.

Katie distinctly remembered a lecture she had once attended where the profiler said, *Even if the detective has a pretty good narrative of the crime in mind—none of it means anything unless solid evidence could be developed...* That sentiment, or working advice, had stuck with her. Even though some aspects of the cases she worked began with theories, in the end, it all came down to the proof, evidence, and solid police work. These current serial cases, the copycat version of Simon Holden's, and the events surrounding Chad's disappearance had many theories, but they needed solid evidence.

She briefly looked at Lane's accomplishments, community work, and buildings he designed and developed.

"It makes you wonder how there's enough time, doesn't it?"

Katie looked at Lane, who was now standing beside her. She wondered where his entourage had gone to and then spotted two men about twenty feet away who were obviously part of his bodyguard crew. "That's one question," she said.

"You know what my favorite charity is?"

Katie forced a smile and shook her head slightly. She was interested in where he was guiding the conversation.

"I love anything that has to do with people. Helping. Supporting. Building. Inspiring."

It reminded her of something that a politician would say. "That's so important. After all, it's all about people and love." She watched how Lane admired his accomplishments. "What do you think about crime and punishment?"

Lane turned to her as a wry smile appeared on his face. "Are you talking about reform? The death penalty? Abolishing bail for those who can't afford it?"

"Any of those," she said watching his eyes closely—noticing that his pupils had now dilated more than they should, which meant that it somehow excited him. "Maybe prison reform?"

Lane appeared to not have heard her as he continued to admire the plaques and articles about himself that were on display. Then he turned his head and took a step toward Katie. "I find that a very interesting question," he said. "Especially coming from a police detective and Army veteran."

It shocked Katie that he knew who she was, but she didn't blink or move in a way that suggested so.

"Detective, I know who you are and I know why you're

here," he said. "You think I don't know that you were at the prison visiting Simon Holden?"

"I can't say that I thought about it."

"I have a responsibility to know about a lot of things. You see, it's my business. I have to know everything that's going on that could affect my work."

"I see." Katie could clearly read that while Lane might not be psychopathic, he was clearly narcissistic. Her main priority was asking herself if he was capable of killing for an incarcerated serial killer. "What kind of business would you have with Holden?"

Lane stared at Katie for a few seconds before answering—it was clear that he was carefully wording his answer. "If you did your homework, I make it a point to speak with any inmate who has a life sentence."

"And that would be because..."

"If we want to improve the criminal justice system, there needs to be some type of accountability."

"And you're going to do that?" she said, realizing that she might be overstepping her bounds.

"If not me, then who?"

"There are more qualified people to assess the prisons."

"And look how well that is doing. Detective, I have many contacts and I want to make a difference by bringing things to light."

Katie remained quiet. He did have a point, no matter how misguided it seemed to be. Her impression was that he was doing his homework before announcing his candidacy for senator.

Lane extended his hand to her. "It was nice to meet you, Detective."

She shook his hand, noticing a firm grip. "Nice to meet you, Mr. Lane."

He smiled one more time and then turned to merge back into the crowd.

Katie quickly glanced at the board again before she went to find McGaven.

As Katie and McGaven left the charity event, they remained quiet until they were inside McGaven's truck.

"Okay, you're killing me here. What did Terrance Lane talk to you about?" said McGaven as he loosened his tie.

Katie relayed everything to her partner. He seemed surprised but fascinated by what she told him.

"I'm still amazed that he knew who you were."

"I know. But after thinking about it, he could have seen a press conference or a news article. We've been in photos before and it wouldn't be unusual for anyone to get access."

McGaven's cell phone alerted. As he took a look, he grinned. "Well, it looks like Deputy Tamblin has some video and a report he's sending."

"Anything?"

"Don't know, but he did say that Butch Turner has some things he needs to explain."

Katie wasn't sure what that meant—about the homicides, or something else? She glanced at her watch. "It's still early. We can get this information back at the department."

"Of course," he said as he started the truck's engine. "Then I'll drop you back at your house."

"Sounds good." Katie felt they were making some progress with the serial cases, but something still tugged at her about the crime scenes—something that they were missing.

As McGaven drove out of the parking garage, he said to Katie, "So tell me, is Terrance Lane a psychopath?"

"The truth?"

"Yeah."

"Well, he definitely ticks some of the boxes for the psychopathic check list, like being charming and with an ego, but with some deceit and manipulation in the mix. But being a definite psychopath? My opinion is no—at least at this point."

"Oh."

"But that doesn't mean that he isn't capable of murder—or hiring someone to do it. All kinds of things could drive someone to kill. It depends on what's at stake as to how far they're willing to go. We need to try to set up an appointment to meet with Lane away from this type of setting and on our terms."

"On it."

NINETEEN

The forensic division at the Pine Valley Sheriff's Department was quiet. John and Eva were out and everything seemed still and silent. It was comforting, the only sound was the filtration system pumping in air.

Katie and McGaven watched the video clips from Deputy Tamblin's surveillance several times from their investigation command center. McGaven had displayed the video on a larger computer screen so that they could study everything closer and slow down anything that looked suspicious.

"I see what Tamblin means about Butch needed to explain some things," said Katie.

"Yep."

Katie had shed her suit jacket and was leaning forward in her chair scrutinizing the video. "Is he buying drugs?"

"It looks like it, but according to Tamblin he couldn't tell for sure."

"Maybe he's buying some kind of enhancer—like steroids, maybe?" she said. "But the real question is, is he involved in abducting and killing women to copycat Holden's crime scenes?"

"There's nothing to suggest that except..." He rewound the video to a place where Butch was in a bar ogling women walking by. "He's a sleazy guy, but that doesn't mean he abducted or attacked anyone."

"True. But it does suggest that he participates in potential criminal behavior." Katie thought about the reach from buying drugs to killing women. It didn't fit.

"This is just one day," said McGaven. "We've got clearance and the go-ahead for Deputy Tamblin to follow Butch for the next week."

Katie leaned back in her chair, still looking at the frozen image of Butch exchanging money for something in a bag in a parking lot. "That's good. It should give us more to go on. Butch isn't out of the suspect pool yet. His alibis are loose around the time of the murders, being at home without any corroborating witnesses."

"And we don't have the time of death precisely pinned down because there's always a two- to four-hour window."

Katie stood up and moved to the murder board. "Okay, what do we have now?" She picked up the marker and added a list of persons of interest.

Bobby Cox, boyfriend of Jenna Day. Had burlap hidden in his apartment. No alibi. Ran from police.

Terrance Lane, visited serial killer Simon Holden several times in prison. Deeply connected. Wants criminal justice reformed. Checked off several traits of psychopathy. Knew about Katie and her cases.

Butch Turner, personal trainer at All Fitness Gym. Knew Gina Hartfield and trained her. Seems to be involved in illegal activities.

Unidentified Man, according to Gina Hartfield's co-worker, Cecelia, there was someone she had met at the gym.

Harry Winslow, building owner of several bars, All Fitness Gym, and several industrial sites. He visited Simon Holden in prison.

"We could also add any of the workers who found the body of Brianna Garcia and the utility guys who found the body of Jenna Day—at least for questioning and background checks. Just so we can exclude them from the suspect pool."

"It'll be easy to check. Then I'll look at the backgrounds of the suspects of interest too," he said.

"What about security videos from All Fitness?"

"I've requested, but it's very limited, unfortunately."

"Why is that?" she said.

"It shows people coming and going, but little in the workout areas."

"What do we know about Harry Winslow?" she said.

McGaven referred to his computer. "Just what you wrote. But, I'm trying to find out if he's a part of these LLCs and what buildings he also owns. He always seems unavailable and I can't nail down his background."

"It's beginning to seem a bit suspicious. And why would he visit Holden? Let's set it up."

"It's not easy. I've left several messages and he or his secretary hasn't returned my calls."

"Maybe we can find out where he's going to be. Like is he going to a certain location—one of his buildings." She stared at her list of suspects. "What would a man like him want to talk to Holden for?"

"Maybe the same as Lane? He seems to be a mover and shaker as well. Big part of the business community. And lots of projects. He seems to have a problem with the criminal justice system," he said.

"Doesn't everyone?"

McGaven laughed. "Especially the criminals."

Katie stood staring at the board. They were making progress but not the headway that she wanted. At any moment, they could be alerted that another body, or two, had been found. It bothered her immensely. The worst thing for a police detective was not finding a killer before there was another victim.

"What's bothering you?" said McGaven. He had looked up from his laptop to watch his partner. "I can tell when you're wrestling with something."

"The call to the apartment building seems out of the ordinary in these cases."

"The killer must know we have something and wanted to waste our time. He's toying with us."

"Yes, I agree with you. But..." Katie looked at the crime scenes, both current and from Holden's stretch. "Everything about Holden's crime scenes are the roadmap to what we're investigating now, but that fake call and whoever was there watching. I don't necessarily think that it was the killer."

"What do you mean?"

"It seems last minute. Almost like a lapse of judgment. Does that make sense?"

"Let me get this straight. You think that maybe whoever was hired to commit these crimes for Holden—I'm just theorizing here—that this person maybe took the empty burlap of their own volition?"

"It was the way the scene was presented. Where the rolled burlap was located. Like someone thought it was a good idea and the fact that they seemed to be there to watch the scene unfold."

"Maybe they wanted to see how we would respond or find out what we knew."

Katie thought McGaven made a good point. But as she studied the photos of the bodies and scenes decades apart, she knew something was off. They were still missing a big piece of the puzzle.

The detectives worked for two more hours. McGaven dug up information about suspects and Katie pulled more information from Holden's trial transcripts. They discussed how they would speak to Harry Winslow.

Katie took copies of the crime-scene photos for the warehouse, Jenna Day, and the park, Brianna Garcia.

"Looks like Brianna's parents will be flying in tonight from Columbus, Ohio, to ID her body. And there doesn't seem to be any other relatives. She went to school here and lived alone," said McGaven reading from an email. "It seems that she was also without any family near."

"And, all three victims had memberships to the gym."

"It's definitely something that we need to look more into," he said. "And I think Butch has some explaining to do."

"After Deputy Tamblin gets done with the surveillance work—we'll have another talk with the trainer."

Katie left the sheriff's department parking lot. She was exhausted and looked forward to going home, grabbing a bite to eat, and getting some rest.

She dialed a number on her phone through her Jeep's hands-free function.

"Hey, Katie," said Evan as he answered his cell phone on the second ring.

"Hi," she said. "What do you have planned tomorrow?"

"Whatever you need me to do."

"How good is Mac at searching open areas?"

"Ninety-five percent on the money," he said.

"Great. I want to search the last two crime scenes. Something isn't sitting right with me. I think we're missing something big. And I want confirmation with a second dog before calling in the troops."

"Sounds good. What time?"

"I'll text you the location and time after I get home."

"Great. See you tomorrow."

"Evan," she said.

"Yes?"

"Thank you."

"Of course, Katie."

"For everything."

TWENTY

Katie arrived at the south area warehouse early, getting there before the time at which she'd told Evan to meet her. The overcast chilly morning made the entire location appear abandoned and long forgotten. It looked almost like the backdrop for a movie set that was ready to film. It was indeed a perfect place to dump a body.

Katie parked in the overgrown drive just before the entrance where the cargo bays were located. She stepped from her vehicle, leaving a very rambunctious Cisco behind for the moment. The dog gave two barks to remind her that he wanted to join her.

She walked fifteen feet and faced the loading area. It didn't take long to recognize where Jenna's body had been placed. The crime-scene photos played through Katie's mind like a picture reel. Something was bothering her. But this was usual when she was involved in a case. It was plaguing her that the killer was more than a step ahead of them, no doubt planning something even more insidious next time. She hated that fact. She needed to find something that would take them further in order to catch the killer.

A slight cool breeze picked up, blowing the weeds and making them sway back and forth. There was a distinct pathway that had been trampled by law enforcement and emergency personnel.

Closing her eyes, she stood still. The only subtle sound was the wind. No birds. No traffic. Taking a deep breath and letting it exit her lungs slowly, Katie tried to imagine the killer arriving at the location and thought about how he might've transferred the body along with the burlap. From the autopsy reports and where the bodies had been left, it was presumed the victims were already dead from strangulation, pinkies removed, and eyeballs detached. It was unclear where the murder sites were located. Was it the killer's home or another building? It was gnawing at her mind. She needed more to go on.

A chill went through Katie's body, causing her to shudder. It was a natural response to standing at the exact area where a serial killer had left one of his victims. She opened her eyes and stared at the empty building and the abandoned cargo bays. She imagined when the company was up and running that there would have been semi-trucks backed up to the openings where they would load or unload.

She tried to understand why the killer chose this spot. It was abandoned. It had privacy. It made a statement. But why *here*? Did the killer have some connection?

She heard the sound of a vehicle approaching up the driveway to the warehouse.

Katie turned to see the tan SUV come into view. She glanced at her watch—Evan was right on time. He pulled up behind her Jeep and quickly got out to meet her.

"Morning," he said. He wore khakis, a dark sweatshirt, and a black baseball cap of his favorite sports team.

It struck a memory chord with Katie because Evan would

always say "morning" when they were training in the military. It brought back many recollections of a period that now seemed a lifetime ago. "Hi," she said.

Evan took a look at the warehouse. "You seemed kind of cryptic about this place. I looked it up and saw that it used to be some type of automotive parts manufacturing warehouse."

"Yes. The company moved out about seven months ago."

"Wow, it looks like it's been abandoned for a couple of years," he said.

Katie nodded. "I agree."

"So what's your thoughts?" he said studying her closely. "When I initially spoke with McGaven he said that you had a somewhat unorthodox way of studying crime scenes."

Katie laughed. "Did he say that?"

"Yep, and he even used those words."

"Well, I don't know about that. Seems like a bit extreme, but I do like to take time after all the chaos from the initial discovery is over. Then I like to step into the killer's shoes—so to speak."

"You've developed another way of investigating crime scenes. Just when I thought you couldn't be more amazing— then you step up and surprise me."

Katie was embarrassed by the compliment and wasn't sure how to respond. "Can Mac track?" she asked changing the subject.

"Yes. Preliminary stuff, but he knows how to search an area —and not just for explosives or bad guys."

"Great."

"What do you have in mind?"

"I want to search this property area. Forensics already took a look around, but there could be something small that they might have missed."

Evan studied the area. "Yeah, and all this overgrowth and weeds make it difficult and time consuming. It would be tough to see something small." Still looking around, he said, "Anything in particular we're looking for?"

"That, I'm not sure."

"Okay. I can live with that." He clenched his jaw as he still surveyed the area.

"I thought Cisco and I could sweep the front while you and Mac take the back area—then we could switch areas. Does that work for you?" she said and turned to face him. There was a slight twinge in her stomach as she made eye contact with him. He had dark and expressive eyes, making it seem like he could read your soul.

"Sounds great. Is this official or unofficial?" he said grinning.

"It's just a follow-up—nothing official *unless* we find something of interest."

"Just checking," he said. "Do we need to worry about anything dangerous like traps or explosives?" He eyed her carefully.

"The sheriff's department, as well as detectives, have been all over this property," she said. "But..."

"But from that time until now could be a different story."

"Yeah. I haven't seen anything to indicate that another vehicle or person recently has been here, but we still need to stay hypervigilant."

"Of course. Do you have any walkies?"

"Yes. I have short-range ones in the Jeep."

Evan walked with Katie and put on his earpiece and mini microphone so that they could communicate. He then left to get Mac as Katie fitted Cisco with his tracking harness and lead.

Katie watched Evan and Mac walk to the back of the building and then the team disappeared. It almost reminded her of an apparition that had vanished—that they had been created only in her mind. She let out a slow exhale.

Cisco nudged her hand with his wet nose.

"You ready, Cisco?" she said and was greeted with happy whines.

As the dog jumped out of the Jeep, Katie readied herself and kept the leash no more than five feet in front of her. She decided to do a strip search instead of a zone, which meant they would walk up, turn about a foot, and then walk back down the area in a "U" formation.

Katie observed the layout of the front area and decided to start at the left, or northwest, area. She gave Cisco the "*such*," or search, command and let him lead her. They worked for about ten minutes when she heard Evan's voice in her earpiece.

"Alpha One, any luck?" he said.

It made Katie smile. "Nothing yet. Lots of garbage and beer bottles though... be careful."

"Copy that."

It was the first time since Chad's disappearance that Katie had really smiled. And it was because she was working with Evan, and Cisco. It was something that she loved and had put so much time and energy into, with Evan's help. It was also a time that she could compartmentalize her life and responsibilities to focus on just one thing—searching with Cisco. Even though her heart was broken, she could still manage to find some enjoyment in her work and activities.

As Katie made her way through half of the front area, Cisco slowed his pace as they neared where the body was. She wasn't sure if he had caught scent of where the body had been or if there was something there of interest.

Katie stopped and took a closer look but nothing came to light. She felt a twinge of frustration, but completed the rest of the front property.

"Hey, Alpha Two, are you about done?" she said.

"Just coming around the building. Anything?"

"Negative." She heard him let out a sigh.

"Negative at the back location as well."

Katie began to think that her idea was a bust and a waste of time hoping that there was a clue for them to find. She saw Evan and Mac approach.

"I can see that you're disappointed. Tell me, what were you hoping to find?"

"I'm not sure, but this killer is several steps ahead of us. I know from experience that every killer makes mistakes. But I see no point in switching search areas and continuing."

Evan appeared to be lost in thought as he took another look around.

"Well, maybe because of... everything else, I'm off my game," she said.

"I find that hard to believe." He moved closer. "This is the second crime scene?"

She nodded.

"What about the third one?"

Katie thought about it and pictured the small neighborhood park in her mind. There were tire marks that came up by way of the private school and a pile of leftover lumber for a retaining wall and playground.

"Maybe we should check that one out?" he said.

"I don't know..."

"C'mon, Katie, we've already come this far. Let's check it out."

"Okay. Follow me."

"Ten-four," he said as he headed back to his vehicle.

Katie drove up to the small park and playground where Brianna Garcia's body had been found. She cut the engine, waiting for Evan to catch up. She wondered if Brianna's parents had flown in and had already identified their daughter's body. That particular reality of being a police officer—dealing with families coming to terms with a murder—was something she tried not to think about often. It left a deep sadness like a crater in her soul. It was the thought of families having to deal with the loss of a loved one that was so painful, especially from such a heinous crime. She knew all about losing loved ones since she had lost her own parents as a teenager. It still left a great hole in her life.

The sadness that crept in made her think of Chad, no matter how hard she tried not to—it was still raw. She tried not to think about the interview when she first filed the missing person's report. It was as if she were talking about someone else —but it was someone she loved and she was planning on marry-ing. The questions and the answers she had to disclose seemed almost surreal, as if it were someone else's life. She tried to come to terms and keep moving forward—but she didn't know if she had enough strength to do so. The lead at the electronics shop might come to something, and that gave her hope that there had to be something that would break open the case and push them in a new direction to find him.

Katie couldn't hold back anymore as her eyes welled up with tears. The stress and reality of what she had been going through for more than a month was simmering just below the surface, and now it overflowed as tears fell down her cheeks.

Cisco sensed his partner's emotions and thrust his head toward the front seat, trying to comfort her.

Katie quickly wiped the tears from her face and took a couple of breaths. She didn't have time for self-pity; she needed to move forward.

Evan knocked at her window momentarily, startling her. She hadn't realized that he had driven up and parked behind her.

"Oh, hey," she said pushing the emotions away. Opening the door, she stepped out. "Okay, this is the little park and—"

Evan took one look at Katie then stepped forward and hugged her. "I'm so sorry..." he said softly, still holding her tightly. "You have so much you're dealing with..."

Katie's first instinct was to push him away, but it felt good to be held in a hug so she let the embrace continue. When she finally let go, she looked at Evan and it was clear that his gesture was genuine concern for her. "I'm sorry," she managed to say.

"Never apologize for going through hardships and pain. That's what makes us human."

Katie forced a small smile, remembering some of his words of wisdom during the military dog training. He had been a tough instructor, but that's what had made her excel and succeed.

The moment lingered and could have turned awkward, but Evan then turned to view the playground. "Seems like something different here for the killer."

"What do you mean?" Katie was intrigued that Evan's observation skills seemed to be in tune with the crime scenes.

"Well, the first two areas were rural and had an abandoned feel, but this is more intimate and part of a small neighborhood. And did you say that the victim lived close by?" He was still surveying the area.

"Yes, Brianna lived a couple of blocks away." Kate followed his line of thinking. She, too, thought it was out of character. "But Holden's third crime scene was in a small park so with following his crime scenes it makes sense."

"But you have to wonder why did Holden choose a location like this?" He turned to look at Katie.

"I think your instincts are right on—there's something about this place." Katie examined the area as her own intuitions kicked in. "I'm going to do a search with Cisco first."

"That's probably a good idea since it is so much smaller than at the warehouse."

Katie let Cisco out.

The dog whined and took a couple of spins before he was ready to go. Whenever there was a job to do, Cisco became extremely alert to the surroundings, ears perked and forward, nose twitching with a heightened sense of smell, and his eyes darted back and forth at the area ahead of him waiting for Katie's cue.

Evan hung back, quiet and watching, but respectful of Katie's search.

Katie was aware of the trainer's scrutiny, but she knew that if she needed improvement he wouldn't hesitate to give the constructive criticism.

"*Such,*" she told Cisco.

The dog took his usual position five feet in front of Katie. This time, different than the warehouse property, he slowed his pace almost instantly. His nose rose up high and he channeled his movement back and forth, heading toward the area where the body had been staged.

Katie's immediate thought was that he was getting the residual odors of the body. But as they moved closer to the vicinity, Cisco seemed more interested in the leftover pile of construction supplies, which was now mostly covered with a tarp. There were wood two-by-fours, cement blocks, and various discarded wood pieces that were going to be recycled. It had been stacked for disposal but still hadn't been picked up yet.

Evan moved closer. "There's something he's detecting around that construction area."

Katie watched Cisco and concluded that the dog had picked up a scent more than just the history of where Brianna's burlap-wrapped body had lain. She followed the dog around the building supplies, scrutinizing everything. Nothing seemed out of the ordinary. And there wasn't anything obvious.

Evan walked up and carefully rolled the tarp away from the construction supplies. He let it fall to one side and backed away from Katie and Cisco.

Katie knew that there were tire marks coming in from the driveway of the private school, which was most likely where the killer had entered. The school was on break and no one would have spotted him unless they happened to be right there at the right time.

Katie decided to take Cisco away from the area about twenty feet and then bring him back around. She glanced at Evan, who nodded in agreement with her decision. Moving near the pile of wood and supplies, Cisco's body stiffened, tail downward, and his nose went straight to the ground instead of staying head height or higher. His focus remained intense at that location.

Katie decided to kneel down, leaning as far forward as she could, and looked at the area underneath the pallet that supported the remaining supplies. The dirt looked different, darker than the topsoil, as if it had been disturbed. Standing back up, she took Cisco around the area and he returned to the exact same spot.

"I think there's something here we need to investigate," she said.

Evan moved quickly to her side examining the area. "Something buried?"

Katie nodded.

"I have a shovel in the back of my SUV," he said and left to retrieve it.

Katie took Cisco back to her Jeep.

Returning to the supply spot, she took photos of the area for documentation.

Evan began carefully digging, taking a few layers of topsoil and then breaking down through the dirt a bit further.

Katie held her breath. In her mind, she wasn't sure what they would find. Evidence? Something from the victims? Something from the killer? Or, was the killer manipulating the police and having fun leaving false clues again? Surely John would have found something the first time? Her thoughts were inundated with too many possibilities.

Evan dropped to the ground on his knees and, putting the shovel down, he used his hand. "Katie," he said softly.

She couldn't see what he was referring to but the sound of his voice was intense and low. He leaned back and suddenly Katie could barely breathe. "That's..." she whispered.

Evan's intense eyes met hers. He nodded and carefully got to his feet backing away from the area.

Katie retrieved her cell phone as her hand slightly shook. She couldn't believe what she saw and what she hadn't suspected. "This is Detective Katie Scott, badge number 3692, we need patrol and forensics to the location at 2600 Baywood Drive, Wellington Park. We have a 10-54." She waited. "Thank you."

The body was right underneath them all the time.

She turned to Evan. "The next victim in the killing series was buried on this property and not at an apartment building. It was right here the entire time. But how?" Pacing, she thought about the probability and the reality of the killer burying a body on the park property. Then, "I would bet that there are two bodies buried here. It would mirror the next crime scene in Holden's murders." The killer was taunting them.

Katie and Evan stood at the supply site staring at a human arm sticking out of the ground. The hand had two rings—one shaped like an ornate silver vine and the other a small dark gemstone set in gold. The appendage still had some flesh, which meant the victim hadn't been buried for very long. Now they had to wait to find out if there was just one body—or two.

TWENTY-ONE

Sunday 1145 hours

Katie stood solemnly at the edge of the park and watched as John and Eva prepped the area where the construction supplies were located. The leftover items had been carefully photographed, moved, and restacked in their same positions about fifteen feet away. There were barriers around the grave site. There wasn't just one victim, but two, just as Katie had predicted. They had been standing at the fourth crime scene and hadn't even known it when they had discovered Brianna's body.

McGaven had been called in to coordinate with patrol for another search and to question the neighborhood in a larger radius, all the way to Brianna Garcia's house. They were going to question employees from D.W. Contractors, which did the renovation. Someone had to have seen something, with three bodies being moved, buried, and dumped in a small neighborhood park.

Evan walked up to Katie. "Mac and I are going to take off unless you need something."

"No, everything is underway. Just need a report from you stating what happened and how you were involved."

"Of course." He hesitated. "Are you going to be alright?"

"I have to be."

"That's not what I asked."

Katie respected that Evan had always been direct. "I will be."

"If you need anything, you know where I am." He paused a moment before he reassuringly touched her arm and then left.

McGaven passed Evan and they exchanged pleasantries before moving on. Katie's partner stood next to her. "I like him."

"Who?"

"Detective Daniels. He's cool."

"Evan is great," she said.

Katie changed the subject. Her mind whirled as she stared at the grave with two victims and the forensic excavation in progress. "Do we know anything yet?"

"Not yet," he said as he readied his iPad. "I have patrol canvassing the area again and contacting maintenance at the school next door. And here is... two views of the area from the drone." He turned it so Katie could see. "This is when we found Brianna's body and this is today's. Notice anything?"

Katie took the computer pad and studied the two videos. She realized. "It's different in how the leftover building supplies were placed after John had searched them. The bodies weren't here when we found Brianna. That means..."

"It means that the killer came afterward. I couldn't believe John wouldn't have found something the first time. And it also means that the killer left two bodies in the same timeline as Holden, just not at an apartment complex."

Katie sighed. "Why is the killer deviating from the previous crime scenes?" The heaviness of the serial case bore down on her like a lead weight. It was the first time in her detective career that she honestly didn't think they were ever going to get ahead of the killer.

"What else is on your mind?" said McGaven. He watched his partner closely.

"This case—these cases—we're no closer to finding the killer."

"I've never seen your stress level this high since I've known you. We will do what we always do. Go through every clue and follow every lead—even if we have to go over them again. C'mon, we've solved every case together. We're an unstoppable team."

"I know. Everything you're saying is true. But I don't want any more bodies. We have five bodies now—and I have a suspicion that the killer has already picked out his next victim."

"Slow down," he said. "It's amazing that you were able to find these two victims. They could've been here for who knows how long. And the fact they weren't wrapped in burlap, this all has to mean something. And I know you, Katie. You will break this new development down with your behavioral analysis and profiling."

The detectives watched as the medical examiners carefully exhumed the first body. The naked victim was lifted onto a gurney and put inside a body bag to keep any evidence intact. Even at the distance at which Katie and McGaven stood, it was obvious to them that the eyes of the victim had been removed, giving preliminary linkage to the other cases.

Katie was already adding to her behavioral evidence list of the killer. He seemed to be enjoying himself, playing the police and watching them run around. It suddenly hit her.

Could the killer be watching all the crime scenes?

Returning to them to watch police?

Could the killer be reporting back to Holden? Changing crime scenes to confuse law enforcement?

"Gav, we need to go over everything about all the persons of interest. I mean everything. I know that there are clues we're not seeing."

"You got it."

Katie watched the second body being exhumed and loaded into a dark body bag. It had the same black holes in its face where the eyes once were. Her grief rose to the surface, her body tingly and her breath catching in her throat. There were two female bodies being retrieved in front of her. Her mind couldn't help but think about what if it had been Chad. She quickly closed her eyes for a couple of seconds to erase such a harsh and horrifying image. The thought was never far from her mind—and that's what terrified her even more.

"Katie... Katie..." said McGaven.

She turned to her partner.

"You okay? Maybe you need to take the rest of the afternoon off?"

"I don't know..."

"They have more to search here and it's going to take a while. Go home. Rest. And I'll update you in a little bit, okay?"

Katie knew he was right, but at the same time she wanted to stay through the entire search. "Okay," she said reluctantly. "I'll take a couple of hours." She headed slowly back to her car, but knew that she would be going over the crime scene list again.

John went to the forensic truck to retrieve some tools and saw Katie. His look was deeply worried as he watched her, but he continued with his work. It was going to be a long afternoon that possibly went on long into the evening.

Katie didn't take a last look at the crime scene. Instead, she got straight into her Jeep. She was concerned for a moment that she would break down, but was determined she wasn't going to let that happen.

Cisco whined and pushed his nose to her.

"Let's go home," she said.

Katie managed to maneuver her SUV around the police

vehicles and a deputy let her through the main barrier which kept any non-personnel out. She saw a small group of people, probably neighborhood residents, congregating about the site and talking among themselves. There was a man to one side wearing a dark gray hoodie that had been pulled up to cover his head. He was turned away so Katie couldn't see his face. Maybe she was imagining things, but the man seemed to be watching the situation while keeping himself hidden.

Katie drove off down the road but once a ways away, she pulled to the side and sent a text to McGaven:

Male bystander, tall, average build, in dark gray hoodie—check him out.

Katie drove home. The closer she got to her house, the more tired she became. Her body was exhausted. Her mind fuzzy. She needed some restful sleep.

Pulling into the driveway, she turned off the engine. Stepping out, followed closely by Cisco, she walked to her porch.

Cisco ran to a plain brown package leaning against her door. His tail wagged as he sniffed the parcel from corner to corner.

Katie bent down to pick it up. There was no address or name. It was a plain brown padded parcel-mailing envelope. It wasn't sealed. She opened it. Inside, she found a framed photograph of her and Chad and a small handbook for fire investigators—both were from his house.

Katie dropped the parcel on the porch. Dread overcame her, and she began to look around her property. There was no sign of anyone or how the package had been delivered.

She stood in her driveway with Cisco at her left side. In that moment she never felt more alone.

TWENTY-TWO

Sunday 1600 hours

Katie and Cisco sat on the couch as McGaven and Nick searched her house and yard for any indication of who might have left the package. They scoured her security video, but there was no image of anyone coming or going. It didn't make any sense.

Katie wasn't scared or anxious, she was numb. The events of everything seemed to absorb into her consciousness to such a degree that she didn't feel anything anymore. She petted Cisco, which helped keep her from crying. She watched McGaven and Nick search her house and converse on what needed to be done. After a while, she didn't even hear them.

On the coffee table were three evidence bags—one for the envelope, one for the fire investigator's handbook, and one for the framed photograph of her and Chad. It didn't seem real, just like when she had woken up in the cabin to find him gone with no indication he had ever been there.

And now, someone had left things from Chad's house at her front door. But there was no indication of who left them or when. It was as if she were living in an alternate reality where nothing was as it seemed.

She heard the sliding door open and then close. McGaven had gone out to check some things out and make sure all security cameras were operational.

"Hey, Scotty," said Nick as he sat down next to her. "You've had quite the day. McGaven and I have been talking and we think someone should stay here with you at least tonight."

Katie looked at him but remained silent. She was too tired to argue. Besides, having someone else in the house would be nice. She never normally minded being alone; in fact, she usually enjoyed her downtime alone. Now, she wasn't so sure.

"I volunteered, if that's okay," he said.

"Of course," she managed to say. "That's fine. The guest room and bath is all stocked up." She looked at the image of her and Chad smiling together and remembered when it was taken.

"We're going to finish up and I'll be back within the hour. Okay?"

She nodded. "That's fine."

Nick rose and then went to the door. "If you need anything before I get back, just call me."

"Okay."

Nick left.

Katie sat alone. For some reason, it unnerved her. She wondered how much heartache a person could take.

The slider slid open and McGaven entered. "Okay, everything is good. All systems are working," he said trying to sound optimistic under the circumstances.

Katie didn't say anything.

"I'm going to get this stuff to John and we'll see what they can come up with. Oh, do you have an extra key to Chad's house? I think John should try to dust for prints and see if there's anything missing that seems obvious." He grabbed the evidence bags.

"He's not going to find any prints or anything else."

"You always say that the perpetrator always makes mistakes —it's only a matter of time."

"He's not making any mistakes anytime soon."

"You don't know that."

She slowly nodded. "Yes, I do."

McGaven dropped the bags onto the table. "This isn't you."

"What do you mean?"

"The Katie I know is tenacious, never gives up, and definitely doesn't sit quietly when there's a killer on the loose."

Katie looked away from her partner. She couldn't bear it, but he was right.

"And the Katie I know doesn't quit."

"You think I'm quitting?"

"What are you doing?"

"I'm trying to make sense of everything," she said.

"That's a start."

"What do you want from me?" She kept McGaven's stare.

"I want my partner back. And I want to find this killer. But mostly... I want to find Chad so that I can have my partner back —happy."

Katie knew that he was right. She should go back over everything and put together a more in-depth profile. There must be more behavioral imprints to the crime scenes still to be found and she knew that a much clearer identity of the killer was slowly coming to light. She still questioned how she could weather these huge emotional storms.

"I can see that the wheels are turning."

Katie stood up and hugged her extremely tall partner. "Thank you, Gav. I can't do this alone."

"We've been through too much together. Fighting those killers and bringing them to justice. He hugged her tight. "You can do this—*we* can do this."

Katie stepped back. "Go. Take that evidence to John and

find out the status of the burial site. Let me know. I'm going to wait for Nick."

"You rest, okay?"

"I will."

"See you bright and early," he said with a smile.

"Of course. I'll see you in the a.m."

"Not if I see you first."

"Please rest and get a good night's sleep."

"I'll try."

McGaven left.

Katie knew that she had great support in her friends, colleagues, and her uncle but it still didn't fill the void of the sadness she felt at the moment.

She was glad when Nick returned and she wasn't alone anymore. Good friends were what she needed right now. They had dinner and conversation that helped her to relax, on subjects that didn't entail crime scenes or Chad's disappearance. It didn't take long. Katie was exhausted and went to bed.

Katie ran along one of her favorite trails through the woods, but her light mood turned uncertain. It was cold and rainy, turning harsher by the minute. The sunlight began to disappear, making the forest seem ominous and foreboding. She tried to find a way out, but every trail seemed to dead-end.

Her heart rate increased. She began to panic as she ran faster. Everything around her turned darker, making it difficult to see the outlines of the trees. She kept running.

"Katie?"

She stopped in her tracks.

Again, "Katie?"

She knew whose voice that was.

"Chad? Where are you?"

"Katie, please don't be sad. You will solve your cases."

"Please, where are you?" She kept turning but didn't see anything except darkness and towering trees. *"Please..."* Her voice wavered as she fought the urge to cry.

"Don't be sad."

Katie strained to hear where Chad's voice was coming from.

"Follow the leads like you always do. Nothing is as it seems."

"Please, I need to see you."

"You will know what to do when it's time."

"Chad... where... I can't lose you..."

"I love you, Katie."

She waited but couldn't hear his voice again. Whispering, she said, *"I love you more..."*

Katie woke with a stifled gasp and sat up in bed. Her breathing was heavy as if she had been running—it took a moment to steady her pulse and calm her dizziness. Perspiration had saturated her nightshirt, but her bedroom was cool. She noticed that Cisco had vacated his usual spot on the oversized chair and was sleeping on the corner of her bed.

She stayed still, listening, but there was nothing. It remained dark—exceptionally dark. There were two low nightlights in the hallway, but it appeared dark around cracks of her closed door. She swung her legs as her feet made contact with the floor, steadying her balance. Opting not to grab her robe, she quietly walked to her door and flipped the light switch.

Nothing. Still darkness. The electricity was out.

Cisco was instantly at her side. He had jumped from the bed without making a sound.

"Cisco, *bleib*," she whispered and made sure that the dog stayed in the bedroom.

Katie put on her sweats and grabbed her Glock from the nightstand, stealthily moving toward the hallway. She quietly opened the door and peered out. The area was dark. The living room and kitchen areas were also dark—no light from the clock above the oven and microwave. Her thought turned to her security cameras—they should still be activated even with an electricity outage for several hours.

She turned and saw that the guest bedroom door was closed —and she assumed that Nick was sound asleep. Contemplating for a moment, she decided not to wake him. She moved toward the kitchen area, carefully stepping with purpose. Goosebumps appeared on her arms and up the back of her neck. It was unclear why she felt trepidation moving through her house. Her dream was still on her mind—she could still hear Chad's voice so clearly.

Nothing is as it seems.

Katie walked into her kitchen where a laptop computer was sitting on the edge of the counter. She flipped it open and waited for it to power up, thankful it was fully charged. Looking at the program that showed all the cameras around the perimeter of her house, she noticed that everything looked normal. Quiet. Nothing looked odd or out of place.

The sound of a bedroom door opening caught her attention.

Katie turned and saw the shadowy figure moving down the hallway.

"Scotty," said Nick. He was wearing sweatpants and a loose T-shirt.

"Yeah," she said softly.

"What happened to the power?"

"Don't know."

Nick stood next to her, looking at the security views.

Katie saw how the light from the computer made Nick's face appear strange and like it wasn't her sergeant from the Army. She watched his eyes scan the screen.

Nick turned to look at her. "You okay?"

"Yeah, just a bad dream that woke me. But now I'm

thinking that there was some kind of sound that woke me instead."

"Where's the electrical panel?" he said.

"It's in the garage."

"Flashlight?"

Katie rummaged through one of the drawers and took a flashlight out, double-checking to make sure it was fully charged.

Nick followed Katie to the garage through the kitchen area. It was a small one-car enclosed garage that she had turned into a storage area.

"It's over here," she said moving to the far side.

Katie fanned the light beam across the area. There were boxes, gardening supplies, and extra pieces of furniture she had taken out of the house.

They made their way to the electrical box and Katie realized that the panel door was open. She directed the flashlight at the area and could see that all the switches were off.

"That's strange," she said. "Why is everything turned off?"

Nick pushed the toggles upward and the electricity came back on. And at that moment the garage door opened.

"That shouldn't happen. The garage door opener hasn't worked in a decade." Katie saw the outside door that had been secured and nailed closed due to being a security hazard was now open a crack. "This door..."

"What about it?"

"It had been sealed shut, but now it's open." She went to the door, readied her weapon, and then stepped outside, fanning from left to right. Walking back inside, she said, "I don't know what's going on here."

"Let's secure this door and I'll unplug the power to the garage door opener," he said immediately getting to work.

Katie assisted him until everything was secure and she was satisfied.

"It's okay. We'll figure it out in daylight," he said. "I'll make sure everything is okay tomorrow."

Katie stared at her garage storage area wondering if anything was missing. Then her mind reflected back to Chad's house and how someone was able to gain entry.

"Scotty," he said. "Everything is going to be fine."

"Someone was in here. Were they inside the house too?" Katie felt violated that her privacy had been breached, but more importantly what was their motive? Again, was the killer closer than she had suspected?

"There's no one here now. We'll figure it out in the morning." Nick tried to appease Katie's concern.

"This has something to do with Chad and..." Her heartache was overwhelming when she thought about him.

"And what?"

"And these homicide cases."

Nothing is as it seems...

TWENTY-THREE

Monday 0745 hours

Katie had been looking through the files for the past hour. She was surprised that McGaven hadn't beaten her to the office. She tried his cell but it had gone straight to voicemail.

She added more information to the killer's characteristics and behavioral evidence: *likes high-drama crime scenes, seems to be toying with police and investigation, shows brazen arrogance, seems intent on re-enacting Simon Holden's crime scenes but moved away for last two bodies, seems to be escalating, takes big chances going back to crime scenes,* and *slightly changing MO.*

Could be related—but can't rule out: break in at Chad's and Katie's houses, tech experienced, notation in fire inspector's text book re explosives page.

Katie sighed. There were so many clues, little hard evidence, and too many subjections and inconsistencies to put it together in a cohesive manner. She still couldn't shake the feeling that Chad's disappearance was somehow intertwined with the serial murders.

But why?

How?

"Hey," said McGaven as he entered the room.

"Hey, yourself. I made it here before you for a change."

"I stopped by your house and you had already left."

"I couldn't sleep much, so I decided to come in," she said.

"Nick filled me in on the electricity thing and showed me what you both found out last night. We did another sweep of your property. And the conclusion? I think you need your security completely overhauled—it's like it's been hacked into. It hasn't been picking up anything—and that garage-door-opening thing. Katie, I don't like this. You could be in immediate danger. You need to take this more seriously."

"So if you can't find anything and the security isn't revealing anything... that means that someone is more than tech savvy and they are somehow overriding my system?"

"That would explain how they were able to get into your garage. But like I said—"

"But why?" she interrupted.

"You're the profiler. Why do you think?" He moved to the board and studied what Katie had recently written.

"Just theorizing here. But the killer seems to be trying to get me, or us, to play his game." She pulled out a chair and sat down.

"That's an interesting point," he said.

"Think about it. Those news clippings left at the crime scenes about our previous cases. Chad's stuff left on my porch. Entering my house as well as Chad's place. And who knows what else the killer has in the works for us." She cringed thinking about someone moving around her place without her knowing about it—just under her nose. Most likely when Cisco wasn't there.

"Let me get this straight. You're inferring that details about Chad, the packet left on your porch and missing books, are somehow mixed into our investigations?" He sat down to face Katie. "I think you need to think more about your security."

"Why and how, I don't know—yet. But I have a gut feeling. One of the articles was about Chad and what he was involved in." Katie looked at her partner. "I know you're concerned about these security breaches. I promise I will be careful."

"Please take precautions and get that security system updated as soon as possible." McGaven looked at his phone. "Looks like John will have some things for us later today and Dr. Dean sent a preliminary report of the buried bodies. They have been identified as Michaela Brown and Cindy Taylor, both twenty-five, roommates in Cedar City, which is about forty miles away."

"Strangled? Missing pinkies?"

"There's no report on that yet. The ME office will let us know."

"Okay, what else do you have?"

"I'm so glad you asked me that. That guy you sent a text about at the park crime scene was no longer there. And the rest of the crowd didn't know him nor had ever seen him before. Not much of a description except he was older—mid-forties or so."

"Where's the good news?"

"Hang on... one of the deputies turned up a lead at the Wellington Park Prep School. The maintenance guy saw someone hanging around at the park late. When he tried to confront him, the guy bolted."

"We need to talk to him," she said. "It seems strange that there wasn't any other report about it."

"Let's go see him."

"He's there now?"

"He should be later today. It's his job to be like a caretaker until the school is in session again in about... two weeks." He referred to notes. "The deputies have statements from D.W. Contractors' employees and they should be coming in email.

Nothing stood out, but Denise will do quick background checks on them too—just to be thorough."

Katie flipped through her notes. "I found out that Harry Winslow owns several warehouses across Pine Valley and neighboring towns. One of his companies is HWI, Harry Winslow Incorporated. It was difficult to unravel with all of the different names he's used in the past, which, to me, seems like a red flag that he might be hiding something."

"What a guy," said McGaven with some sarcasm. "Just making our jobs that much more difficult. But, after talking to I don't know how many people who work for Harry Winslow, I found out that he'll be at a future commercial building site at 200 Pine Crest tomorrow afternoon."

"We'll be there," she said firmly. Thinking about what McGaven had just told her and the information on the board, she knew that there was only one place they needed to go at the moment. She stood up.

"What? Did I miss something?"

"We need to talk to Simon Holden again—there's too many unanswered questions that have to do with people of interest on our list. This time I won't play nice." She made the arrangements so that they could talk to him later that day and then quickly left to speak with Terrance Lane.

After answering a phone call from Lane's office, she said, "We've got an appointment with Lane in twenty minutes at his office."

McGaven looked at his watch. "We've got to hurry."

TWENTY-FOUR

Monday 1050 hours

Katie didn't like driving to downtown Pine Valley as they made their way to Terrance Lane's office. The handful of tall buildings always seemed to be looming and overpowering the rest of the landscape. Even though the architecture was impressive and the high rises housed many companies and businesses, it still seemed to be a scar on the beautiful area. She drove in silence. Glancing at McGaven, she saw that he too was contemplating the investigation. One of the many things that she liked about her partner was that they could co-exist in quiet—each contemplating everything they had learned so far. It was a respect aspect to their relationship, an unwritten bond they both shared when investigating the latest case.

Katie parked in a nearby parking garage and the partners made their way to Pine Towers, where Lane had the top ten floors for his businesses and his campaign headquarters.

She remained quiet, gathering her thoughts as they entered the elevator. Watching the doors slowly close and while the car hummed upward, it reminded her how everything in life goes on no matter how much her life hurt. While she watched the numbers climb, it finally stopped at the seventeenth floor.

The doors slowly opened.

Katie stepped out, glancing left and then right. It was deserted. There was no receptionist and it was unclear if there were any employees.

"Where is everyone?" said McGaven.

"Don't know. It looks like a private floor, but why were we given access?"

"That's because you were allowed access," said a man who seemed to just appear. It wasn't Terrance Lane but one of his employees.

"And you are?" said Katie eyeing him closely. She glanced at a security camera that showed the main entrance and inside the elevator.

"Hyde."

"Well, Mr. Hyde. Are you Mr. Lane's assistant?" she said.

"I'm his security advisor," he said flatly. "This way." He turned and walked down one of the hallways, moving with purpose and authority. His hair and clothing were perfectly in place.

Katie scrutinized the man's well-fit suit, but knew that he had at least one weapon tucked in a holster underneath his buttoned suit jacket. She turned to her partner and raised her eyebrows to indicate this. McGaven subtly nodded in agreement.

The security guard stopped at large double doors. There was no identification or number. He stepped in and opened the doors.

The office was huge, with large windows looking out at the city revealing in the distance the beautiful vista of Pine Valley's forest. It was spectacular and Katie paused for a moment to admire the view.

It was clear that an interior decorator had designed the

office. There were few pieces, but each made a statement. The immense walnut desk and oversized leather chairs. There were two stained-glass floor lamps, two small tables, each with a small metal sculpture, two immense abstract paintings in black and reds, and a large neutral sisal rug. Everything was deliberate and minimalist.

"Detectives Scott and McGaven," said Lane as he rose from his massive desk. He was dressed casually, unlike his security advisor, in slacks and a dark navy sweater. It was reminiscent of what he had worn at the charity celebration.

"Mr. Lane," said Katie. "That's quite the view."

"Isn't it?" He sat back down, not bothering to gaze out the windows. "Please take a seat," he said referring to the two leather chairs in front of him.

Katie and McGaven sat down.

Katie took a breath before she began. She watched Lane's mannerisms and kept his gaze. "Mr. Lane, we have just a few questions."

"Go ahead. I've nothing to hide."

Katie thought that was a strange thing to say—it was as if he thought he was a suspect or under scrutiny. "Of course." She glanced at Hyde, who had positioned himself to appear as though he wasn't paying much attention, but he was definitely interested in the conversation with his torso facing them and his gaze straight ahead.

Lane patiently waited, tapping his right index finger lightly.

"It's come to our attention that you've visited Simon Holden in prison on five occasions." She watched Lane's reaction.

"I see. Is that a crime?" he said, now leaning back in his chair, changing his demeanor from casual to suspicious. "Detective, we've already been through this. I told you at the gala that it was about criminal justice reform. I make it my business to visit anyone with a life sentence or the death penalty."

"Yes, you did," she said.

"I thought you had other questions."

"I do."

He chuckled. "I can see you're proficient at word games."

"Mr. Lane. I could see visiting once or twice, but why five times? What could you have talked about?"

"I don't have to tell you anything, but... since I have nothing to hide, his appeals were running out, so it took more times than the usual. We talked about the case."

"I see. What was Holden's attitude? Did he say anything about his murders? Or anything about the recent murders?" Katie knew that she was treading in volatile areas, but she wanted to know the truth—if Lane was being honest or if there was something more sinister about the visits.

Lane looked at McGaven. "Is she always like this?"

"You mean good at her job?" said McGaven.

"I suppose that's one way of describing it. Detective Scott, Holden seemed like he always was. A little showy and full of questions of what could be done."

"Is that it?"

"Pretty much. And no, he didn't say he killed those women from twenty years ago or last week. The guy had a one-track mind to get his sentence overturned, or at least shortened."

"Was there anything that seemed out of the ordinary or seemed strange to you?" she said.

Lane looked at his security advisor. "What do you think? Anything strange?"

The stolid man shrugged his shoulders.

"See, even Hyde didn't think there was anything unusual." He stood up. "I'm sorry, Detectives, but I don't have time to answer the same questions over and over. If there's anything else?"

Katie rose. "Not at this time. But I hope that I can reserve the right to come back." She smiled.

"Of course," he said, returning her smile.

"We appreciate your time," said McGaven.

"Hyde will show you out." Lane sat back down and flipped opened a file, not looking at the detectives again.

Katie's thoughts swirled with more questions and the intense gut feeling that there was something she was missing.

The detectives dutifully followed the security advisor to the elevator, where he waited until the doors shut and the lift began to move, taking them back to the main entrance.

As usual, Katie and McGaven didn't speak until they were back in their car. It was routine and they never knew who might be listening, either in person or with security cameras.

Katie got behind the wheel and waited.

"That was interesting," she said.

"More than interesting."

"What do you mean?"

"Can't put my finger on it... as lame as that sounds, but Lane knows something more," he said.

"You mean like he knows about the murders—or at least if Holden is behind this?"

"Lane has a weird tick."

"The movement of his jaw? I saw it too."

"But did you notice that he did it every time you mentioned Holden's name?"

Katie thought for a few seconds. "That can indicate someone is giving half-truths."

"Yep. I agree with that."

"But which ones are the truth... and which ones are the lies?"

TWENTY-FIVE

Monday 1300 hours

The drive to Mansfield Prison didn't seem as long as the previous trip. Katie kept her eyes focused on the road, but her mind was busy flipping through everything that had transpired in the past twenty-four hours. The interview with Lane unsettled her, but she had to forge on, keeping the investigation in order and following every lead.

Katie may have been hasty in her realization of not having enough pieces of hard evidence. Whenever she was stuck in her investigations, she would think back to some of the advice she'd gained from mentors and the conferences that had made an impression on her over the years. They would always stress that if an investigator thought they didn't have enough information or clues, they just weren't looking hard enough for them. There were always pieces of evidence right in front of them. Refocus and look harder. That's what she was going to do.

"Are you going to fill me in on your private brainstorm?" said McGaven.

"Just going over everything that transpired in the past two days."

"And?"

"And... we need to push harder."

"Which means everything points back to Holden," he said.

Katie nodded. "That's what I'm thinking. He's playing a game, but it's going to get real for him now."

"He's not going to just open up to you."

"That's because both of us are going to have a chat with him."

"He's not going to go for it."

"Oh, he's going to tell us what we want to know."

"What makes you so sure?" he said.

"Psychology."

"Don't you think he's going to see it coming?"

"Maybe, but his lack of impulse control won't allow him to be upstaged," she said. Katie had thought long and hard about how to get through to Holden. Everything came back to the fact that she needed to play his game—and win.

McGaven smiled. "I like it. What do you need from me?"

"Just be you—do what you always do when I'm interviewing. Just keep Holden off balance with your movements."

"What if he refuses to talk and wants to leave?"

"I'm taking the chance that he won't let it go, that he'll want to brag and feel like the most important person in the room." Katie turned off the road and headed up to the prison.

The detectives once again went through all the security checkpoints, parking and entering the prison, and finally found themselves standing outside the secured meeting room.

Katie had everything set in her mind, but now standing at the door she had some doubts. She couldn't show any weakness or hesitation, then the interview would be over and she wouldn't get the chance again.

Taking a couple of breaths, Katie harnessed the tough

police detective characteristics and tried to push aside everything in her mind just for this moment.

"You ready?" said McGaven. His demeanor was calm and it was clear that he was comfortable in his zone. His expression remained neutral.

"Yes."

The guard who had been waiting patiently inserted his key into the two locks and opened the door. The detectives entered. The same sound of the double locks securing behind them still made Katie shudder.

There was just one empty chair, so McGaven took his cue by moving toward one side of the review room. It was just the three of them in the room. There was the usual guard standing in the corner as before.

"So you can't control yourself alone with me and you brought your bodyguard," he said. "That's pretty weak, Detective. Alright, I'll play along."

Just as before, Holden sat across the table, shackled, with his fingers laced and his forearms resting on top. This time he kept eye contact with Katie. A wry smile was on his face. He didn't seem to notice McGaven or didn't care.

"Mr. Holden," said Katie.

"Please, we're past the formalities. Call me Simon."

"Alright... Simon."

He leaned back, taking his arms from the tabletop. "So I'm guessing that you're stuck in your investigation and you've come back to see me, right? Or, is it because you find me attractive?" Holden raised his eyebrows as if he were being shy or bashful.

Katie could read him clearly and she was going to get what she needed. "Were your parents ever proud of you?"

"What do you mean?"

"You know, proud of their son like any parent would be. Even after you graduated from college?"

"I see what you're doing."

"Good. So were they proud of you?"

"I thought you wanted to talk about your cases."

"I do. But I had a few other questions first." Katie decided to sit down across from Holden so that she could get a better look at him and his mannerisms.

"I don't want to answer that question."

"I see. Does that mean they weren't proud of you?" Katie was keeping her focus and settling in with her examination.

Holden held his tongue and didn't answer as he turned his head away.

Got him.

"That's okay. I don't need to know anyway."

"What do you want, Detective?"

"The truth."

"That's all up to interpretation."

"No, I think the truth is the truth. Fact. Certainty. Reality."

"I'm aware of what it means."

"Okay. Why did Terrance Lane visit you after you were sentenced?" She waited patiently, never taking her eyes away from him. She could see McGaven in her peripheral subtly shift his weight and pace slightly.

"I'm sorry, who?"

"Terrance Lane."

Holden shook his head as if he didn't know who that was.

"Simon, he came to visit you. He's a prominent person who likes to help lost causes."

"Oh, the guy who wanted to know all about me. How I grew up. What I did for fun. Just the usual stuff. I figured that he was doing some type of true-crime angle."

"Did he ask you about the murders?"

Holden didn't answer right away. "Detective, really?"

"I think it's a pretty straightforward question." Katie wasn't going to repeat it. Holden knew what she wanted and she was going to keep pressing.

Holden made a dramatic sigh. "No, he didn't. He was more interested in my history and not the crimes I was accused of."

"Do you usually talk to people who want to know about your background?"

He shrugged.

"So what about Butch Turner?"

"Ah, Butch. What a funny guy, not really smart, but funny."

"So, your dad knew his uncle?" she said.

"Yeah. Butch just came here to see how I was doing. How considerate, right?" He averted his gaze. It was clear that speaking about his father made him uncomfortable. It wasn't in his comfort zone of trying to shock and be the center of attention.

"Maybe. You sure he wasn't here to do you a favor?"

"Favor?"

"You know, doing something nice for someone."

Holden shrugged. He raised his hands and began to bite his nails. A nasty habit but it seemed to be a stress response.

We're getting somewhere.

"Katie, just spit it out. What are you trying to say?" Holden appeared to be losing interest.

"Did you ask or imply in any way that Butch should kill for you?" Her words hung in the air. The room almost appeared to become smaller. The mere mention of the word "kill" changed his demeanor—he was cautious, nervous, and wary of Katie.

"No."

"You never talked about your kills."

"Detective, I maintained in court that I didn't do it. I'm sure you read the transcripts."

"C'mon, Simon, I don't know why you won't take credit. Imagine all of the notoriety you would receive for these crimes. Planned. Well-executed. Intelligent."

"You can flatter all you want, but... I. Didn't. Kill. Those. Women."

Katie leaned back and studied the man. He didn't flinch or waver. His stare wasn't intense. "If you didn't, then who did?"

"I'm not at liberty to say."

"So explain to me, to us, why was there DNA evidence from you at the crime scenes, as well as impression evidence from *your* car, and the timeline fit your schedule?"

"I can't."

"Whoever is killing these women now is copying your crime scenes." Katie slammed her fist on the table. "There's going to be more victims. Give us something." She didn't like losing her temper but lives were at stake and it was her responsibility as a police officer and detective to keep the citizens safe.

Holden began to laugh—it grew in intensity as his voice rattled around the room. It was eerie and bizarre.

Katie would never forget his laugh for the rest of her life. "Want to fill us in on what's so funny?" she managed to say.

McGaven moved forward closer to the table.

Holden's demeanor changed. His face clouded, his eyes narrowing, mouth tensed, and his shoulders rose. As he spoke, spittle flew from his lips. "Finding killers is your job, Detective. My job is to sit in this hellhole and do my time. Any questions?" He leaned forward and pitched his arms with fingers outstretched at Katie.

"Hey, settle down, Simon," said McGaven.

"Very good, Simon," she said. "You've given us a lot of information."

"What are you talking about?"

Katie laughed. "You know exactly what I'm talking about."

"I don't know what you think you've accomplished here... but—"

"But you've told us more than I ever expected to know." She smiled and stood up.

"Where are you going?"

"To follow up our investigation."

My job is to sit in this hellhole and do my time.

"You can't leave," he said. "You leave when I say you can leave." It was as though he was struggling to keep his place as an alpha personality, but failing.

"Sorry, Simon. We're done here." Katie moved to the door followed by McGaven. She knocked. Moments later the locks were disengaged.

"You can't leave! You won't find him!"

"Find who?"

"Now I've got your attention."

"Quit playing games. It's so boring."

"Don't you want to find Chad?" he said.

"What did you say to me?"

"Chad. Haven't you wondered about him?"

"Whatever you know, you need to tell me *now*."

He leaned back and laughed. "I don't know anything. Except... you need to be careful."

Katie shrugged. "Bye, Simon." She wasn't in the mood for his games. He wasn't going to answer any questions—but she got what she needed. It was difficult not to fall apart at the mention of Chad's name, but she wasn't going to do anybody any good, including Chad, if she didn't stay focused and do her job.

"No! You can't leave!"

The detectives left the meeting room while Holden was still yelling obscenities.

Katie and McGaven didn't discuss anything until they were outside the prison and walking to the car.

"You okay?" said McGaven.

"I will be."

"So I guess you got what you needed," said McGaven. "Are you going to let me on it?"

"I didn't see it before," she said.

"What?" He turned to face his partner. "He didn't tell us anything."

"That's because he doesn't know."

"You've lost me."

"When I asked him about who is killing, he said that it's our job and his was to sit in prison."

"Okay."

"There's one thing for sure."

McGaven waited.

"Holden is right. He didn't kill those women a decade ago."

"Wait. What are you saying? He's innocent?"

"I believe, from our two visits with him, he's not the killer. That doesn't mean he didn't have any part in the crimes, but he's not the killer."

"He's the accomplice?" McGaven glanced around. "So if what you're saying is true, that means..."

"That means that the real serial killer is still out here—killing again. And the killer is pulling all the strings—including Holden's." Katie opened the car door.

"So let me get this straight, when we solve these cases then we'll solve Holden's cases. The cases he's in prison for."

"That's correct," she said. Katie knew that she was taking a big step to push her theory based on what a convicted killer told them. She knew that it was what made sense. Holden was only the pawn and whoever was out there killing more women made sure he would stay quiet.

"Well, let's get busy then," said McGaven.

TWENTY-SIX

Monday 1500 hours

Katie and McGaven continued to debate her new theory and profile while they grabbed a quick bite and lots of coffee. They were still discussing it when they pulled up to the Wellington Park Preparatory School. Katie parked on the road—she wanted to check some things out on their walk up the driveway.

The detectives got out of the car.

"Okay, I'm still saying that I need more convincing—proof and evidence," said McGaven.

"I appreciate that," she said. "It keeps me on my toes."

Katie stopped for a moment. She studied the school. She could see that during the vacation time it appeared almost abandoned, almost like the warehouse. The difference was that it was maintained. It hit her hard. She knew that the killer must have used the school's driveway to enter the park, knowing that the school was on a break.

"Katie? What's wrong?" said McGaven now next to his partner. "You okay?"

"I'm not sure." She began to put together what they had so far.

"Clue me in, partner."

"It's just... looking at the school right now made me think of the warehouse."

"Jenna's crime scene?"

Katie nodded. "Did you say that the maintenance security guy didn't see anything, according to the patrol officer's canvass of the area?"

"Yes."

"But the killer has been here at least twice and spent time." Katie walked to the property lines in between the two areas. "I just can't seem to believe that no one saw anything."

McGaven nodded as he was following Katie's reasoning. "Meaning that no one would say anything if they saw someone they recognized. We were asking if they saw anyone looking suspicious."

"Exactly." She walked in between the properties and looked at the places where the killer would have been seen.

"Let's go speak with..." he said looking at his cell phone, "Denny McAdams. He's listed as the maintenance and security guy. Been working for the school for twelve years. No record."

"He should be familiar with the area around here."

"The deputies' reports didn't say anything unusual."

"Let's find out what he knows from him directly," said Katie.

They walked up the drive to where they could see a white pickup truck parked at the far side of the property. There were some buckets, gardening tools, and an open toolbox next to the building.

"Someone's here," she said.

They moved toward the side entrance, which had a sign indicating it was for maintenance only. The door was wide open.

Katie stepped up to the opening. "Hello? Mr. McAdams?"
There was no response.

"Sheriff's department," said McGaven.

"Hello?" Katie turned to McGaven. "What do you think?"

"After you."

Katie entered the building, suddenly remembering the maintenance area at the apartment complex where someone had left two rolled-up burlap rugs. She slowed her pace. "Hello?" she said again.

It was the largest and most neatly organized maintenance area that Katie had ever seen. She caught a faint whiff of fresh paint. The interior had been freshly painted and the tools were organized along one wall. The placement of the hooks, pegs, and hangers had been thought out carefully for ease and accessibility.

"I need someone to organize my garage like this," said McGaven.

Katie kept walking into the area, expecting to see Mr. McAdams at any moment.

"Maybe he's in the school. Let's go around."

They retreated and walked around the area. It was a two-story building with two large doors for the main entrance. The doors were locked.

Katie jogged up the stairs and peered into the windows. "I don't see anything."

"Maybe we should call him," said McGaven as he searched for the contact number and pressed the call button. He shook his head. "Voicemail... Yes, Mr. McAdams, Detectives Scott and McGaven are here at the school waiting to talk to you. Thanks." He ended the call. "We should hear from him soon."

Katie stayed on the steps and looked out at the property. She could easily see the drive in for cars and buses, but she could also see the small park next door. In fact, the park was easily seen from many places at the school. "Let's search the school."

They decided to split up. Katie took the areas around the school and behind. McGaven doubled back to search near the maintenance area.

Katie didn't see anything out of place, but her intuitive senses were heightened. It could simply be due to everything they had experienced so far on these cases. And she could still hear the haunting laugh from Holden so it was reasonable to assume that her nerves were stretched.

She was going to turn around and head over to where McGaven went, but decided to walk behind the buildings instead. There was a high retaining wall behind the school intended to keep the erosion and drainage from the sloping ground above the property from damaging the grounds and building.

Katie noticed some water dripping off the building, coming from the roof area. She considered the rooftop and gazed up. Thinking McAdams might be on the roof, she made her way back around to the front of the school again. She didn't see McGaven anywhere. The front doors were open—they had been closed before. She glanced up to the corners and eaves and saw that there were security cameras and wondered if they were working—and why the deputies canvassing hadn't mentioned them.

There was a crashing sound from inside.

Katie spun around and cautiously moved to the double doors and stood listening. There was only quiet. She used her cell phone and sent McGaven a message to meet her at the entrance. She waited.

There was another strange sound coming from inside the building.

Katie took several steps inside. Instinctively, she didn't call out, but rather kept her senses sharp and hearing alert. She dared another few steps, glancing back at the door expecting McGaven any moment.

Another sound emitted as if someone had run into a piece of furniture—with a thump and scraping of the floor.

Katie moved through the main area where several couches and folding tables were stationed as if they were expecting some type of event or registration. That's when she saw him.

A male figure moved quickly across the end of the hallway and disappeared into another area. The person was dressed in dark gray sweatpants and hoodie with the hood pulled up. His face was obscured and there weren't any identifiable features—but he resembled the man Katie had seen when she was leaving the excavation at the park. Medium height. Average body build.

"Stop!" Katie pulled her gun. "Sheriff's department!" She ran after the man and found herself in the middle of a maze of rooms and cubicles located in the central area of the building without windows. The man could be anywhere. She was just about to retreat and wait for McGaven when the electricity went out.

Katie stopped and stood completely still—listening and slowly turning, trying to become accustomed to the dark. There were no windows in the immediate area, making it difficult to gauge where everything was located. Not wanting to be ambushed, she stayed very still.

There was a strange scraping sound like fabric running down a wall.

Katie's first thought focused on burlap.

"Katie!" yelled McGaven from the entrance. There was an urgency in his voice that she had never heard before.

Katie retraced her steps until she met up with McGaven. He had his gun ready as well. There was a look of relief on his face.

"What happened?" he whispered.

"Gray hoodie guy," she said quietly.

"Bystander from the crime scene?"

She nodded. "I think so," she said.

McGaven retrieved a small flashlight from his pocket and flipped it on. The light cascaded a large, but weak, arc, making the vicinity appear like funhouse lighting.

Katie let McGaven lead with the light as she covered them from behind. She swept her weapon left to right and back again. She kept her focus razor-sharp. Every shadow and darkened area just out of view seemed ominous.

McGaven moved faster, but something told Katie to slow down and be more cautious. She tapped her partner on the left shoulder. He slowed and stopped.

The noise she heard earlier seemed familiar, but she couldn't place it. The scraping. The sound of heavy fabric. The thump. The crash.

"Gav—stop," she said.

They were in an open hallway area with classrooms along one side, a small amount of light peeking in through the outside windows. Ahead were more rooms, but just where they stood the hallway suddenly narrowed. Bulletin boards and colorful posterboards detailing classroom assignments and future school events adorned the walls.

McGaven stopped but didn't turn around; instead, he stood his ground, fanning the flashlight beam around them, making objects on the walls glint in bursts. Something shiny caught the light. It seemed to be a fishing line, strung horizontally about a foot from the floor, and to Katie's horror she knew exactly what it was.

"Gav—don't move," she said.

He stayed extremely still.

The line that reflected from the weak light beam was a trip-wire—for an explosive device. She couldn't tell if it was live as she wasn't able to see where it was connected. She had seen all types of booby traps and hidden explosive devices when she was in the military. And this was definitely something to be concerned about.

"We need to retreat, retrace our steps, and call this in," she said. "Be very careful." Katie put her left hand gently on his shoulder so that he knew how close she was behind him. Her traumatic memories began to kick in of the time she'd spent in Afghanistan going through terrifying experiences and explosions. They were memories that she pushed away most days—until now. Images came rushing back. The tripwires. The bomb detonations. Loss of life. Heavy gunfire. The smoke. The insurgents. It all came hurtling back at once slamming into her spirit.

They turned slowly, now facing the opposite direction. Katie led them slowly out of the vicinity and toward the entrance once again.

There was the sound again—a faint scraping noise.

Katie turned just in time to see something small and shiny drop next to them with a low metal sound. There was no mistaking what the silver canister was.

"Cover your ears!" she yelled.

Detonation. The deafening sound and blinding light was from the flash-bang that landed less than three feet from them.

The noise left a strange buzzing in Katie's ears and made her ribcage vibrate from the sound. A heaviness in her chest followed. Her vision had been reduced to a white light, which only slowly began to return to normal.

The detectives tried to recover for about fifteen to twenty seconds before gaining their bearings.

"You okay?" she said.

"I think so. Never had a flash-bang thrown at me before."

Before Katie could respond to her partner, another loud explosion ripped through the building. The sound was overwhelming, coming at them both like a runaway train and earthquake combined. She didn't realize it in that instant, but McGaven had shoved her out of way of the immediate fallout of the blast ripping past them. Pieces from the walls and ceiling turned to jagged confetti as the cubicles, desks, chairs, and filing cabinets blew out at them in a tornado-like movement.

The loud blast became a white noise as Katie fought to stay awake against the heavy pressure of the explosion. She realized that she wasn't standing any longer, but lying face down with her head turned to the left and her arms outstretched. There was pressure against the back of her legs and back, so she couldn't move.

Pieces of the building were still falling and scattering around them. After the main onslaught, the building still shook with a strange swaying motion.

Katie tried to say something, but her voice seemed to be lost in her throat. Her eardrums hummed like she were underwater. She strained her eyes to see around her as she tried to push herself up. Her arms couldn't hold her weight and something seemed to be holding her down.

"Gav," she croaked.

McGaven was lying face down as well with his face aiming away from her. He wasn't moving and didn't answer her.

TWENTY-SEVEN

Monday 1630 hours

"Gav?" Katie said again, freeing her legs after several painful attempts. Clambering her way toward him, she pushed some pieces of sheetrock and other debris from her path. Not letting her fears overwhelm her, she kept crawling toward her partner until she could touch his back. "Gav, you okay?"

He didn't move.

"C'mon, Gav," she said through welling tears. "We've been through worse... Gav..."

Katie pulled her partner toward her. He had a gash across his forehead, blood covered his face, and his eyes were closed.

Katie shed her jacket, tearing a sleeve off to make into a temporary bandage. Pressing it against McGaven's forehead to stop the bleeding, she looked around them as the dust cleared to make sure there wasn't anything else that was imminently dangerous. The roof looked unstable and the wreckage was all around them. She knew that they needed to get out immediately and couldn't wait until help arrived.

Katie saw her weapon lying nearby, grabbed it, and stuck it into her waistband.

McGaven mumbled.

"Gav," she said. Relief filled her, hearing him respond.

"You okay?" he barely muttered.

"I'm okay. We need to get out of here now."

"Okay."

"Can you get up?" She knew that she couldn't carry or drag him to safety, so she tried to help him up.

McGaven slowly rolled over and then struggled to get up.

"I got you," she said.

The sound of the building groaning and shedding more of the damaged debris rattled all around them.

"We need to go now."

McGaven pushed himself and stood up. His balance wavered and he touched his forehead.

"Can you walk?" she said.

He nodded.

Katie hooked her right arm around McGaven's waist to steady him as they began to move through the wreckage. They fell once, but managed to get to their feet again. "C'mon, just a bit farther."

Katie saw the entrance and it appeared to be intact. She could see the outdoors, the trees, and a glimpse of the park. It struck her as odd. Not quite sure why, but she filed it in her memory.

"Hey, nice view," said McGaven.

"We're almost there. I'm sure someone has already called the police after that explosion." She gripped her partner tighter, feeling his energy weakening. "C'mon," she said as she pushed open one of the doors. The fresh air greeted them. She hadn't realized that they had inhaled a lot of dust and whatever was in the building rubble.

Katie guided McGaven to an area with three large pine trees and made him sit down leaning against a large trunk. She had the feeling that whoever set the explosive charges was still nearby. Readying herself, she watched the area in a one-hundred-eighty-degree view, keeping guard with her gun directed, carefully looking for any movement.

McGaven said something that she couldn't understand and slumped to the side closing his eyes.

Katie checked her cell phone, which had miraculously made it through the explosion. The cover was cracked, but there was a signal. Her heart pounded and she wasn't sure if she could speak coherently. Too many personal tragedies rolled around in her head making it difficult to organize her thoughts. Chad's disappearance was never far from her attention.

She pressed 911 and waited only seconds.

"Nine one one, what's your emergency?"

"This is Detective Katie Scott, badge number 3692. I'm at Wellington Park Prep School. There's been an explosion. More bombs are unknown at this point. My partner is down and needs medical attention. Send bomb squad, fire, and ambulance now," she said breathlessly.

She waited as the dispatcher was contacting all the necessary first responders.

"Please hurry." Katie ended the call. Now she had to wait. Her exhaustion was camouflaged by the intense adrenalin running through her body making her hands shake and breathing rapid. She turned her attention to McGaven and noticed that the cut on his forehead had stopped bleeding. She knelt next to him.

"Gav," she said softly, wiping blood from his face. "Can you hear me?" She looked for any other wounds but didn't see any. Still glancing around them, she kept vigilant for any traps or someone drawing down on them.

What seemed like an hour was only seven minutes when Katie heard all the sirens approaching their location. She let out a sigh but her anxious symptoms didn't diminish. Her body felt strange, almost buzzing, and her hyperalert vision became slanted and dizzy. Not wanting to leave McGaven's side, she opted not to search the area for the rogue person who had set the charges.

"Hey, partner," said McGaven staring at her.

"Gav," said Katie. "You okay? They're almost here."

He grabbed her hand. "I'm fine. Thanks to you."

She hugged her partner. If anything had happened to him, she didn't know how she could live her life right now.

Two deputies ran to them.

"There's the possibility of the perp still on the property," she said winded. "Treat him as if he's armed and obviously very dangerous. There is possibly a civilian on the property we couldn't locate, security maintenance, Denny McAdams. The inside needs to be cleared by bomb squad."

Two more deputies arrived. The four of them conversed and split up in pairs to search the outside of the building and nearby grounds.

Firefighters along with EMTs arrived.

They began tending to Katie's minor cuts and bruises. "No, please take a look at my partner. He's been fading in and out of consciousness."

The EMTs began to take care of McGaven.

Katie got up and walked toward the four deputies returning from their search. "What's up?"

"Found him," one of them said.

"The outside area is secure, Detective," said another.

"Where is he?" she said.

"He was DOA," the deputy said.

Katie took off to see the killer, or an innocent victim—her

legs sore and muscles tight, making her move more slowly than usual. She wanted to see the body to confirm her suspicions of where their cases were going. She felt that it was staged like the crime scenes by a clever killer who seemed to be a couple of steps in front of them. It was difficult not to picture McGaven hurt and unconscious—she would get back to him to go to the hospital as soon as she saw the body. She neared the side of the building where the damage was almost nonexistent. Smelling smoke and a mixture of building components, Katie slowed her pace. She could hear voices of the first responders and thought they would probably call out Detective Hamilton to head the investigation.

She came to an area where there seemed to be bomb-making tools and several flash-bangs lying on the ground. She slowed her pace. There was a man's body lying on his back, legs sprawled, with a fired gun in his right hand. There appeared to be a self-inflicted gunshot wound to the right temple. He committed suicide? What stopped her in her tracks was that the man appeared older than she remembered of the man she saw, slightly overweight, out of shape, unlike the man she had seen at Brianna's scene, but he wore a dark gray hoodie. The sweatshirt was slightly askew and zipped only partway, as if he had been dressed by someone else. She knew that the man lying before her was the school's maintenance and security man by the driver's license photo they had viewed before coming to the school.

Katie shook her head. "No," she said out loud.

She knew that this man wasn't the mastermind behind the explosion. Plus, the man she had followed who had worn the gray hoodie wasn't the same man. She looked around and scrutinized her surroundings—as a staged scene. The way the body was lying seemed to be almost symmetrical rather than random.

"Katie."

She turned to see her uncle standing there. "I was..." she tried to explain.

"You were inside the building during an explosion. This is now a crime scene. You shouldn't be here," said Sheriff Scott. "And you need to be checked out immediately."

"I will be," she said, still looking at the body and the clothing.

"Katie, I mean it." The sheriff was clearly upset but he did everything by the book. "Get to the hospital now."

Taking one last glimpse, she turned to leave. "I want to go on record. This is clearly a staged scene. This is the security guy and I bet that he was dead before the explosion. Should be easy enough to check the time of death."

"Detective." Her uncle was losing patience and had a stern tone, but at the same time his eyes said how concerned he was about her.

"I'm going. And I'm fine." It hurt her to see how her uncle was worried.

Katie left the sheriff and passed Detective Hamilton on her way to the ambulance, which was being loaded up with McGaven. She hurried to the open ambulance as they were giving McGaven fluids.

"You doing okay?" she said to her partner.

"Yeah. Just a really bad headache." He looked at Katie and touched her face. "You need to be checked out."

"I'm fine." Katie put the back of her hand to her nose and discovered blood running down her face from a nosebleed. She quickly wiped it away.

"There's something troubling you," he said.

"We'll talk about it later. Let's get you to the hospital and get rid of that headache." She leaned in and took his hand. It pained her that he was hurt. They were just lucky that they hadn't been injured worse—or killed.

Katie saw the firefighters prepare to enter the building to

ensure that any fires were properly extinguished after the bomb squad cleared it and made sure it was safe. Seeing the fire investigator speaking with police officers and firefighters made her think of Chad. She closed her eyes and held her emotions tightly.

The ambulance was readied, the back doors were shut, and it took off to the hospital.

TWENTY-EIGHT

Monday 2015 hours

Katie sat up from the hospital bed where the doctors had examined her earlier. She had been left alone in a small room adjacent to the emergency area as the nurses went to attend to a trauma alert. She felt fidgety and wanted to go home, but she had to go through the protocol for when a police officer had been injured on the job. She couldn't leave until she had been officially discharged.

Katie stood up. Her ears had finally stopped ringing and her nosebleed had stopped. She felt a little unsteady on her feet, but walked to the doorway and looked around. There were voices and she saw nurses farther away, but it was quiet around her. She decided to find McGaven to see how he was doing. Moving to the left, she casually began to search for him.

There was a room off the intensive care unit where she finally saw McGaven. He was alone and appeared to be resting. There was a uniformed police officer stationed at the door. He nodded to Katie.

Katie tiptoed in, deciding whether she should disturb him.

"I know you're there," said McGaven.

"How do you do that?" she said moving to his bedside.

"I'm a detective, remember?"

"It's hard to forget." Katie smiled.

"Why are you still here?" he said.

"They haven't officially released me yet." She pulled up a chair. "Besides, I wouldn't leave without knowing you're okay."

"I will be. Whatever they gave me has eased my headache. But..." he said, "they want to keep me overnight just as a precaution and I can't return to work for another twenty-four hours after that."

"Is Denise coming?"

"Yes, she and Lizzy are on their way."

"I'm glad. She's really amazing."

"Some days I think, how'd I get so lucky?"

"Because you're an amazing guy, that's why."

McGaven took Katie's hand. "I know you're hurting, Katie."

"I'm—"

"I know you keep saying you're fine. You're the strongest person I know... but you have to lean on the rest of us sometimes. You don't have to always be the strongest person in the room."

Katie didn't know what to say. She remained quiet. It was true her heart ached and sometimes during the day she had a difficult time breathing when she thought about things.

McGaven chuckled. "I don't mean to make you feel uncomfortable, but I just don't want to see you hurting so much and dealing with it alone."

"Thank you," she said softly. Katie knew that McGaven could read her well since they had worked together for so long now, but she didn't want to be a deficit to the partnership and investigations because of personal tragedies. Changing the subject, she said, "The more important thing right now is that you need to recover and get some rest. I need my partner back."

"Detective Scott," said a nurse standing at the doorway. "We were looking for you. You need to let Detective McGaven rest and we're working on your discharge."

Katie stood up. "I'll see you tomorrow." She walked to the doorway. "I'm on my way," she said to the nurse.

She left McGaven's room, returning to her own to wait for the final okay to leave.

After a patrol officer dropped Katie off at the department, Katie got into her Jeep. Her uncle and Nick were at her house with Cisco. She sat behind the wheel. McGaven was right, there were so many people who cared about her and wanted to help. Just that thought was overwhelming as well.

Before she started the engine, her thoughts went back through Wellington Park Prep School. She would receive the reports tomorrow, but it was clear, at least in her mind, that the scene was staged to put the blame on McAdams. It left the unanswered question of the identity of the bomber. It also seemed that the killer and bomber seemed to know the moves of where the detectives were going to go. How was this possible?

After another few minutes, Katie was driving home. The closer she got, the more tired she became. She was worried about McGaven, but she was also worried about the next potential homicide victims if they didn't find the killer. The heaviness in her chest didn't seem to lessen as she thought about everything going on.

Katie pulled into her driveway and saw Nick's truck and her uncle's SUV parked. It made her feel comforted that they were there with Cisco. She parked and got out, feeling the aches and pains setting in from the explosion.

As she approached the front door, she remembered the envelope that had been left. All of these clues and the killer toying with them made her more motivated to find the killer. She could hear voices inside along with some laughter.

Katie opened the door to see her uncle and Nick sitting in her living room enjoying a beer together. She hadn't realized that they were friends, but it made her happy to know that they liked one another.

"There she is," said her uncle.

"You okay?" said Nick.

"I'm fine. Just really exhausted."

"How's McGaven?"

"He's resting comfortably. They're going to release him tomorrow," she said going to the kitchen. "He'll have to be at home another day before coming back officially from a medical clearance by the department. Not sure how he'll take that."

"That's for his protection, making sure he's ready to return to duty," said the sheriff. "And you should be off tomorrow as well." He stood next to her.

"I'm fine. Just a bit sore, some scrapes, and really tired."

"Katie, you need to slow down."

"We're right in the middle of serial cases. There's no time to slow down," she said, opening the refrigerator.

"We have takeout. There's a chicken vegetable bowl if you like," said Nick.

"Great," she said, taking the to-go box out of the fridge. "Thank you."

Katie's uncle leaned against her kitchen counter with his arms crossed. "I think we need to talk about what you did at the crime scene today."

Nick decided to go back into the living room with Cisco.

"We have. And I don't think there's anything to talk about until the reports are in and Detective Hamilton has completed his assessment."

"That's not what I mean."

Katie began eating.

"You shouldn't have gone back to the crime-scene area since you were a part of it. And bomb squad hadn't finished clearing the area. It was reckless and dangerous."

"I'm sorry, but—"

"Katie, I've known you your entire life and you have always been impetuous, stubborn, and ambitious. But you have to follow protocol. Understand?"

"I understand."

"You better. Otherwise, I may have to take official action and it will affect your professional file."

Katie wanted to protest. She knew in her gut and from her experience with serial killers that Simon Holden hadn't killed all those women almost twenty years ago. But she knew that he knew who did. And whoever was killing women now knew that she and McGaven were getting close. If the killer wanted them dead, they would be. The explosion today was a serious warning. But Katie kept her opinion to herself—for now—until they had hard evidence.

"I do understand," she said.

Sheriff Scott took a breath and softened his demeanor, back to being her uncle. "I've got to go, but I'm glad you're okay. I've ordered Nick to stay."

"He doesn't have to."

"He is staying. And I've set up for a new security system to be installed tomorrow."

"Okay." Katie leaned in and gave her uncle a quick peck on the cheek. "You don't need to be worried. I'll be fine."

"I'll feel better when these cases are over with."

Sheriff Scott said his goodbyes and left.

"I'm going to bed," she said.

"No way, Scotty," said Nick. "I know you're planning something and I would bet that you haven't told anyone else what you've theorized."

"Am I that transparent?" She sat down on the couch.

Cisco jumped up and nestled next to her.

"I wouldn't say transparent, but you have gumption."

"Gumption? Wow, I haven't had that word used to describe me." She smiled.

"You know what I mean—you're resourceful and courageous. You get your mind on something and you don't let go—'tenacious' is a better word."

"I know, I can be," she said petting Cisco. "I can't help it. We're under the gun here. If we don't start making serious progress, someone else is going to die."

Nick sat for a moment as if contemplating. "What can I do?"

"You've done so much."

"No really, use me to help."

"I don't know... things have changed since the explosion. It's getting really dangerous and I don't want anything to happen to you—or anyone."

"Scotty, from everything that I know that's going on—you could use all the help you can get."

"Can I tell you something?" she said. It was important for her to get these things out in the open but not let it leave the room.

"Of course," he said leaning forward in his seat.

"I can't prove this yet, but I think that Chad's disappearance and these homicide cases are connected."

"What do you mean?"

"I mean I think that the person behind this is the same person responsible for the murders and the disappearance." She felt better putting it out in the open. There was more but she would keep it close until there was evidence to back it up.

He sighed, clearly contemplating what she had just told him. "But if the person killed those women..."

"I know what you're thinking. Then what makes me believe that Chad is alive?" Her voice cracked a bit.

Nick nodded keeping Katie's gaze.

"Call it a gut instinct. There's been some way that the killer has been tracking us... the articles about our investigations... the comments about Chad from Simon Holden... There's a few things. It's like... a way to keep the game going..."

"You think that the killer intentionally kidnapped Chad, like the beginning of a game or a challenge?"

Katie thought a moment about being challenged in a game. "That's exactly what I think is happening."

"Well then we have to beat the killer at his own game."

"We have to get ahead of him and that's exactly what I intend to do."

TWENTY-NINE

Tuesday 0945 hours

Katie had already spoken with McGaven on the phone first thing that morning. It was just as she thought, he was bored in the hospital and wanted to get to work. She had the preliminary reports from yesterday's explosion at the prep school sent over for him to read through while she kept the investigation going by visiting the medical examiner's office and seeing what John had to say.

She stood in the medical examiner's office alone. It seemed strange not having McGaven with her, but she would make sure to update him as soon as she could. The office was extra busy, with technicians wheeling bodies in and out of examination rooms.

She noticed that her sensitivity to sounds and smells was elevated. Everything seemed slightly brighter, louder, and even more pungent than usual. The familiar odor of cleaning solutions seemed stronger than normal. Katie thought that it had something to do with the previous day's experience. It had revived the history of intense stress that had become a part of her after her tours in the Army, along with the symptoms of PTSD from which she still sometimes suffered. The PTSD could definitely still make her days a challenge. She also noticed today that her startle factor when something suddenly presented itself was more pronounced than usual, so she tried to take slow breaths to calm down.

Dr. Dean jetted out of an examination room wearing a blood-spattered lab coat—underneath he was dressed in his usual colorful Hawaiian shirts and loose-fitting khakis with neon running shoes. His expression brightened when he saw Katie.

"Detective Scott, thank you for coming out at the last minute."

"It looks like you have quite the full house here," she said.

"It's just one of those days. Just sorry that you have to be thrown into this mêlée." He moved down the hallway. "C'mon, they are in the last exam room."

"Okay."

"Where's your partner?" he said over his shoulder.

"He's out today." She didn't want to explain everything to the doctor.

Katie followed the medical examiner, passing several rooms where bodies were opened up and internal organs were being documented and weighed. The sight of the bodies and blood made her feel woozy—she didn't know why. Her stomach became queasy and her mouth went dry. She glanced into one of the exam rooms as she passed and her attention was captured by the body of a man. It made her stare, unable to look away.

"Chad?" she whispered. She burst into the room, surprising two morgue technicians who were preparing the body for autopsy. She pushed them aside. "Chad," she said again. When she reached the body and looked at the man's face, it was obvious that it wasn't Chad. But the experience still shook her deeply.

"Detective Scott?" said Dr. Dean standing in the room. "You alright?"

"Yes, I'm fine," she said, realizing that she had been saying that a lot recently. Glancing back at the man lying on the stainless table, she thought about his family, friends, or even girlfriend or wife, and the grief they must be feeling. That same type of grief could be what Katie would have to experience. She tried not to think about it.

Katie turned and left the exam room. "I'm sorry, I thought that man looked like someone I knew," she said to Dr. Dean.

"It's quite alright. I know you have been very busy with these cases and I heard about your fiancé. I'm very sorry. You seem to have more than you should have to handle on your plate right now, Detective." He hesitated a moment. "Please, this way," he said.

Katie tried to shake off her trepidation and concentrate on the cases. She pushed all the things out of her mind that weren't related to the investigation. It was difficult, but it was the only way she could move forward.

Just inside the small exam room, there were two gurneys. On them were laid the bodies of two women without sheets covering them. Those women were the last victims of the serial killer. Katie looked at them and felt overwhelming sadness again that McGaven and she hadn't been able to get ahead of the murderer to save their lives.

"Okay," said Dr. Dean. "They've been identified by family. We have Michaela Brown and Cindy Taylor. Both are twenty-five years old, good health. Brown had her upper wisdom teeth removed recently, but other than that they're both healthy young women."

Katie studied their bodies. "They seem to have more decomp than the others."

"Good eye. That's because they died more than seventy-two hours ago."

That new piece of evidence made Katie realize that they were killed around the same time as the first and second victims. "Cause?"

The doctor moved closer to Michaela Brown and motioned to her neck, which was heavily purplish and some of the skin was decaying. "Cause of death, strangulation. Manner, homicide." His voice lowered more than normal as if he was tired of saying this.

"I see."

"Same for Cindy Taylor. Strangulation. I'm also ruling a homicide."

"Is there anything that seems different than the other women? Besides they weren't rolled up in burlap."

"One thing," he said.

Katie moved closer as the medical examiner lifted up Michaela's arm.

"Their pinkies are still intact. All digits are intact."

"But their eyes have been removed," she said, wondering why their little fingers weren't removed. Was the killer evolving? The eyes represented what watched the killer, but he didn't remove digits until later.

"Yes, but it seems, at least to me, that the precision wasn't there on these women."

"Meaning?"

"It simply means the technique was sloppy and hurried."

That was interesting to Katie. "Could you say that the killer was practicing?"

"That wouldn't be very medical of me—but yes, my opinion is yes. It looks as if someone was practicing or perfecting their skills."

The killer was evolving...

"Were they sexually assaulted?"

"There are no indications of sexual assault."

"Were the eyes removed post-mortem?"

"Yes."

"They were both strangled numerous times," he said. "As if they were rendered unconscious and then strangled again. You can see several areas where someone put their hands around their necks." He showed Katie the necks from both bodies.

Katie was overwhelmed. These victims were at the beginning of the killing spree. Did that mean there were more bodies that the killer was waiting to dump or for the police to uncover? There could be many more.

"Detective, I can see something is troubling you."

"I was just thinking that if these women were murdered a few days ago, then it's possible that there are more buried somewhere."

"It's possible, of course. But you would need to get inside the killer's head to find out where more bodies could be located," he said.

Katie stared at Dr. Dean's bloody lab coat, realizing that the killer had made sure that there was the least amount of blood expelled. "Thank you. I don't want to take up more of your time. If we have questions..."

"Of course, Detective. Unfortunately, I'm always here. Call me anytime."

Katie forced a weak smile, took another look at the bodies.

"I've sent the reports to both you and your partner."

"Thank you," she said and left the room.

Katie hurried from the medical examiner's office, this time not deviating to look into any of the examination rooms. She held her breath all the way back to the car, finally exhaling. Looking around the parking area, it was just filled with cars and those going about their duties. Even with people around her, she still felt extremely alone.

THIRTY

Tuesday 1200 hours

Katie hurried into the forensic division at the sheriff's department, now armed with new information to help identify the killer. It was quiet. She didn't hear John or Eva. They were either at lunch or at a crime scene.

Katie entered the main headquarters for their investigation. The room seemed to be extra cool and it made her shiver slightly. Her senses still seemed askew from yesterday. Her body temperature seemed a bit off as well.

She retrieved her notes and stood at the murder board. She added the two buried victims to the board—totaling the number of victims linked to this killer to five. The number five rattled in her mind. She began to write, adding to the list.

Possible First Victims*:*

Michaela Brown, Cindy Taylor*, buried at third crime scene, both twenty-five, healthy, single, background (under* *investigation), strangled multiple times (practicing?), missing eyes (not practiced), fingers all intact, first victims?*

Killer:

Practicing? Learning? Apprentice? Holden accomplice not killer? Who is orchestrating the murders? Killer on radar? One of persons of interest?

More bodies? More buried bodies?

Taunting police? Explosion warning to detectives?

Killer has possible military background? Use of explosives? Surveillance? Obtaining classified information?

Technology trained? Able to enter buildings and bypass security?

Studying. Learning. Evolving.

Significance of burying? Is killer escalating to explosions?

Katie's phone alerted her to a text message from Nick.

Security guys here installing your new system. All OK. Took Cisco for nice long walk.

Katie smiled and was glad that Nick was there. She responded to his message with her thanks and appreciation.

"Hey," said John from behind her.

Katie startled.

"Sorry, didn't mean to sneak up on you."

"It's fine. I've been a little jumpy lately," she said.

"No wonder, after that blast yesterday." John walked into the room and immediately read the murder board. "How's McGaven?"

"He's fine. Just bored and wanting to get home."

"That's good to hear he's going to be okay." John stared at Katie. "How are you? You've got some cuts and bruises."

"Just superficial. We were lucky—very lucky," she said remembering the moment the flash-bang went off and the explosion that had swiftly followed.

"Wow." John was reading the board.

"If you don't have anything helpful to say..." She laughed, trying to lighten the heaviness that tried to consume her.

"We're still working on the evidence from the two buried victims and the security guy McAdams."

"Okay."

"But, I do have tests back on those fibers you brought back from the crime scene from Lookout Trail."

Immediately Katie perked up. "And?"

"You were correct in assuming that they are natural and not manmade. They're natural grasses, what's called broom corn."

"Like a soft garden broom?" she said.

"Pretty much. The fibers are generally found in central Africa, but it can be found in the US."

"And you can buy these brooms anywhere, right?"

John nodded. "Right."

"But it does tell us that the killer likes natural fibers and soaps." Katie was disappointed, but it did give a better personality picture of the killer. Unusual, but distinct.

John stared at Katie. "Katie," he said gesturing to her nose. "You're bleeding."

"Oh," she said, grabbing a Kleenex and dabbing.

"Are you sure you're alright?" His face clouded with concern.

"Yes. The doctors said this was normal when we received

such an impact. I might have nosebleeds for a couple of days."
She saw John's worry. "Really, I'm doing okay."

He gave her a look like he wasn't convinced.

"Is there anything else?" she said.

"I received some more security footage of Chad from Detective Daniels. It was from the same day but different angles from other businesses. We're checking it."

"Oh, okay," she said. "Let me know if you find anything."

"You'll be the first," he said. "You need anything?"

Katie smiled. "No, but thank you. Just going to keep pushing on these cases."

"If you do, let me know." He smiled at her and then left.

Katie could hear muffled voices and a door closing. She knew that they were working hard to discover anything that would either help the serial homicides or Chad's disappearance. She was lucky to have such thorough forensic technicians working the cases.

Still holding the tissue to her nose and looking at the board, it struck Katie that Chad had been at Dayton Electronics, a retailer that sold high-tech computer components, which included security and surveillance equipment.

She opened her computer and began to search for anything about Dayton Electronics. There hadn't been any issues with the store or employees. She spent time looking into employees, but nothing seemed out of the ordinary.

Then she thought about the building. After running several background checks, she decided to check property searches. It was strange. Katie doubled-checked the address and even pulled up a computer map of the area, but there didn't seem to be anything on record for that location.

"Where is the address?" she said. McGaven would usually search for these types of things and always knew how to work around hiccups in the searches.

Katie picked up the phone and pressed an internal extension.

"Hey, Katie," said a perky voice after two rings. "Are you okay?"

"Hi, Denise. I'm fine."

"You are working solo today. You couldn't take a day off too?"

"We have to keep these cases going. I'm having some trouble finding out who owns a building in the Sacramento area. Gav always worked his magic and I'm flailing." She laughed.

"No problem. Give me the address."

"It's for Dayton Electronics, 1277 Arch Street, Sacramento."

"Got it. Give me a bit but I'll get back to you before the end of the day."

"Thank you, Denise."

"No problem. Bye." She disconnected the phone.

Katie leaned back and took another read-through of the board. Soon there would be more photos of the excavation and victims.

Her cell phone rang. She saw it was McGaven.

"Hey, how's the patient?" she said.

"Ready to break out of here any moment. I may have to call SWAT."

"It can't be that bad."

"It's not. I'm just ready to do something. Sick of staring at this room."

"When do they release you?" she said.

"The doctor wants to talk to me before they sign the discharge papers."

"They're just trying to be cautious. We were in a building that blew up."

"I guess you're right."

"So what's up? You called?"

"I wanted to remind you that Harry Winslow was going to be at that commercial building on Pine Crest today. You should try to go talk to him and see what he says about Holden."

Katie had completely forgotten about Winslow. "Thanks for the reminder."

"Just be careful. And don't be the usual Katie, okay?"

"Whatever that means," she said chuckling.

"You know exactly what that means. Don't take any unnecessary risks. Maybe you should bring Detective Hamilton with you?"

She made a slight frown.

"Or call Detective Daniels. You shouldn't go out to that project by yourself because you don't know what you might be walking into."

"I'll be fine, Gav. You get some rest. I'll see you soon."

"Katie..."

"Bye." She ended the call still smiling. Maybe she would call Evan.

THIRTY-ONE

Tuesday 1400 hours

Katie hurried from the sheriff's department building in the parking lot. It only took a moment and she saw Evan. He was leaning against his truck, arms crossed, looking across the area. She wondered what he was thinking about. Watching him now, it reminded her of the military. His body language was always a reflection of what he was thinking. If she had to guess—his thoughts were on the case and the location she had explained to him.

As she moved closer, Evan turned his head and saw her approach. He smiled and walked to meet up with her. He had dark sunglasses, beard stubble, and wore a black baseball cap.

"Detective," he said nodding.

"You know, you're not a detective here in my jurisdiction." She knew he was carrying his weapon concealed.

"I understand. I'm like a detective on hold playing a civilian in your investigation."

Katie heard a familiar bark. "You have Mac?"

"Yes, of course."

"Would you mind driving?"

"So you ask me to tag along with you on a criminal investigation as a pretend civilian and I have to drive?" he said smiling.

"Yes."

"Okay, just checking. C'mon."

Katie followed him to his SUV.

Mac stuck his head out of the window.

"Hey, Mac," said Katie petting the dog.

Once inside, Evan turned to her. "Address?"

"200 Pine Crest Drive."

Evan put in the address on the GPS.

As they drove closer to the location, Katie felt awkward and wondered if she should have invited Evan. It wasn't that it was against department policy because he was a police detective, but rather, she hoped that he didn't get the wrong impression.

"I think this is the area," he said.

Katie was surprised. The land hadn't been graded yet and it seemed to be too far out of the main city areas to be a regular site. There were backhoes, excavators, loaders, and other construction equipment parked along the pathway, which was no more than dirt. It had rained a couple of days ago, making the area muddy.

"Are you sure about the location?" he said.

"Yes. It was the address that McGaven gave me. He had spoken with several people who work for Harry Winslow." She looked around. It didn't seem like a regular location for construction. There were still trees that needed to be cut down, the ground needed proper grading, and there didn't seem to be a manager's trailer that would help identify the project.

Evan stopped. The road ended and there didn't seem to be access around it. "What do you want to do?"

"What I wanted to do and what's available here are two different things," she said craning her neck trying to see if there was any area that would indicate a project in progress.

"What were you looking for?" he said.

"I wanted to talk to Harry Winslow and his office said he would be here all afternoon. So Gav and I thought we'd come here unannounced and try to talk to him. He's been unreachable and no one would return our calls."

"I can see why. What do you know about the guy?"

"We know that he owns various properties around the area —mostly commercial. And the main reason we wanted to talk to him is about him visiting the serial killer Simon Holden."

"That's right—you said that you had talked to Holden?"

Katie nodded.

"So what was that like?"

"Probably like you would expect. Creepy. Narcissistic. He played games. Not answering my questions. But I got him to admit some things that I think will help the investigation."

"Interesting," he said as he surveyed the area. "And this was the address that Winslow's office gave you where he would be today?"

"Yep." Katie nodded. She felt that the office was giving them the runaround.

"Then we should check it out."

"Really?"

"Absolutely. We can't see past these trees. Maybe there's a foundation or structure."

"But..."

"You mean there's something that Katie Scott is scared to do?"

"Very funny. I just think it's a waste of time."

"Let's check it out. We're already here."

Katie realized that he had a point. It was a strange piece of property and an even weirder building project. "Okay, but we're just checking it out."

Evan put the SUV in reverse and backed up the road they just drove. "I think it might be best to park off the property."

Katie didn't argue.

"I hope you don't mind getting your shoes muddy."

"I'll manage."

Evan parked in an out-of-the-way area, so the SUV wouldn't be easily seen if someone were to drive up.

Katie shed her jacket and left her personal things in the vehicle—except her badge and gun. She adjusted her belt and looked at her boots. Not wanting to admit it to Evan, she hated the fact that she was about to ruin a very comfortable pair of shoes.

"You ready?" he said.

"As I'll ever be."

Katie led the way, wanting to take the perimeter to check things out first. Why would they pick this location? And why was Winslow not wanting to talk to them?

"Walk the perimeter. Smart," he said.

Katie trudged through the area. The mud was more difficult than she originally thought. She climbed up the drive and walked along a weeded space, which gave her grip and helped to keep her balance. The height made it easier to see across the property as they weaved around trees.

She finally saw a small trailer that was being used as a meeting area. There were three large cement foundations that had been poured and one tall structure like an office building was underway. It was unclear if the building project was recent or had been halted some time ago. There were three men talking. Katie halted and turned to Evan, making the motion to stay quiet.

He nodded.

Katie knew what Harry Winslow looked like and it was obvious that one of the men that were talking was indeed him. The office assistant was correct that he would be at this location. She watched the men but couldn't hear what they were saying, but it was clear they weren't socializing. Two of the men were siding against Winslow, leaning closer to him and backing away again. It didn't look friendly, but Winslow remained calm and seemed to be explaining something that wasn't what the two other men wanted to hear.

Winslow was late forties to fifties and was dressed in casual clothes of jeans and long-sleeved shirt. He looked average, receding hairline, dark hair, clean shaven, and wouldn't normally stand out in a crowd.

Katie turned to Evan. "What do you think?" she whispered.

"They obviously didn't hear us drive in."

"I need to talk to Winslow," she said.

"The guy with the long-sleeved shirt and jeans?"

She nodded.

They couldn't hear the entire conversation, only when there was a heated exchange about money owed. The words "we've given you more than enough time" repeated several times. It seemed that Winslow owed a lot of money to various people.

"The other two look like some kind of muscle or debt collectors," said Evan.

"And not from a bank," said Katie with slight sarcasm.

Katie thought Evan's observation seemed accurate. She wanted to hear more, and maybe the two men would soon leave, leaving Winslow alone. "We need to get closer." She surveyed the area and decided they could go around the property and come in behind the men.

They carefully walked along a ridge winding around trees through thick brush and muddy spots. Katie noticed that they could hear the men's conversation clearer. They definitely heard the men arguing about contracts and monies that had been exchanged.

They approached closer and stopped.

Katie waited and watched. She could see two dark vehicles— one sedan and one SUV. She could also see the building project in progress. Something seemed weird about it. The framing was haphazard, with beams not matching in style and size. She quietly pointed in the direction to alert Evan to her observations.

He studied the construction and then his gaze rested on the men.

Winslow began making gestures with his arms, complaining that the building project was expensive, supplies had gone up, employees had quit, and that he had no choice. It wasn't clear what that meant. Then he said that he was working on it and he would get back to them when he knew.

Katie was beginning to think that she and Evan had stumbled on some type of organized crime activity and not anything connecting Winslow to Holden or the murders. She slowly scanned the area, wanting to make sure she wasn't missing anything.

The two men suddenly returned to their vehicle and drove away.

"Here's our chance to talk to Winslow. And he's alone," said Katie.

Both detectives began moving down the hillside.

Before they reached the bottom, Katie felt the soil slip underneath her footing, so she slowed. That's when she saw the heavy burlap tarp spread out in front of them. Suddenly, Katie and Evan fell through the fabric into a large hole.

Katie tried to scratch at the sides as she slid down and hit the bottom. There were a couple feet of water that had pooled making it a sinking mudhole. The landing was soft but extremely wet and cold. She flailed for a moment until she could stand up.

"Evan?" she said.

"Yeah, I'm okay." He stood up, assessing if his cell phone and gun were still usable.

Katie immediately looked around. The hole had been dug recently. It was about fifteen feet deep and twenty feet wide.

The light was dim due to the depth of the pit and the shade from the tall trees above them. The walls were slick from the water draining into the pit. The pungent smell of wet earth and forest was strong, making it almost unbearable.

"Well," she said. "Can we climb out?"

Evan made several attempts to climb out, but he slid back down. "It's not going to be as easy as it looks. Let me see if I can boost you up."

"Okay," she said.

Evan moved close to her. "See if you can climb up?"

Katie was already feeling her energy dwindle from being soaking wet. The cold zapped her body, causing her muscles to contract and making her weaker. She grabbed at the sides and was able to grip a thin root, pulling herself upward. Evan held her and pushed her up.

"I can't quite reach the top," she said.

Evan was strong and she felt his hands hold her weight, so she grappled with the vines and roots until she was near the top. "Almost." She didn't feel Evan's assistance as she neared the top. She grabbed the last root, but it snapped. Katie slipped and fell backward—dropping into the pit again. Instead of hitting the muddy waterlogged bottom, Evan grabbed her, easing her landing.

"Thank you," Katie managed to say. She was breathless and shivering.

Evan didn't immediately let her out of his arms. There was a moment between them, but it felt so wrong to her.

Katie backed up and looked away. "Okay, let's try this again. I know which tree root not to grasp. Let's do this." She tried to sound optimistic, but the situation and Winslow made her dread what was going to happen next—in the homicide cases and her own life. Dizziness momentarily overcame her and she stumbled.

"Whoa, you okay, Katie?" said Evan as he caught her from falling back into the water.

Taking a deep breath and steadying herself, she said, "Yeah, just a little dizzy." Her body shook and her teeth chattered, but she could feel the warmth from Evan's body.

"Take a moment," he said.

"No, we need to get out of here now. Let's do this." Her instincts kicked in so her focus cleared.

There was a sudden loud noise as an engine started up.

Katie looked questionably at Evan. "That's one of those backhoes or excavators."

"That's not good."

"They must know we're here. Why would they suddenly start one of those machines?" she said. "C'mon, help me up."

Katie and Evan worked together again and this time she was able to get to the top. It was slippery. She fell a few times, but was able to gain a foothold and get up over the top.

Realizing her gun must've dropped, she kneeled on part of the burlap and yelled into the hole. "My gun, it must be down there."

Katie looked around. She heard the construction excavator, but didn't immediately see it. She smelled the diesel fuel that floated in a wispy cloud around her and could see the large earthmover coming around the corner ahead.

"Coming up!" said Evan.

Her gun landed next to her. She quickly assessed it, making sure it was operational. To her relief, it was. "I'll be right back," she said.

Evan yelled back, "Be careful!"

The bulldozer revved and shifted into another gear. It began barreling down on Katie.

She stood her ground, aimed her weapon, and yelled. "Stop! Pine Valley Sheriff's Department! Turn off the engine! Now!"

The excavator kept coming.

Katie squeezed the trigger, but her gun jammed. She tried again. Her gun wouldn't fire.

The bulldozer continued its charge, the engine racing as the big tires rushed toward her.

Katie had no other choice, she had to stop it otherwise it would run her over and bury Evan alive. She ran as fast as she could along the edge of the path.

Steering the roaring equipment was Harry Winslow and he had the look of absolute determination. Katie knew she couldn't stop him any other way, so she readied herself, estimated her distance, and jumped.

Katie's distance was slightly off. She grabbed on to the seat as Winslow tried to push her off. She fought him and kept her balance. Her hands were wet and she was covered in mud, making it difficult to hang on.

Winslow's average build didn't convey how strong he was, and he could handle himself physically. He shoved her with his left hand while he still kept the excavator moving forward.

"Stop!" she said, fighting him to try to turn the machine off.

Katie was able to get her left leg up and braced herself before she could give a final blow. She felt the impact of Winslow's fists, making it difficult for her to take a breath. With difficulty, Katie managed to get the upper hand and shoved Winslow off the seat. She took control of the excavator and shut it down.

Wasting no time, she went to Winslow, who was shaking off his fall.

"Harry Winslow?" she said with her gun drawn. Even though it jammed, it still got his attention.

The man nodded slowly.

"Get down on your stomach! Now!" She caught her breath. "Let's see your hands. Keep them out."

He obliged, obviously realizing his defeat.

Katie didn't want to leave the man, so she got her wet cell

phone out and hoped that it would still function. She pressed the button and was relieved to hear police dispatch.

Katie watched as a deputy sheriff loaded Harry Winslow into the back of a patrol cruiser. He stared at her through the window as he sat handcuffed in the back seat. There was anger behind his gaze.

The fire rescue pulled Evan out of the pit, trampling the surrounding area. Katie wondered if there was anything they could have used as forensic evidence.

Detective Hamilton was called in to search the area with two deputies. He went inside the trailer that was being used as an office area. Some of the materials and office paperwork would be boxed up and taken back to the department.

Evan walked over to where Katie was standing.

"You okay?" he said. "Did they check you out?"

"I don't need it. Just a few more bumps and bruises."

"I have to say that being around you isn't dull by any means." He chuckled.

Katie looked at him—he had dried mud all over. He even had mud across his cheek. "I'm going to need a ride back to the department."

"No problem. I have some towels in the car."

"How's Mac?" Katie suddenly realized that the dog was in the SUV listening to everything going on.

"Mac is tough—don't forget he's ex-military."

"He is tough. So is Cisco."

"Let me know when you're ready to leave," he said.

"I just need to speak with the detective to update him and see what they've found. But I'm going to be the one interrogating Winslow. He's my perp."

Evan smiled at Katie. "I wouldn't want to argue with that."

Katie finished up at the Pine Crest construction site. She

would receive reports in the morning and re-evaluate at that time. She wasn't sure if Harry Winslow was indeed a person of interest in her serial case or someone who was just caught in an illegal activity. Soon she would have some answers and she wasn't going to end the interview until all the answers were revealed.

THIRTY-TWO

Katie had returned home and quickly showered before returning to work. She entered the Pine Valley Sheriff's Department barely an hour and a half later and headed to the detective division. It was strange for her to go alone to interrogate a suspect—it was standard for both Katie and McGaven to take turns on who would do the questioning.

Katie stood in the hallway for the interview area. There was a uniformed officer standing in front of the first room.

"Is Harry Winslow waiting?" she asked.

"Yes. No one has questioned him."

"Great. Thank you."

Katie opened the door to find Winslow seated at the table. He wasn't handcuffed, but he sat at attention with his arms resting on the table facing her. He still had dried mud on his clothes, but it was clear from the smears that he had tried to clean up his shirt and face.

As she watched the man she had pushed off the excavator,

he appeared calm and collected. It was unusual behavior for a man in that position after being so angry and lashing out earlier. The background information didn't seem to fit him.

She didn't know quite what to expect, but she was ready. The main priority was that he had visited Holden and Katie wanted to know why.

"Mr. Winslow. Do you know why you're here?" she said casually, looking on the other side of the room for McGaven out of habit.

He remained quiet but kept intense eye contact with Katie.

She smiled. "Mr. Winslow, you realize that you tried to kill a cop, right?"

He sighed.

"And you realize that you tried to bury another cop—that's trying to kill two cops."

He leaned back in his chair with a smug look on his face.

"And you are wanted in questioning for five murdered women."

"Murder?" he said.

"*Now* you decide to talk."

"What murdered women? You mean the ones in the news? That's supposed to be a serial killer." His eyes grew wide in disbelief. "You think I'm a serial killer?"

"I have some questions, Mr. Winslow."

He began to laugh.

It reminded Katie of Holden, but without the macabre tone. "Is there something funny about murder?" she said.

"I find it ridiculous that you think I'm a serial killer." He looked away.

"Then enlighten me. Why would you visit Simon Holden?"

Winslow didn't immediately answer. It was clear that he knew Holden. Her question rattled him and she knew she was getting somewhere.

"I've chatted with Holden. In fact, twice. He had some very interesting things to say," she said.

"About what?"

"About his work. About his visitors. Just stuff."

Winslow fidgeted in his seat. Suddenly he was uncomfortable, looking around as if trying to figure out how to escape.

Katie smiled. She had him. "Look, with everything we found in your office trailer, you're in a lot of trouble."

He stared at her.

"And, I'm a homicide detective and not organized crime, but I'm guessing you're in deep to the wrong types."

"Look, I don't know what you're angling for."

"I think it's pretty obvious." Katie stood up as if she were going to leave. It was an old-school way of interrogating a suspect, but it worked under certain circumstances.

"Okay, okay," he said. "What do you want to know?"

Got him.

"Why did you visit Simon Holden?" Katie took a seat sitting in front of him, waiting for an answer. "What was the reason?"

"It wasn't my idea."

"What do you mean?" she said.

"I received a message that I needed to visit Simon Holden in prison. I knew who he was but have no connection—at least I don't think so."

Katie studied him. He had unwavering eye contact, didn't fidget in his seat, and his hands remained still.

"I'm telling you the truth."

"How did you get the message? From who?"

"It was a message written on a plain piece of paper instructing me to go visit Holden—at a specific day and time. It was handwritten and I don't know who it was from."

Katie hesitated as she thought about what he'd said. "You could have declined and just gone about your day. Why did you go?"

"Well, let's just say that it was in my best interest." He leaned back in his chair.

"Blackmail? If you didn't comply, then your business would be at stake?"

"Something like that. But yeah, I would lose everything."

"And you have no idea who sent you that note? Was it mailed?"

"No, it appeared on my desk at one of my projects. I really don't know who sent it."

"What did you talk about with Holden?"

"That's just it. Nothing."

"What do you mean nothing?" she said.

"I waited for him in the meeting area for inmates and attorneys, but he came in, saw me and then left. It was strange."

"Did he say anything?"

Winslow shook his head. "He looked at me and I assumed he knew who I was. Then he smirked and turned around—and left."

"You expect me to believe this?"

"I don't expect anything. It's the truth."

"And you never heard later what it was all about." Katie pressed him.

"No. You can ask me a million times and my answer would still be no."

Katie stood up. "Oh, and why did you try to kill two cops?"

"I didn't believe you were cops. I thought you were one of them."

"Them?"

"Let's just say that I'm behind on my payments."

Katie had enough information. She would turn over Winslow to the organized crime division.

"Thank you."

"That's it? Hey, wait a minute."

"Thank you, Mr. Winslow. Detectives will be with you shortly."

"Hey, this isn't what I signed up for."

Katie opened the door. She paused and looked at Winslow before leaving. Her takeaway was that she believed him. Now she needed to figure out what it all meant.

THIRTY-THREE

Wednesday 0714 hours

Katie stood in the front yard of the cabin watching the sunrise. The air was crisp but it was clear that the day would bring abundant sunshine. The streams of morning light in yellows and oranges squeezed in between the tree limbs cascading a veil of light. Mornings were always a promise of a new day with new expectations.

Katie took several deep breaths, breathing in the incredible forest smells. She closed her eyes and let the beautiful outdoors speak to her. As she did with crime scenes and listened to the area, she tried the same technique at the cabin.

Cisco ran up and happily barked, making Katie open her eyes. She watched as her overzealous black dog bounced and spun then checked out nearby bushes and trees. After several moments of joy, the dog returned to her and took his rightful position at her left side.

Surprisingly, no one had stayed at the cabin since she and Chad had their romantic evening there. Maybe it was the result of a slow season. Or maybe it was because the cabin wasn't going to have any guests until the mystery was solved. At least that romantic notion was what Katie would like to think and it kept her going.

The sun crested the horizon, bathing her in morning light. It was beautiful. Katie wanted to stay at the cabin. It strangely felt safe, but it also represented the beginning of everything that she had to work out.

Katie turned around, feeling the warmth on her back as if Chad were still with her. She went back inside with Cisco trailing behind. Having been at the cabin several times after Chad's disappearance, she felt something pulling her back there. She had permission from the owners to visit again, and they had given her their blessing to try and find what she was looking for.

In fact, Katie didn't know what she was looking for, but she was going to try and figure it out. This was the first time she had brought Cisco, on the off chance that he might be able to catch a scent—even after all this time. She wanted to search the cabin again before heading to work.

As she stood at the door, she found it difficult to step inside. Her breath halted to a shallow inhale. She felt dizziness settle into her head making her vision tunneled. Her feet remained stuck, almost like they were permanently cemented to the floor. Her eyes welled with tears as she fought hard to stop any outward emotional reaction. As she closed her eyes, she still couldn't block out the memory of her and Chad at the cabin. That special time together would forever be imprinted in her mind. If she tried hard, she could almost feel Chad's warmth, hear his voice, and watch him move across the room.

Why?

Why him?

Why now?

Katie's mind was always rearranging what they currently knew and no matter how she shuffled it, it would come back to her intuition that Chad's disappearance and the five homicides seemed to her to be connected. There were overlapping areas. Holden's comments. The explosion and the arson investigator's handbook, which could explain the explosion at the school. The news articles highlighting Katie and McGaven's previous cases. Someone entering Katie's and Chad's houses without being detected.

She was sure that there was someone pulling all the strings. It was someone who managed to orchestrate the serial killings a decade ago and was beginning the rampage again. Why? It seemed clear to Katie that Holden reveled in the spotlight but didn't talk about the murders, as if he wasn't sure. It made her think that he was the accomplice and not the primary killer. The big question was how she was going to link everything together that would lead them to the killer and finding Chad.

Katie took a couple of steps into the cabin. For a second, she thought she could catch a whiff of Chad's soap but it was only her imagination. Remembering his kisses and embrace made her even more devastated—and alone.

Cisco moved around, sniffing random things without much interest.

Katie moved through the areas as she had done a couple of times before. The décor, furniture, and accessories seemed to be exactly the same. Nothing had changed. But it had changed that night when she was sleeping—from a sedative slipped into the wine. She assumed that was how someone was able to take Chad against his will. He would have fought with everything he had.

Katie was going to leave and drive to work to meet with McGaven to try to figure out their next move. She heard Cisco whining and went looking for him. As she entered the bedroom, she saw the dog his nose poking under the bed. It was on Chad's side.

She decided to investigate. "What do you have, Cisco?"

Katie knelt down on the floor and flipped up the quilt. Still feeling some aches and pains from the explosion and fight with Winslow, she didn't see anything at first as her mind went to the image of some food that had spilled making the dog interested.

Cisco didn't retreat his position, which she thought was strange behavior for him. He began using his nose and then sitting as if he was alerting her to something.

Katie managed to pull the dog back and peered under the bed. She couldn't see what the fuss was, but ran her hand over the area and there was a thin piece of fabric approximately two inches square that had been tucked under the bed. It hadn't been there before when the cabin had been initially searched.

She sat back and studied the fabric. It appeared to be some type of natural fiber—similar to burlap or a type of linen that was used for anything from bags to home décor to various types of art. Returning to the kitchen, she was able to find a small bag that she dropped the fabric into it as potential evidence.

Katie's mind wandered back to the crime scenes and couldn't find a connection as to why the killer used burlap to roll the victims in, and the pink velvet to cover the eye orifices. Was he concealing them, taking away the victim's ability to see him? Was it a mercy killing? Was the killer covering for some unresolved trauma? There were many reasons why a piece of fabric could be found under the bed, but the type was something worth looking into. She took the evidence and secured the cabin.

"Good boy, Cisco," she said as she walked out of the cabin.

As she neared her Jeep with Cisco in tow, she abruptly stopped. Not believing what she was seeing, her stomach plunged and she thought she might faint.

Folded neatly on the hood were the clothes that Chad was wearing that night at the cabin.

Snapping out of her distress, Katie returned to her police trained mode. She pulled her weapon immediately and searched the area for any signs of the person who left the clothes. Keeping Cisco close, they moved together systematically, just like when she was in the military, until she had covered most of the area. There were no footprints, tire tracks, or anything unusual that someone had been there besides her. She checked the two security cameras at each corner of the front of the cabin, but they had been blacked out. She also wondered why Cisco didn't hear anyone approach.

The creeping feeling that she was being watched never abated. She looked everywhere and even re-entered the cabin. Nothing. If she didn't know any better, she would have thought she was going insane.

Without wasting any more time or touching the folded clothes, she called into the Pine Valley Sheriff's Department, requesting assistance and forensics.

Katie sat down in a chair on the porch with Cisco at her side waiting for a police team to arrive.

THIRTY-FOUR

Katie stood to the side of the cabin property with Cisco as Detectives Hamilton and Ames worked the scene along with John. They had already documented the clothes, which were now in evidence bags along with the piece of fabric.

Three deputies were canvassing the area and conducting a search of both inside the cabin and the surrounding areas outdoors, but they found nothing new. The cabin property was fairly isolated and it would have been easy for anyone to sneak around without leaving a trace.

It made Katie distraught and uneasy. It seemed unproductive as the police conducted their investigation and searches. Both detectives were quiet and didn't seem to acknowledge her or ask her any questions after the initial discovery they had made when they arrived. She had a turbulent history with Hamilton, but Ames was in charge of Chad's missing person's case. He seemed to be tired of being bothered by all the inquiries and had told her he would contact her if anything changed.

Her emotions escalated as she thought about Chad and what he could be going through—but she managed to stay professional. It was the alternative scenario she didn't want to think about—and what it meant that Chad's clothes were left at the cabin where it had all began.

John had finished dusting for prints from Katie's Jeep without finding anything that would assist the investigation. The SUV had been wiped clean—there weren't any of Katie's prints visible except on the inside proving that whoever left the clothing never got inside the vehicle. The perp was thorough and knew what he was doing.

"Katie, we are not going to take your vehicle. There was no indication that anyone was in your car," said John. He spoke with concern, but kept his professionalism. "I will have Eva comb through the clothes for anything foreign."

"Thank you, John," she said.

He moved closer to her, just out of range so the others didn't hear what he had to say. "Katie, I can stop by this evening to make sure that your new security system is operating properly."

"That would be great." It was a relief that John would be taking a look at her new system. She trusted him and his expertise since he had helped with the installation of the old one.

"And I was thinking that maybe you might need some decoy cameras. It couldn't hurt."

Katie nodded. "Thanks, John. I'll see you later." She took Cisco and got into her Jeep.

Detective Hamilton approached. "Scott, if we need anything more from you, we'll be in touch."

She nodded and watched him walk away.

Katie needed to get away from the cabin. She most likely wouldn't return. She had done what she could and there wasn't anything more for her to do. In the back of her mind, she still thought that when she and McGaven solved the murder cases it would then lead to what had happened to Chad. That was her hope.

As she sat quiet for a moment and Cisco settled down for the ride, she thought about what John had said about a decoy security camera. They were easy to install.

A decoy.

The word resonated with her—throwing people off track. Her mind raced.

How could the killer know their moves?

How would someone know she was at the cabin?

Unless...

Katie popped the Jeep hood and got out of her vehicle. Pulling on gloves, she then leaned into the engine area and began searching. She wasn't sure where or what the device might look like, but started scanning everything. Then she began running her hand around the wheel wells.

John watched her for a moment and then he seemed to realize what she was doing. He immediately joined her. "You're looking for a GPS, aren't you?"

Katie stood up and faced the forensic supervisor. "It makes sense. Think about it. How could the killer know I was here, or anywhere Gav and I were going? Like at the school?" she said. "And I wasn't followed when I rode with Detective Daniels in his vehicle. Right?" A renewed energy filled her.

Hope.

Drive.

Moving ahead.

"Let me help you look. I've seen where these tracking devices can be attached to areas where it would be quick and easy," he said. He joined Katie and they began looking around the car. It didn't take him long. "I got something." He pulled his body partially underneath the back bumper. "Here it is," he said. "We need to document it before I remove it." He crawled back out.

Katie felt relieved to have found it but angry at the same time. Now she understood how the killer had known their next steps. "We're going to need to have the detective sedan and other vehicles searched for GPS devices as well."

Detectives Hamilton and Ames were interested in the car search and watched John as he documented and collected the evidence.

"It's just a cheap tracking device that anyone can buy. About twenty or thirty bucks."

"I think all the police detective vehicles should be searched," she said.

John nodded and took control of coordinating the searches.

Katie took one last look around for her own interest and left. As she drove back and headed to the police department to meet up with McGaven, she cried.

THIRTY-FIVE

Wednesday 1300 hours

Katie walked along the vacant path with Cisco at her side. She couldn't go into the office just yet. There was something she needed to do and it was long overdue. With everything she had been struggling with, she needed this break for reflection and peace.

She stopped and stared down. Waiting a moment, she decided to take a seat on the grass.

The gravestone read: *Roger Neil Scott & Evelyn Nicole Scott in loving memory.*

Closing her eyes, she sat for several minutes, remembering all the times she had shared with her parents. The fun times. The laughs. The barbecues at the house. The vacations. The Saturday morning breakfasts.

Cisco pushed his long sleek body closer to her as if he felt her pain.

"I miss you both every day," she began. "You taught me so much before you left me, but now, I don't know if I have the strength to persevere." She took a breath, fighting back the tears.

"I feel like I'm losing so much more than I can bear. First it was you both. Now, Chad. I don't know what to do. I'm afraid to stay still but I don't know if I can move forward."

A breeze kicked up, blowing through the trees and making that wonderful sound through the pine needles. It blew across her face and she felt like she had been heavenly kissed by her parents. The chirping birds had suddenly quieted and she couldn't hear any traffic in the distance. It was as if she were the only one left on earth.

Katie petted Cisco, who gently panted beside her. He kept a vigilant watch, but at the same time, he was supporting her emotions waiting patiently for her to continue.

"All I ever wanted was to have a marriage, a partnership like the two of you had, but now, I'm not so sure." A tear rolled down her cheek and she quickly wiped it away. "So many people rely on me and I'm terrified that I can't keep doing my job. My heart is broken and I don't know whether it can ever be healed."

Katie hung her head, trying to regain the strength that she desperately needed. She recited a prayer that her mom had taught her when she was a little girl. It comforted her and helped to lift some of the burden she had been carrying the past month.

She waited another ten minutes before she spoke again. "I love you, Mom, Dad, and I count the minutes until we will see each other again. I know you're always with me and knowing that helps to comfort me, along with my faith."

Katie got to her feet, taking another moment before she and Cisco walked back to the car.

THIRTY-SIX

Katie dropped off Cisco at the sheriff's department K9 kennels then picked up lunch at the request of McGaven. They were going to be in the office for a while trying to put together all the puzzle pieces they had acquired.

As she entered the forensic division carrying food and beverages, she could immediately hear voices. It was odd because it was usually as quiet as a grave when she entered. Some people referred to the area as a tomb, but that suited Katie just fine. They were able to think, focus, and connect clues together in a quiet environment.

When Katie got closer to their working office area, she heard McGaven and Eva laughing and talking, but also another voice that she didn't immediately recognize. As she stood at the entrance, she saw that Evan was inside as well. It surprised her, but he must've received special approval from the sheriff to be there, so she was okay with it.

"Hey, food," said McGaven. He had a bandage on his forehead, but looked well.

"Hi, everyone," she said. "I have enough food for an army." Katie thought it was a fitting description and brought the food into the office, where she set everything down on the side table. "Eva, I know how much you like vegetarian food, so I got you this great sandwich that I think you'll love."

"Thank you," said Eva. "Yum." She turned to Katie. "Awesome find with the GPS."

"It's a start. I hope that we can learn something useful from it," she said.

"We're going to see if we can track it, finding out where it was purchased and what cell phone and tower was reading it."

"You'll probably find it was a burner phone," said Katie.

"You never know," Eva said, taking a bite of her sandwich. "I'd better get back to work. John will be back shortly." She took her sandwich with her and left.

After the food was dispensed, everyone engaged in idle chitchat for a few minutes before getting down to work.

McGaven smiled. "Okay, we're going to begin with what I found out about the prep school explosion." He flipped open his laptop. "They sent over some preliminary stuff from the arson investigation and Hamilton's report. And, the body that was found belonged to the maintenance/security guard, Denny McAdams. Never been in trouble with the law except a few parking tickets and one moving violation from five years ago. And it seems that he didn't have gunshot residue on his hands—only residue on his hoodie."

"I doubted he was the hoodie guy who I originally saw when I entered the school," said Katie. She realized that they probably weren't going to learn anything that would blow the entire investigation wide open.

"Hoodie guy?" said Evan.

"It's a man who was seen at the crime scene at Wellington Park during the body excavation," said McGaven.

"No other description?"

"No, just basic build, height, and the way he moved," said Katie. "Which boils down to average. I couldn't get a pinpoint of age—maybe thirty to fifty?"

Evan studied the murder board and the photos of the crime scenes.

"Okay, now to the good stuff," said McGaven. "Ready for this... the type of explosives was C-4."

"C-4?" said Katie and Evan.

"It was a relatively small amount. But yeah, try being there," said McGaven.

"If it wasn't properly measured, it could've taken out an entire block," said Evan.

Katie went to the board and began writing. "Okay, we know it was deliberately set with C-4 by someone who knew what they were doing. I don't think they were trying to kill us—just scare us, injure us, send a message, of course, but not kill us—at least for now."

"Are you sure about that, Katie?" said McGaven. "One of us could have died."

"It's just from everything I've seen, the behavioral evidence, and what was left, or not left, at the crime scene indicates the killer is clever and prepared—organized." She paused. "The killer seems to be enjoying spying on us and being a step ahead, while we react to the crime scenes. He's enjoying this like watching an interactive game, which makes him a double threat —he's not going to quit."

"From Holden's crime scenes, the next was another industrial warehouse area," said McGaven reading a copy of the reports. "It was a cement plant."

"We don't have anything like that—so it could be any industrial type of area."

"It could be another explosion," said Katie quietly. "What do we know about anyone who has access and training in C-4?" She turned to Evan who had been quiet taking in everything.

"Well the obvious is a military person and combat engineer," said Evan.

"Demolition experts and maybe some branch of government like the FBI and AFT?" said McGaven. "The tripwire we saw hadn't been activated, sort of like a scare tactic, and there wasn't anything explosive attached to it. It was like a decoy."

Katie thought about it. "So what you both are saying is that our killer has either been in the military, is a demolition expert, and has access to C-4." Katie scanned her board again pulling together all the facts. "The killer seems to have an affinity with natural things—burlap, soap, and fabric. And he is versed in security technology."

"And then blows stuff up," said McGaven with slight sarcasm.

"Complex killer," said Evan.

"It tells me that it almost sounds like a team of people—or at least more than one person," she said. "As if someone in charge is calling all the shots. I'm just giving you some theories here..."

"I hadn't thought about it like that."

"It was what Holden said at the last interview. He said, 'my job is to sit in this hellhole and do my time.' His *job*," said Katie. "Interesting choice of words."

"He's smart and tried to be clever. Maybe it was just a way of dramatizing it?" said McGaven.

"Maybe. What do we have on Butch Trent and Bobby Cox? Anything new?"

McGaven shook his head. "Nothing, just two weird guys. Actually, Butch has been around some unsavory people. He will most likely get arrested sometime soon. But Bobby, nothing."

"Do you think the burlap was really a coincidence? Or could someone have planted it there as a way to distract us?" said Katie.

"I don't want to say one way or another. It's possible."

Katie studied the crime-scene photos of the victims. "Maybe we're not looking at this the right way." She pulled down Gina Hartfield's and Jenna Day's photos. "These young women look very similar, close in age. What if, now this is a what-if, the killer was targeting young women who looked a certain way because they remind him of something?"

"Like a person or loss?"

"Yes. But something more specific—a person or event. We all have defining moments in our lives that make us who we are. People-involved moments are the most common," she said.

"You mean like a daughter or sister?" said McGaven.

"It could remind the killer of some loss—that manifested into a killing spree. It's possible that the cleaning and burlap might have to do with a funeral?" she said. "Or maybe a cleansing?"

"That might make him older."

"Like around Harry Winslow or Terrance Lane ages," she said.

"You still think it's possible it's one of them?"

"It would make sense why they visited Holden."

"Wouldn't it be public record that they were related to one of the victims?"

"Maybe. Maybe not," she said. "Has there been anything on the properties owned by them?"

"Nothing that stands out. I'll keep checking."

Katie knew why Evan was quiet. And she knew why he was there, but didn't want to acknowledge it. He had some things to share about Chad's disappearance. She sat down so that she wouldn't lose her balance when he shared what he had. "Evan, I'm guessing why you're here. It's more than being a witness and almost a victim at Winslow's property. Tell me."

Evan didn't immediately speak up, but glanced at McGaven, indicating that he had already spoken to him.

"Please, just tell me." Even though she was scared to hear what he had.

"It's not what you think," said Evan.

Katie was about to say something but decided to keep quiet and listen.

Evan nodded to McGaven.

Her partner opened a laptop and hit the keypad. A video came into view.

It took every ounce of energy for Katie to keep her eyes glued to the screen. The video was from two other businesses near Dayton Electronics. It showed clearer images from several angles of Chad walking into the electronics store and leaving, but more importantly, it showed the man in the dark truck.

The facial outline of his profile became sharper. The man appeared to be in his forties or fifties. His coat collar was turned up obscuring the lower part of his face. It was unclear if he was clean shaven or had a beard or mustache. What was clear was the outline of his nose.

Katie had been holding her breath, but now she exhaled. It was like having a knife plunge into her gut every time she saw Chad. The man who had been watching and possibly tailing him was coming more into focus, but there was still not enough for identification.

"We know that the black truck pulled into the parking lot right behind Chad," said Evan. "It's become more obvious that this person was following him based on these other angles. We still can't see the license plates though."

Katie watched the footage and she would have to agree with the assessment.

"I know this must be very difficult, but we are getting closer to finding out who this man is."

It wasn't much of a comfort for Katie, but she remained stoic.

"Katie, what do you want to do next?" said McGaven.

She turned away from the detectives and gathered her thoughts. "I think we need to do a more in-depth background check on Lane, Winslow, and Turner to find out if any of Holden's victims were related or close to them. We need to dig deeper on these men's backgrounds. And... what about the people who are the closest to them, like best friends, a family member, or an employee."

"I'll see what Denise can find out and I'll perform some data searches as well," said McGaven. He looked at a text. "Winslow was released yesterday on his own recognizance."

Katie frowned. "We saw that coming."

There was a knock at the door.

John leaned in, breathless. "We have a lead. The serial number on the GPS tracker on Katie's Jeep has been traced to a store."

"Where?" said Katie.

"Dayton Electronics."

THIRTY-SEVEN

Wednesday 1605 hours

Katie didn't completely agree with the decision for her and Evan to go to Dayton Electronics together, but since the store was in the Sacramento area and in Detective Daniels' jurisdiction it made sense. She really wanted to dig through more of the transcripts from Holden's trial and work up the profile more. At least that was what she kept telling herself. Of course, she wanted to go to the last place he was seen, but the emotions might prove difficult to handle.

However, it was decided that Katie would be the best person to go with him. McGaven stayed behind in the office to run through databases, trying to dig up more information on the three main suspects since his recovery still wasn't a hundred percent after the explosion.

Evan drove and managed to break every speed limit on the way to the electronics store. "I'm taking the silence as you don't agree with this assignment," he said.

"Not a problem."

"Katie, I can't begin to imagine what you're going through

or pretend that I do, but I am sorry. You're one of the strongest women I've ever known. You'll get through this. And... we'll find out where Chad is."

Katie was hearing Evan, but her thoughts were on the man who followed Chad—and why.

"Do I make you feel uncomfortable?"

Katie almost forgot that Evan didn't mince words and was very direct. Under most conditions she found it refreshing, but she kept imagining the kiss they shared when they were in the military. She found herself grappling with so many emotions and memories that it was dizzying and confusing.

They were minutes from the electronics store.

Mac paced in the back and gave a few whines, which made Katie think of Cisco.

"I'm sorry, Evan. These cases as well as Chad's disappearance are a heavy load."

"You know that I think the world of you. I'm here for you—as a friend. I hope you know that," he said.

Katie knew that he was sincere. One thing she'd known ever since she'd known Evan was that he was honest—almost to a fault. "Thank you. I appreciate that."

"I know that there's something else bothering you."

She gazed out the window. "Why someone went to all this trouble to kidnap Chad—and all the special details. Usually when someone is taken it means that they want something—money, revenge, or the thrill of the kill."

"We don't know that he's..."

"No, but the longer we don't know what happened to him... I have to accept facts and the longer we don't know or hear from him—it means..."

"We don't have facts that support that."

Katie knew that as well, but she was going to have to face reality at some point. Maybe they would find out who the man was watching him—and why.

Evan tried to keep to the investigation. "Chad went to the electronics store based on information about an arson investigation of a house that burned down under suspicious circumstances. Walton was the name."

"That's right," she said.

"The store didn't know anything about Chad's visit, but now they're going to answer who bought the GPS that you found on your car."

"I'm not leaving until we get some answers," she said, gritting her teeth and trying to muster more energy.

A few minutes later, they pulled into the parking lot that supported several businesses: hardware store, discount shop, sandwich shack, and the electronics store.

Katie scanned the area to see from the video perspective where the truck had waited and watched. She spotted the parking space where the man had set up to watch the electronics store.

Evan pulled into a parking space and cut the engine. He didn't immediately get out, but turned to Katie, putting his hand on her arm. "You ready?"

"Absolutely," she said.

Evan lowered the windows for Mac and then the detectives left the vehicle and headed toward the electronics store.

Katie was anxious and relieved to be out of the SUV and walking outside. It was an overcast day, but the air was heavy, making her tired and her arms and legs feel overworked. She had forgotten about the big city's noise and pollution. It made her homesick and glad that she had decided to join the Pine Valley Sheriff's Department instead of going back to Sacramento PD.

Katie slowed her pace and quickly surveyed the area. She noticed that in front of the hardware store located over to one side there were two small metal tables and an area where cigarettes had been extinguished. It suggested that either the owner or one of the employees took their breaks out there.

Evan watched her and gazed at the area she was looking at. "Maybe someone might have seen Chad or the black truck?"

It was as if he had read her mind. "We'll check it out before we leave."

Evan pushed the glass door open. A chime alerted employees that someone had entered.

The store was small but well organized and had sale signs affixed to the front windows. Along one side were all types of security items ranging from doorbell cams to larger more complex security systems. There were other computer and digital items behind locked cabinets. The other side of the room consisted of laptops, iPads, and e-book reading devices. There were also various add-on gadgets and accessories promoted throughout the store.

It was an older building, but well kept. The windows were clean and the old low-pile carpet was dirt-free without any noticeable spots.

Katie and Evan stood in the middle of the store. A young man with a name tag reading Tyler came out from the back. "Hello," he said. "What can I help you with?"

Evan took lead and showed his badge. "Tyler, I'm Detective Daniels from SPD and this is Detective Scott PVSO."

The young man looked disappointed and slouched his shoulders. "What can I do for the police?"

"A friend of ours came here with some questions and he has since disappeared," he said.

"I'm sorry to hear that. But what can I do?"

"For starters, have you seen this man?" said Evan as he showed the salesperson a photo of Chad from his phone.

The young man studied the photo and shook his head. "Sorry, I've never seen him before."

"What about this guy?" Evan showed the photo of the man in the truck.

"I think I've seen him. I remember the black truck—it was a nice ride."

Katie turned to face him. "Where?"

"I've seen him in the parking lot."

"When?"

"I don't know... a couple of weeks, maybe a month ago."

"Have you seen him regularly in the area?"

"I think I've seen him three or four times."

"Can you describe him?"

"That's the thing. The guy I'm thinking of usually had sunglasses and a baseball cap. I couldn't see him clearly. But that photo seems like the guy."

Katie pushed. "You never saw the first guy?"

Tyler shook his head. "No, I'm sorry. He never came in here that I saw."

"Did you hear your boss or anyone say anything about a fire investigator Chad Ferguson?" she said.

"No. And I would remember the name because Chad is my brother's name."

Evan said, "Is there anything else you remember about the guy in the truck? Anything unusual? Anyone talking to him?"

"Detectives, I'm sorry but that's all I know."

"One more question. This was a GPS bought from this store," said Evan showing the photo. "We traced the serial number here. I'm betting whoever bought it also bought one of those burner phones." He waited for Tyler to answer.

"Look," he said lowering his voice. "People come in here and buy stuff like this but they always use cash. They never give their zip codes or names for the computer. I have no way of giving you anything about the person who bought them. I don't recall. It was probably one of the other salespeople."

Evan frowned. "Is it possible to get more security footage? It would be for Sacramento PD."

"Yeah, Chris can help with that."

Two people walked in and Tyler went to help them.

Evan leaned in to Katie. "C'mon," he said as he steered her to the back area.

"Uh, excuse me?" said Tyler when he noticed the detectives going to the back room. "You can't go back there."

"It's okay, we're just leaving," said Evan.

Katie hurried with Evan as they went through the storage room and to the back entrance. The area seemed typical of the type of store with lots of labeled boxes. They kept moving to the delivery entrance and opened the door. Katie half expected the security alarm to blare but it stayed silent.

Standing out in the back alley, Katie once again felt the cool air and smelled the car exhaust. She looked around but nothing seemed to capture her interest, until she saw a large dumpster filled to the rim with some of the contents oozing out. She walked to the dumpster.

"What do you see?" said Evan.

"I'm not sure." Katie flipped open the lid. The contents weren't just bagged garbage, but loose pieces of paper. "Strange. Don't most people bag their garbage and shred everything else?"

"What are you looking for?"

"Something that might be connected to Chad or our investigations. People, places, connections? I don't know." Katie hoisted herself up and swung her leg over the side of the dumpster.

"Okay," he said as he looked both ways in the alley and then assisted Katie.

Katie looked at the mass of hastily dumped papers and felt her pulse increase and her anticipation skyrocket. It was the first time during this entire investigation that she felt close to something—something big. Her usual drive and tenacity began to surface.

Positioning herself in the dumpster, she began digging through the paperwork. The person who had disposed of the papers didn't bother tearing or shredding them. They were still attached by paperclips, which Katie thought was unusual. Someone had been in a hurry to get rid of them.

Evan watched to make sure that no one saw them or sneaked up from behind. "Need a hand?"

"Nope." She found some interesting invoices dated both before and after Chad's disappearance. They were all types of surveillance equipment. All paid with cash with the same initials printed at the top: SMH. She grabbed all of the receipts she could—not wanting to spend any more time in the dumpster than necessary.

Katie handed the invoices to Evan and climbed out of the dumpster.

"I bet when you got up this morning you didn't think you would be in a dumpster."

She chuckled. "I have a confession. It's not my first time." She jumped down. "Let's go see what's going on at the hardware store."

Evan took the paperwork and quickly ran to the SUV before returning to Katie. She sat down at one of the tables, wondering if the person who smoked had sat there and seen the man in the truck. Katie tried to piece the events together.

Evan casually sat down next to her. "Good view of the parking lot," he said.

Katie nodded. She had almost forgotten how perceptive and intelligent Evan was, one of the main reasons she had always liked him. She kept watch on the lot in hopes that the truck would drive in, but no such luck.

"Let's go inside," said Evan.

Katie followed him into the hardware store. It wasn't a

typical chain store, but family owned. Like the electronics store, the building was older but well maintained. The aisles were organized and the inventory was well-stocked.

A middle-aged man with a gray beard approached them. "Hello, folks, what can I help you find?"

"Are you the owner?" said Evan.

"Yes, is there a problem?"

"I'm Detective Daniels and this is Detective Scott," he said. "We have a couple of questions regarding a missing person's case."

"Of course. I don't know how I can help," he said.

Katie noticed a young man with blond hair and tattoos down his arms walking across the small tool aisle. He was dressed in the same T-shirt as the owner. The guy watched the detectives as if he wanted to know what was going on—or he knew something.

As Evan spoke with the owner, she decided to take the opportunity to talk to the young store associate. Katie walked down the aisle and peered from left to right. She then continued and started systematically going down each area until she found the man stocking the shelves.

"Hi," said Katie.

He turned, pushing his bushy blond hair from his eyes. "Can I help you?" He eyed her badge and gun.

"Maybe." She glanced at his pants pocket and saw an outline for a cigarette pack. "Do you take a smoke break out front?" She saw his nametag said Tim.

"Yeah."

"Can I show you some photos to see if you recognize anyone?"

He stood up. "Sure."

Katie reached into her pocket and retrieved her cell phone. She pulled up the photos and then turned it to Tim. "Do any of these guys look familiar?"

"Why? What did they do?" He looked carefully at each photo.

She waited patiently not answering him.

"Yeah, I've seen them."

"When?"

"I don't know. I saw that guy probably a month ago," he said, referring to Chad. "I think he went into the electronics store."

Katie tensed, hoping that Tim saw more—at least something that would help identify who took Chad.

"And, yeah, I think I've seen the guy in the truck, but I couldn't be sure though."

"Why not?" she said.

"He always seemed to cover his face. I dunno know for sure. I'm sorry."

"That's okay. About what time have you seen the guy in the truck?"

"Afternoons."

"What makes you so sure?"

"It's when I take my afternoon smoke. I just saw him before you guys got here."

"Right now?" she said. "Thank you." Katie turned and ran through the store and headed for the exit.

Evan watched her dash by and then fled out the front door.

Once outside, Katie scanned the parking lot. At the far corner, she saw the tailgate of a black truck. That was all she needed—she took off at a full run. She ran by several people just exiting a car and then made her way toward the truck.

An engine roared to life.

Katie saw the black truck, which had backed in its space, jet forward. She ran as fast as she could but the truck managed to make its way ahead of her and left the lot, revving its engine.

Katie stopped. She couldn't see the driver and there were no plates on the vehicle.

"No!" Her frustration boiled over.

Why was the truck guy following them?

She turned around to go back to the hardware store.

Evan jogged up. "Who was that?"

"The guy in the black truck. I couldn't get to him before he bolted." She was still breathing hard.

"What was he doing here?"

"My guess. He's following us."

"Then that would mean..." Evan jogged back to his SUV and took a few minutes until he found a GPS attached to the undercarriage. "Here's your answer." He had the same type of GPS in his hand that Katie had on her Jeep.

"There's one thing we know," she said.

"What's that?"

"We now know that the guy in the truck was most likely the person who attached the GPS to our police vehicles. But what about Chad's disappearance?" She struggled with the connections and the fact that not only did she want to know—she needed to know in order to set things straight in her mind.

THIRTY-EIGHT

Wednesday 2010 hours

Katie sat in her living room spreading out the invoices she found in the dumpster behind the electronics store. They were fanned out like a jumbo card game. She began putting them into piles of specific categories of security equipment—then by dates.

She kept her concentration and finally felt like they were moving forward with the investigation. Maybe it was wishful thinking because she needed direction for getting to the truth. Or, perhaps it was because she needed a strong distraction.

"You know that there's still a uniform parked outside on the street," said Nick. He sat down drinking a beer.

"You know that you don't need to stay here. Don't get me wrong, you're always welcome, but I'm sure that you have other things to do." Katie put down some of the invoices to look up at the sergeant. "Really, I'm okay."

"I know you can handle anything, but I think it's important that you have the support from your friends."

"I don't know how I got so lucky. Thank you," she said.

"Don't you have someone special you should be spending time with?"

He laughed. "You read me so well. Well, I don't know about special—yet."

"Fill me in," she said smiling.

"Well... I had coffee with my physical therapist, Christina."

"Christina?"

"She's amazing. Funny. She did four years in the Marines, but I won't hold that against her." He laughed.

"It's nice seeing you smile and laugh. I hope Christina sees what I do."

"Thanks, Scotty." He downed the last of his beer. "So tell me, what do you have?"

Cisco pushed his way in between Katie and Nick, making himself comfortable.

"I've found most of the GPS devices that match up with the ones found on our vehicles. They're cheap—about twenty-five dollars each. The burner phones bought were used to track them, so it makes it impossible to trace with any accuracy. Everything was paid for with cash, making it that much more difficult." She picked up a stack of paperwork. "But almost all of the invoices that were sold have SMH written on them."

"Initials?"

"That's what I thought. But trying to find out who that is makes for a million possibilities. Maybe not quite that many, but too many to figure out." She looked at her notes and then opened her laptop. "We have time and date stamps from the invoices against the security footage sent over—I can't believe how fast they got back to us. Look at this," she said, turning the laptop to Nick.

"That guy," he said, eyeing the man dressed in dark sweats, hoodie, and a baseball cap pulled down. "Can't see his face."

"Yeah, he's making sure that he can't be identified."

"Which means that he knows where all the security cameras are located," he said.

"I'm forwarding to Gav and John to see what they can come up with." She pondered a moment. "But these invoices with SMH..."

"Couldn't just be random letters? Maybe the transaction won't go through unless it has someone's name or initials?"

"It could. But this is consistent. If it's the killer, I would say it's significant besides consistent."

"I'm not sure where you're going with this. Do you know who it is?"

Katie picked up several files and flipped them open. There were lists of suspects, victims, and names of friends and family. "All these names from the investigations are on these lists. All the people, anyone we've talked to, suspects, people connected to everyone, and even cops who've worked on the cases and crime scenes."

Nick raised his eyebrows in question. "That's a lot of people."

"Yes. But guess what. Not one of these people on the list has those initials. What are the odds?"

"I don't know. I'm not really a statistic kind of guy."

"There's only one person matching the three initials. SMH. Simon Marcus Holden."

"Holden?" he said.

Katie nodded. "It's another way the killer is toying with the investigation. It's another way that he's asserting his mastery of control—letting us know that he can do whatever he wants and not get caught. He's actually toying with us. It's part of his personality profile and plays into his mastery of control."

"That's quite a theory."

Katie leaned back, petting Cisco. "I know it's a theory, but it's also a gut instinct. And..."

"And?"

"It leads me to believe that Chad's disappearance isn't random, but connected. Those news articles about our previous investigations. It's a clear sign that he's pointing things directly at us—while controlling us."

Katie thought about all the large amounts of information they had, which seemed to be growing by the day. "Everything points back to Holden. But I know that sounds crazy—because he's in jail. I don't think Holden is a killer. He's part of it but not the one in charge of everything. I believe that someone else is pulling the strings and orchestrating everything."

Nick contemplated what she said. "How are you going to find out who that person is?"

"That's the big question. Everything is in front of us—we just have to put the pieces in the right order so it will lead to the killer." She let out a breath as her anxieties rose. "This case... these cases..."

"Scotty, it's okay. Take a breath and slow down."

"Gav and I have to solve these cases before another woman is murdered." She closed her eyes for a moment. "I feel like time is running out—for everyone."

"You have to give yourself a break. You're doing everything you can. McGaven is back to full duty. You'll figure it out. I know you guys—you'll find the connection and zero in on the killer."

Katie worked for another hour before she couldn't keep her eyes open any longer. She didn't want to go to bed because she was afraid of what she might dream. Whenever she was in the middle of a case, the victims haunted her dreams—helping and pushing her forward. Now she was even more terrified that one of those victims in her dreams would be Chad.

THIRTY-NINE

Love inspires. Love heals. Love gives life. Love lingers in everything. Love never completely disappears, but rather grows exponentially never leaving you abandoned. If you're blessed enough to have it from those around you, cherish it, be grateful for it, and never do anything to tarnish that love. Always tell those close to you that you love them, allowing it to grow. One thing that love never does is teach you how to live without it.

Thursday 0830 hours

Katie stood at the murder board with her hands on her hips. She'd studied everything so many times she could see it in her mind throughout the day, when she was driving, and when she closed her eyes at night. She knew every inch of the crime scenes and the victims' injuries. The extracted pinkies and eyes made horrifying images, but it was a telling sign of the killer— wanting the victims to be sightless and weakened just like wanting the police to feel powerless. But Katie wasn't going to let the killer win—at any cost.

"Interesting. I've read all your updates to the cases and what happened at Dayton Electronics yesterday. SMH. You really think that stands for Simon Marcus Holden?" said McGaven.

"I think everything revolves around Holden. Think about it. The crime scenes. The victims. He's still setting a dramatic scene." Katie took a closer look at some of the images she'd taken of the photos of Gina Hartfield that her office had posted in her memory. She was smiling in them and looked to be somewhere cold with snow, like the mountains. She wore a scarf that was navy and beige.

"Wait a minute."

McGaven remained quiet watching his partner.

"The third crime scene at Wellington Park was where the fourth and fifth victims were found buried. I think that our sixth victim is at Sampson and Crawford Real Estate Developers."

McGaven stood up and walked to the board.

"Look at this," she said, indicating to the scarf in the photo. Then she pointed to one of the ravines behind the real estate developers and what looked like a piece of similar fabric.

"That's a stretch, but I see where you're going with this," he said. "You think Gina was taken at her work. Maybe the killer had been watching her and then when she came out, he was already in her car? Or followed her home?"

"Or the killer used a GPS to keep track of her by following her home."

"What about the scarf?" he said.

"It couldn't have fallen out of her car innocently. The killer could have taken it from her and left it as a clue for a previous victim." She turned to her partner. "I have a bad feeling about this, Gav. It seems that the killer has had all these murders carefully planned out and he's leaving clues of the already dead women."

McGaven grabbed his jacket. "Let's get over there and hopefully prove your theory wrong."

"Have I told you how much I've missed you?" she said. "Let's go."

FORTY

McGaven drove into the parking lot for Sampson & Crawford Real Estate Developers, heading around back. Katie was anxious, with many things spinning through her mind and constantly wondering if she was indeed on the right track or just grasping at baseless theories out of desperation against the serial killer's ticking clock.

"Where is everyone?" said Katie.

The back parking lot as well as the front area were deserted. There wasn't one car.

"That's weird. It's Thursday. There should be someone here today." McGaven called the company but the call went to voicemail with no special message that they were closed.

Katie got out with a pair of gloves and headed directly to the ravine.

"Wait," said McGaven. "We need to figure out what's going on." His words didn't stop his partner.

Katie had already begun making her way down into the ravine. It was still wet and muddy from rain a few days ago so she placed her feet carefully, still remembering the deep hole at Winslow's property. The smell hit her first. It was the usual odor of old garbage and a small dead animal. As she scanned the area before setting another foot deeper, she tried to ascertain if things had been moved recently or if it was the outcome of months of accumulation.

"Hey," said McGaven. He lowered a short spade to her.

"Where did you get this?"

"It was in the trunk. I thought it would make it easier to move stuff around. Be cautious, okay?"

"I will." Katie began to scrape things out of the way where layers of garbage had settled for a while. She started to think that it was futile, but she doggedly kept going, carefully moving across the area.

McGaven descended a few feet in case she needed help, but he decided not to immerse himself in the hole in case it was too much weight. It was unclear if the ravine was stable or just a part of a much bigger and deeper crevice. "Be careful," he stressed.

"I'm okay. Just taking one careful step at a time." Then she saw the area where the navy blue and beige scarf was located. She used the spade to gently pry the garment up from the rest of the debris. She showed it to McGaven, who nodded in recognition that it looked like the one that belonged to Gina Hartfield in the photograph.

Katie put the scarf aside so that they could document and then bag it as potential evidence. She looked back down and noticed something that was out of place. It was a piece of broken-down cardboard box that appeared to be new. The card was of the sort that would most likely be used for heavy commercial items. Next to it was a small burlap bag with a drawstring used for something small.

"Anything?" said McGaven.

"I'm not sure." Katie moved the small bag. She hesitated for a moment and then used her gloved fingers to pull the string. Once it opened, she still moved slowly.

"What is it?" said McGaven again—this time he sounded impatient.

Katie looked inside. She stared at the contents and then moved back. "It's..."

"What?"

"It's... a... severed finger, looks like a pinky, and... two eyeballs."

"Get out of there. We need to call this in."

"Wait," she said. She knew that she needed to carefully backtrack and climb out, but her instincts were telling her to look underneath the cardboard. She was obsessed with knowing, but anxious at the same time. With her heart racing, she didn't move slowly, but quickly flipped the piece of cardboard.

McGaven moved closer to try to see what Katie was seeing.

Katie sucked in a breath. She wanted to be wrong, but she was right. Just a couple of inches from the top, she saw the forehead of a woman with partial facial features and there appeared to be more of her body buried under debris. The empty dark holes of where her eyes were haunted Katie. "We need everyone here now. It's the next victim."

"I'm on it," said McGaven. He called in their location and what they had discovered.

Katie backed up from the crime scene and carefully climbed up out of the ravine. She waited for McGaven to finish coordinating the police call, making sure that there were no sirens.

She looked at her partner. "Gav, what's going on?"

"I don't know. This is one of the most disturbing scenes I've seen yet."

Katie looked around the area. "Where is everyone?"

"It does feel eerie being here alone," he said.

"So has the killer already murdered his victims and is now

burying them at previous crime scenes and victims' places of employment?" Katie was trying to make sense of everything. She'd had a hunch about the ravine, but she didn't imagine anything like this. Looking at the office building, she saw a back door. "I'm going to check it out."

"Everything is too weird. I think you should wait here until backup arrives."

"I'm going to just check things out and see if I can figure out why no one is here," she said.

"Katie, wait," said McGaven.

She turned to face her partner.

"I have to insist you stay here."

"Insist?" she said.

"There are too many variables with these cases. We need to sit tight and re-evaluate."

Katie could see his point, but she still wanted to snoop around. There might be some type of notice posted as to why the employees weren't there. "I'm just going to walk around the building and see if there's something indicating why no one is here."

McGaven didn't argue, but he was clearly annoyed with his partner. "Fine. No one will be here for fifteen to twenty minutes since it isn't exigent circumstances."

"Okay," she said and started walking to the building.

"But…"

She stopped again, turning to look at McGaven.

"I'm going with you. We're partners. You know, part-ners… allies… associates… got each other's back."

"Okay, okay. Let's check it out." She couldn't help but smile, but it soon faded as they approached.

There was a handwritten sign in black ink on an eight-and-a-half-by-eleven piece of paper. It said: "Broken water pipes. Office closed today."

"Broken water pipes?" said Katie.

"It happens."

"Of course. But where's the crew to fix them? Or the city?" she said.

"Good point."

"There's no one here. And look at the date, it was yesterday." Katie began looking around, almost as if there was someone watching them. It made her unconsciously shiver—it was the same feeling when someone is about to go into a dangerous situation and their body reacts to surrounding unnatural circumstances. She felt that same sensitivity when she was on patrol in the Army when the enemy was hidden close by.

"There could be a logical explanation," he said.

Katie reached out her hand and touched the doorknob. It turned and she pushed the door open a few inches. "Hello?" she said.

McGaven instinctively took a few steps back. "Something isn't right." He put his hand on Katie's arm.

"Hello? PV Sheriff's Department," she said, turning to her partner. "We need to check it out."

McGaven shook his head. "We need to wait. It could be rigged with explosives. Again."

"We need to know what we're up against so we can relay it to reinforcements. The door is unlocked and there are no cars in the parking lot. It couldn't be maintenance or a security guard—they would have a car."

McGaven looked around and tried to stall.

"Let's just take a quick sweep to make sure it's safe so we have something to report."

"Let's go." He took his weapon out of the holster.

Katie did the same. "Sheriff's department." She nodded to McGaven and entered first followed closely by her partner.

They walked inside and entered a hallway. They moved carefully, fanning their weapons making sure that there wasn't anyone hiding or waiting to ambush them, alert for tripwires.

Katie went left and McGaven went right. They kept quiet but their gestures communicated to the other what was needed to know.

Katie moved on as she heard her partner take the other direction. She stopped at what appeared to be the break room. There were two round tables and various chairs. A long cabinet with a sink and a refrigerator at the end—everything appeared to be clean and empty. It was as if everyone had retrieved their stuff and left for the day.

Two coffee cups caught her attention. They were rinsed and in the sink. It seemed odd that there were two cups as if two people had shared a beverage recently. She touched the coffeemaker and it seemed to be warm.

The creeping feeling swam up her back and neck.

She recalled everything they had seen and wondered why someone would be in the building even though it was clear that the employees were already gone.

"No."

Katie moved quickly, backtracked, and went to find McGaven. She knew why the building was unlocked and waiting for them. She could barely breathe as she frantically searched for McGaven. Not wanting to yell her concerns or alert anyone else, she hurried looking into various offices until she reached the main area they had seen when they had spoken with the manager, Jeff Braxton.

She stopped at the coffee and water area, which was where there were photos of Gina Hartfield smiling broadly as if someone had said something funny.

"Hey," said McGaven. "No one here. It doesn't appear that anyone has been here."

Katie raised her hand to her mouth.

McGaven immediately stopped talking or moving.

She didn't know why she did that, but it seemed like the

right thing to do. Motioning to go back toward the back entrance, they moved with swift synchronicity.

There was a strange scraping noise—the same as the one she had heard at Wellington Park Prep School.

"Move!" she yelled.

The detectives took off running and both made it out the door heading to the police sedan. Katie crouched and took cover on the opposite side of the car. McGaven was next to her and he helped to shield his partner.

Within seconds, the explosion ripped through the inside of the building. It seemed to stay contained in the middle of the building, but the blast blew out the windows. The ground shook and the concussion pressed hard against Katie's body. For an instant, she felt like the building was lying on her chest.

McGaven sat up and was instantly on his cell phone calling in the emergency to have everyone stay away from the property except for bomb squad and SWAT. He and Katie were going to meet the emergency vehicles at the entrance of the driveway near the street.

"You okay?" said McGaven, still shaken.

"Yeah, I think so." Katie slowly got up and stared at the building.

"How'd you know?"

"I heard that same weird scraping sound. And I wasn't taking any chances." Her pulse and adrenalin were still racing. The sound of the blast brought into focus her time in Afghanistan, which made her shake a bit longer. The memories seemed real as if she were transported back there and she could smell the smoke and expelled ammunition. The fears. The uncertainty. The reality. All came rushing back.

McGaven started walking and he turned around to see his partner still standing at the car staring at the building, which was now pluming smoke. "Let's go. Katie?"

"I'm coming," she said.

. . .

Kate stood at the edge of the property and watched the coordinated efforts of the bomb squad and the fire department making sure that the building was safe—no more bombs or fires. Forensics and the medical examiner's office stood by waiting for the okay to go in and document and collect evidence, as well as recovering the body in the ravine.

McGaven also coordinated with deputies and the first responders. He gave and gathered information. The deputies fanned out and conducted a search of the area.

Katie watched everything almost like she were in an audience and the efforts playing out were a movie. Voices. Sounds of heavy boots trampling the area. The rolling sound of the gurney. Everything was working together like a finely oiled machine.

"Katie," said the sheriff as he approached.

She turned to him and gave a weak smile.

"You okay?" he said, trying not to sound like a concerned uncle but a sheriff in charge. But it was obvious behind his eyes that he was worried.

"I'm fine."

"What do we have?"

Katie explained what had transpired when they had arrived.

"That was quick thinking on your part and that you both got out in time."

Sheriff Scott took another moment to give Katie a reassuring look before he left to oversee the rest.

Her cell phone interrupted her heavy thoughts. Katie answered. "Detective Scott."

"This is Cecelia Randall from Sampson and Crawford," the caller said.

"Cecelia, are you alright? Why isn't there anyone at the building?"

"We were told yesterday to go home until the pipes were

fixed," she said weakly.

"Is everything okay?"

"No, not really. I think someone has been following me. And I think it has to do with Gina."

"What makes you say that?" Katie heard the frightened woman's voice. She knew there had been more to her story the day they were interviewing her.

"Gina had said she thought that someone was following her from work and the gym. But I just thought that she was being overly suspicious. She had men bothering her all the time."

"Cecelia, where are you?"

"Home."

"Stay there. Lock the doors. I'll send a deputy, but my partner and I will be right there," said Katie. "What's your address?"

"Uh... it's 1477 Spreckles Way."

"I know where it is. Stay inside. We'll be right there." She hung up. "Gav!" She spotted him nearby.

He approached Katie.

"We've got to go. Cecelia just called and she said someone has been following her. She sounded really scared."

"Let's go. Deputies are scarce right now because of this call, so we need to get over there now."

FORTY-ONE

Thursday 1400 hours

McGaven drove with the siren blazing as they made their way to Cecelia's house. He was gripping the steering wheel and taking the corners too fast, but Katie could see that he was extremely concerned and had a renewed energy.

Katie waited as patiently as she could while looking out for Cecelia's house. When they finally pulled into her driveway, everything seemed normal. There was a small compact car parked on the left. The landscaping was neat and nothing appeared to be out of place.

Katie hurried to the front porch and began knocking, but the door was open. She stepped inside. "Cecelia?"

McGaven was behind her. "Cecelia? It's Detectives McGaven and Scott. It's okay."

There was nothing but silence.

A kitchen stool was lying on its side and mail and paper-work were on the floor. There were dishes soaking in the sink. Katie touched the water and it was still warm.

"Gav, she had to have been just here."

"Something happened here," he said, focusing on the stool and papers.

Katie spotted a piece of paper, just like the one taped to the door at Cecelia's work, lying on the floor. She picked it up, reading the dark black letters:

Now you have everything you need. Come find us.

"Gav," she said showing him the paper. Her blood ran cold and her heart jumped. She couldn't allow the killer to take another life, but it seemed that they were still a step or two behind. Now it was personal, the killer was making it a challenge for the detectives.

"Where would he take her?" he said. "I hope that's what he means by us—that Cecelia is still alive."

Katie didn't know anything for sure, but she thought the killer was right. They did have everything they needed to identify and catch him. "We missed something."

"What do you mean?"

"There's something we've missed or aren't seeing clearly." She looked around. "We need to have John and Eva sweep this place for anything that might belong to the killer, and especially for fingerprints."

"This killer is smart—probably won't find anything."

"We have to try—no one is perfect one hundred percent of the time." Katie had to believe that. She saw a photo of Cecelia with an older woman who she assumed to be her mother and hoped that her mom wouldn't be identifying her daughter's body in the morgue.

No.

Katie and McGaven took a preliminary look around the home and it appeared that the only visible disturbance was in the kitchen area; Cecelia was most likely washing dishes and was caught by surprise.

The small cottage was neat and tidy. Cecelia lived alone and had an impressive skill of keeping everything in its place. Most of the furniture seemed to have been refinished and painted in bright colors.

"They are going to be busy at the building site for a while and we won't know anything until later today or maybe tomorrow. We need to go back to the office—to square one. We need to look at *everything*."

McGaven checked his phone. "Looks like John sent a text message and it says: 'Young female victim, brunette like the others. BTW, explosion was C-4.'"

Katie thought about it. "C-4 indicates someone in the military or with special military training. So what are we missing?" She had to stress that question again. "These cases are piling up. What an investigative mess." She had been so filled with pain that her anger had taken a back seat and now she wanted let her fury out in order to find the killer.

"Okay," said McGaven. "Let's get back to the office."

FORTY-TWO

Thursday 1720 hours

The forensic division was quiet as a midnight crypt, but that was a comfort to Katie. It was a place where she was safe and which no one could enter without being invited. The silence made it easier to concentrate and to see investigations with some clarity. John and Eva were still at the office building and the work areas were like a ghost town.

McGaven sat in the chair with paperwork spread all around. "So let's go over this again with our three main suspects. Should they be our top three?"

Katie stood at the board in her usual place, eyeing each case, studying what they had found out with forensics and autopsies —trying to gain linkage in the cases to the perp. She perused her criminal profile and realized that the killer likely wasn't completely a psychopath—some traits, of course—by the way the murders were carried out. It seemed that there was lingering paranoia to the killer's behavioral evidence. There seemed to be a type of persecution stemming from a type of loss. She added to her original profile.

"Maybe we're wrong looking at this as the psychopathic tendency, and it has more of a paranoia quality," she said. It helped to say things out loud rather than keeping it inside her head.

McGaven studied the board. "So a paranoid individual goes through the persecution complex with imagining everything around them is a threat and conspiracy."

"Basically, yes."

"It still doesn't help with the list, but I get it."

"I believe that whoever the killer is..."

"He's going to strike again. We need to have a plan if we're going to save Cecelia. Time is ticking..."

Frustration setting in, she said, "Of course. But we need to be better equipped than we are right now." She looked at the two buildings where explosives were used. "Why does the killer want to bring more attention to himself by blowing up buildings? It's risky."

"It's taking a chance. The C-4, GPS trackers, and burying bodies at previous crime scenes."

"That's what the killer wants," she said. "It has Holden's signature all over it. At least that's what the killer *wants* us to think."

"Okay," he said. "Here's the latest list of the people who are the closest to Terrance Lane, Harry Winslow, and Butch Turner from Denise." He read down the page.

"Tell me." She turned to look at her partner, hoping for some news.

"Terrance Lane's best friend and bodyguard, Sean Hyde. Harry Winslow's longtime friend and business partner on most of his acquisitions, Rex Starr. And Butch Turner's best friend from high school, Randall Leche."

"All longtime friends. Okay, I'm surprised there aren't any siblings or cousins as their closest friends. What are the backgrounds?"

"Nothing out of the ordinary, but I haven't checked all data bases yet."

"My gut says keep digging on their friends' backgrounds—especially for Winslow and Lane. If I had to guess—which I won't."

"Go ahead. Who do you think would be more than likely?"

"Any of these three *could* be a killer. But, Butch doesn't seem to have the wherewithal to plan, coordinate, and pull off these killings."

McGaven nodded.

"Now both Lane and Winslow are a different story. We already know that Winslow wouldn't and didn't hesitate to run down two police detectives. But Lane... he's an entirely different type of personality." She recalled the conversation with her at the charity event. "He's arrogant, smug, and narcissistic. He likes to be in charge and lets everyone know it."

"So are a lot of people."

"But there was something almost creepy about him. He knew who I was—and seemed proud of himself."

"But our solved cases have been public."

"Who owns all these properties where we've had the crime scenes?" she said.

"I haven't been able to verify a few of the companies so I'm still not sure if Lane or Winslow are the owners. But... All Fitness and the building where Sampson and Crawford was located are owned by Winslow. There are other of the same types of buildings around the area too that I need to double-check."

Katie thought for a moment. "Who would have access or training in explosives? Been in the military?"

McGaven read through another report. He shook his head. "Nothing indicates that any of the three men had been in the military, but Winslow's first daughter had been killed when she was eight years old—hit by a truck. It was a hit and run."

"Is that enough to avenge her death? It was too long ago. And the age is wrong." Katie thought about it. "But... he does do some demolition work for his commercial properties. He doesn't do it personally but he would have access to explosives, I'm sure. We need to check it out."

Katie felt her anxiety rise as she glanced at the clock. "It's been two hours since Cecelia disappeared. We can't even file a missing person's report yet because technically through the eyes of the law she isn't missing. We need to get ahead of the killer..."

"Holden?"

"We're done with him. He played his last card and I don't think that he'll even meet with us now. There's no more show. When we're done with these cases, I think we'll find that Holden wasn't the killer but the accomplice." She looked at the locations for the bombs. "No, the explosives are the clues for now that have become front and center."

"The Wellington Park Prep School and now Sampson and Crawford Real Estate Developers—a school and an office building. What's the connection?"

"It's not the location—it's the crime scenes."

"Isn't that the location?" he said.

"Yes and no. Look at this killer, whether it's the same as a decade ago remains another story, but the killer has taken it up another notch. It's flair or drama, or whatever you want to call it. Now the killer is begging us to play his game. That's why the two explosions were just the beginning... right before the grand finale." She looked at the crime scenes.

"Meaning?"

"Meaning, the industrial building and the crime scene for Jenna Day is the next target. I would bet on it."

McGaven gave a stern look. "I know what you're planning."

"This time we're going to be ready and be prepared," she said. "We need the okay before we start and..."

"Katie?"

She began stacking paperwork and thinking about who would help. "Yes."

"What about the book at Chad's with the page marking explosive investigation?" he said.

It was always something on her mind, but she wasn't going to verbalize it due to the fact that intense pain would come barreling back. "I know... that there might be a connection... Believe me I know..." Her sadness continued to stay with her.

Now you have everything you need. Come find us...

FORTY-THREE

Thursday 2010 hours

Katie and McGaven had managed to coordinate and receive the go-ahead from the sheriff to do a building search of the warehouse where Jenna Day's body was recovered. It wasn't feasible to have a regular search of the building due to the possibilities of explosives, so deputies weren't given access. Katie had been given special access due to her military experience.

It was already late and the light had long gone away—so they were operating in darkness with the use of flashlights and outdoor lighting.

There had been no word about Cecelia, and Katie didn't think there would be under the circumstances. The killer was challenging them to his game. Stakes were high. Safety was of the utmost importance.

After speaking with Evan first and seeking his advice, Katie relayed the plan to Sheriff Scott. He was hesitant at first, but having been given all the facts and learning that Cecelia was missing, he agreed. They had to act. SWAT and bomb squad were on high-alert and would be available if necessary, but their

ETA would run anywhere from a half to a full hour. There were other calls in the county area that they were attending or for which they were acting as backup.

Katie got Cisco then drove up to an old auto garage to which the team had got interior access. It was within walking distance to the warehouse. Their staging area was in the process of being remodeled so it was empty and a perfect place to get ready.

As she parked, she saw that McGaven, John, and Evan were already there. Obviously they were coordinating the operation with their expertise. John, ex-Navy Seal, and Evan, Army military working dog trainer and military police, were both military veterans just as herself. McGaven had proven himself over and over with his skills. They would be a great team and she trusted each one of them with her life.

Her idea sounded great when she was relaying it to her uncle, but now as she sat in her Jeep she had some second thoughts. Dragging the three men into her plan might have been a mistake. She didn't want anything to happen to them.

Was she on the right track?

Would the killer have already set the traps for them?

Would they be able to rescue Cecelia in time?

Katie got out of her car. She was dressed in combat gear, pants, shirt, and boots along with a bulletproof vest. She thought about the missions that she and Cisco had led. It still left her a bit breathless until she focused on the greater good. The dangerous and tight situations they experienced would forever be engraved in her mind, forming a defining moment in her life. Even through some of the most treacherous proactive assignments, there were always both good and bad encounters.

Cisco whined, bringing her back to the present.

Katie outfitted Cisco in his vest and made sure everything fit properly and the lead was secure. She would fix his safety goggles as well as her own when they were about to leave.

"Stay here," she said and shut the Jeep door.

Katie could hear the men talking in low tones. She walked in and found the three of them leaning over a folding table with the plans of the warehouse spread out. She could instantly see the notations of where the entrance and exits were as well as where the power was located. The symbols of windows, air ducts, air-conditioning units, staircase, and weak structural areas were visible.

"There she is," said McGaven. He too was dressed for a military maneuver just as John and Evan were. The Sacramento PD had worked out an agreement to lend Evan to Pine Valley Sheriff's Department in order to complete this operation.

She nodded her greetings. "How did SWAT and bomb squad take it that we're doing this op instead of them?"

"As well as you would expect," said McGaven with a slight frown. "I'm actually a bit surprised that Sheriff Scott signed off on this because we're three detectives and a forensic supervisor."

"They don't have the expertise like two military K9 bomb units," said Evan.

"Are we all okay with this?" she said, looking at each one of them.

They all nodded.

She searched their eyes to make sure that they were absolutely in agreement. Each of the men had intense eyes, especially Evan.

"The search warrants are in place. Okay, show me the exact plan," said Katie.

Evan stepped up because he had experience of being instrumental in similar missions but from a military perspective. "John and McGaven will be our cover officers and our eyes and ears outside. They will be stationed across corners, John in back and McGaven in front." He turned to Katie. "You and I will clear the property first. Mac and I will take the back and you and Cisco the front—we will meet at the entrance here. Even though we've been there before, the killer seems to like to return to the crime scenes."

Katie could see clearly how they would enter the building. Her trepidation and jitters dissipated as she concentrated on what they would be doing.

"We will enter together, Mac and I will clear the first level, and you and Cisco will go straight ahead up the stairs to clear the second level. Now underneath the stairs is where power boxes are located and that would be a great place to plant a bomb device. I will sweep that before you go up the stairs. Okay?"

Katie nodded.

"It's very important that we stay focused and move slowly and deliberately. From what I've been told and read in reports, this killer wants to bait us," said Evan.

"He's been a step or two ahead of us the entire time," she said. "And we're still not sure who owns this building."

"And that's what makes him so dangerous," said McGaven.

"We also have a victim who's possibly with him—and hopefully still alive," said John.

"The sheriff wants to be kept up to date with everything we're doing—and I'll handle that," said McGaven.

"We retreat if anything is unsafe. Understand?" she said.

"After the entire property and building are cleared, there will be a security detail to keep watch just in case the killer wants to make it an explosion zone," said McGaven.

"Alright, let's go over everything one more time," said Evan.

Katie had prepped both her and Cisco with protective gear. She now had a fitted helmet, goggles, and communication microphone and earpiece so that they could all keep in constant contact. It was the only way that the building sweep would work efficiently and keep everyone safe. She had extra rope from K9 training just in case.

The group headed toward the building.

Katie's mind bounced back and forth from the murder board to where they were heading at the moment. She couldn't get the killer's note out of her mind.

Now you have everything you need. Come find us...

There was something about it that made her think that the killer wasn't talking about Cecelia. Was he referring to someone else or one of them?

Katie and Cisco led the group. She watched ahead for anything that could prove to be a trap or something out of the ordinary. It was nerve-wracking, but she had done this so many times in Afghanistan that it felt almost familiar.

The night was settled in darkness—no moon or stars lit the way. Instead the group made their way in almost complete blackness.

Katie glanced down at her side and could barely see Cisco— just a general outline of the black dog. He was quiet, no whining, no pulling. He knew they were on an important mission and he had been trained for situations such as this.

McGaven followed as her cover, then Evan and Mac, with John as cover at the end of the group. They moved well together, giving each other ample space but keeping a watchful eye at the same time. Katie kept her weapon leading the way as the others fanned from side to side—and John periodically fanned behind, where they had come from.

The air had cooled, making the slight breeze extremely cold. There was no sound of traffic. The nearby commercial businesses had long closed for the day. It was isolating and felt as if they had been quarantined.

"Stay frosty," whispered Evan.

Katie upped her pace slightly as she saw the roadway leading up to the warehouse. When her boots hit the road, her steps made a slight crunching noise beneath her feet. She noted that the others barely made a sound behind her. To her relief, her vision became more accustomed to the dark as they didn't want to use flashlights at this point until inside the building.

She slowed her pace as they approached. McGaven took his position at the left, or north, corner of the property and patrolled in a small area keeping a watchful eye.

John jogged behind the building to take his position at the right, or south, back corner. Katie watched him disappear into the night.

Katie and Cisco moved to the north area to begin a proper search and clear a path to the main entrance. She glanced to the right and saw Evan and Mac disappear around the building. His silhouette as well as the dog's imprinted in her mind. She could see his weapon ready and the dog's alert ears perked.

Her mind wandered momentarily and as she remembered.

Watching Evan working with the various military dogs was unlike any experience Katie had before—learning a new skill that originally made her uneasy doubting herself, but the more she watched, the more she respected and understood the team-work-building process with handler and dog. It was similar to a well-oiled machine and a secret language that only handler and canine fully understood. She saw Evan move his body, shifting his weight from side to side, moving forward and back, as the intended dog couldn't take their eyes off him. Neither could she. Evan's body tensed and released, his remarkable hands moved with fluidity at the perfect time whenever the dog responded and their correct behavior marked for the intended outcome. As the dog was released for scent detection or obedience drills, the K9 team was perfectly in sync...

.   .   .

Katie took a breath and began her search in a strip-like fashion, keeping to a tight path and then a sharp turn to return in the other direction. She allowed Cisco only a couple of feet in front of her—keeping a shorter leash ensured that she had control and could keep the dog close in case of danger.

As she worked the area, watching Cisco's body language, he was relaxed, his nose down and occasionally up to catch any blowing scent, and Katie was relieved. She wondered how Evan and Mac were doing behind the building.

"Front area clear," she whispered for everyone to hear.

Within two minutes, "Back area clear," said Evan.

It was a relief for Katie to hear. She closed her eyes for a moment to gain her bearings before going into the building.

Katie and Evan advanced toward the main entrance until they met.

"In position," said McGaven indicating he was ready.

A moment later, "In position," said John.

Katie heard her colleagues' tense voices as she watched Evan cut the lock, tossing it to the ground. It took a moment for him to completely free the door for them to enter. There was no alarm and no cameras to deal with, which Katie thought was strange.

Evan slowly opened the door wide enough for them to pass through.

Both dogs were beginning to get antsy because they seemed to know they were going to get to work—the outdoors was one thing but getting to go inside a large building was something else for them.

Katie and Cisco were the first to enter the building. She stepped across the threshold and immediately saw the metal staircase ahead of her, but waited near the first step as instructed while Evan and Mac passed her, heading to the electrical area.

The illumination of a flashlight bounced around the area giving flashes between the stairs.

Tensions were high. Katie felt it and sensed Evan was carrying the weight of the pressure. She continued to wait, keeping Cisco against her left thigh. She heard Evan giving Mac the search command and then silence. No movement, no sound, not even a whisper.

Finally, "We have a problem," said Evan. "Katie, *don't* move."

She froze.

FORTY-FOUR

Thursday 2145 hours

Katie felt her stomach twist and her heart rate hammer as if it would burst out of her chest. It made it difficult to hear with the incessant pounding inside her ears. She kept Cisco steady, still next to her side. She didn't have to ask what was wrong—it was obviously a bomb issue. The fear had become a reality. Evan was experienced with the dismantling of bombs and she knew that he could likely figure it out. But the thought of being this close to danger made it almost too much for her to take. She and McGaven had already experienced two explosions—and now this. Her nerves were on edge and every muscle in her body was tense.

"It's a compression type," said Evan. His voice was husky and low, but even in tone.

The sound of his voice almost startled her, but then she realized that he was letting everyone know what was going on.

Katie tried to breathe normally with deeper breaths, but the air kept getting caught in her throat causing her head to pound. So she decided to think about the murder board along with

Lane and Winslow. It suddenly captured her attention that Lane had had a best friend who was a bodyguard. How had that individual become a bodyguard?

Being involved in military maneuvers, even as a police officer, had always made her exceptionally alert. When she was in a stressful or life-threatening position, she could often see more clearly and be able to infer details better. She realized there were missing details about the bodyguard. Was he a police officer? Security detail? Or, was he in the military?

"Gav," she whispered not moving a muscle except to talk. "Check Sean Hyde, to see if he was in the military. Search those Department of Defense databases. See if his prints are on file."

"Copy that." McGaven's voice was low and barely resembled his usual upbeat personality. She knew he was equally tense about the situation they were in.

Katie continued to wait, not uttering another word. She knew that the sheriff's department records division was working twenty-four hours and someone would be able to search for him.

There was a clunk sound.

Katie held her breath and squeezed her eyes shut, expecting the worst.

A few tense seconds ticked onward. She heard movement that sounded like Evan retrieving something from his ballistic vest and what sounded like him taking a footstep. The noise of Mac lightly panting now filled the area. Then everything went silent, making her hold her breath again. There was a snap like a wire being cut and then quiet for more than a minute.

"All clear," said Evan.

She breathed a sigh of relief. There were some sounds over the radio as though McGaven and John also let out a tense breath each.

Evan and Mac came into view and he gave her a thumbs-up

sign with a smile. He took another couple of seconds looking at Katie before they parted ways.

Katie took the first step on the stairs with gentle care and then she allowed Cisco to lead the rest of the way. Her boots hit the metal steps, causing a slight ringing sound. She pushed her pace to get to the top, not entirely sure what she would find. She only remembered what she had seen on the building plans, which showed the second level of offices down each side with an open area in the middle like a mezzanine to give a direct view below.

There were numerous offices along the front and back of the building. Some of the doors were open while others were closed. She had no way of knowing what was or wasn't inside them. There were so many doors with opaque squares of glass in the middle with possible areas for traps and hiding places among them.

Katie stood at the top of the stairs preparing her moves. She was going to start with the offices facing the front of the building first. She stepped to the hallway, which had a railing opening to the first floor below. Catching a glimpse of movement below, she saw a flashlight sweep back and forth. She knew that Evan had begun his search around the working areas and some machinery that had been left behind.

"Cisco, *such*."

The sleek black dog immediately began to systematically search the perimeter of the first office door, which was closed. His highly sensitive nose sniffed the cracks around the door and the knob. His ears were perfectly straight up and forward. Eyes trained on where he was about to enter, waiting for his okay command.

Katie put her hand slowly on the door handle and turned it, directing the flashlight into the small space, mindful of tripwires or other types of triggering devices for explosives. She gave Cisco some direction to let him know that he needed to check out the room. She remained at the entrance, keeping an eye on both sides of the hallway.

Cisco cleared the empty room.

Katie continued through the next offices with the same procedure until they reached the end of the building. She couldn't yet relax, but she did feel a sense of relief as they made progress. She knew they weren't out of the woods yet, since the killer had set a compression bomb at the entrance. This also indicated that the whomever it was had some military background.

"First side clear, second floor," she stated.

"First side clear, first floor," said Evan minutes later.

"You were right," said McGaven. His voice was hurried with exhilaration. "Sean Hyde was in the military—Marines. His expertise was... explosives."

Katie stopped cold.

She closed her eyes and tried to imagine this bodyguard carrying out the work of a proficient killer—and why. As she opened her eyes and looked around, she realized that she carried the victims with her wherever she went. She needed to let them go—freeing her own soul of sadness and grief.

Cisco nuzzled her hand, bringing her back into the present, encouraging her to move on with what she had to do.

Katie passed the end section where there was a built-in wooden ladder going up to the roof. She figured it was for main-tenance of the air system or for any other work-related safe-guard for the building.

She and Cisco rounded the corner preparing for the back-facing row of offices. Leaning over the railing, she could see Evan and Mac clearing various work areas, manufacturing storage units, and employee work zones. He was proficient and moved with ease, reminding her of his training techniques of reading the dog's behavior—making sure that Mac searched everything before he moved on. It was difficult for her not to see him as the military working dog trainer whenever she saw him and Mac working.

It was clear the second floor was for the management to watch production and to keep an eye on workers meeting deadlines. She knew that the previous owner and business had moved to a more modern facility, leaving this one behind—a perfect backdrop for a serial killer.

As Evan worked the areas, she was still in awe of how he could read, mark, or spot certain definitive behaviors, and transform dogs into the remarkable working animals they became—a soldier's bonded partner. The training of these special dogs was extremely important to protect lives and keep areas secure, and in general didn't get the recognition and exposure that it truly deserved—for the dogs, handlers, and trainers.

There was a crash in one of the offices, breaking the quiet of the building. She thought she heard a whimpering sound.

She didn't move at first. Her body stiffened. Heart hammered.

Cisco lowered his body and let out a low guttural growl. She secured his lead by attaching it to her belt, keeping him next to her body.

Katie readied herself with her weapon and flashlight.

"Sound coming from office on east side," she said to alert everyone of a potential danger and so they would know that there was a threat.

The radio went into silent mode until she had cleared the room.

Katie moved toward the office with Cisco. Their steps in sync, they progressed with purpose like they had on so many previous missions.

She took a breath and turned the doorknob.

When she opened the door, that was when she was hit by an incredible light. All she saw was a glaring white radiance, making her momentarily blind. She stumbled back and could feel Cisco's warm body still at her side. He too had been blinded and whined in pain and confusion.

"Bravo!" said a man's booming voice with the sound of clapping hands.

Katie heard static on the radio, or what might have been the clamoring of her teammates—it was difficult to ascertain, but she knew that they had her back.

"Detective Scott, I knew you couldn't resist coming here," the voice said. "You're actually quite interesting. A bit predictable. So broken. So vulnerable when you think no one is watching. How painfully pitiful..."

As Katie's eyes began to focus, she saw a man, dressed in gray sweats and a heavy leather jacket, standing in the room. She recognized his dark hair with streaks of gray and his profile. "Sean Hyde," she said.

"Aw, you don't look surprised. But a super detective like you, I'm not at all surprised you solved this whodunit." He chuckled, clearly amused with himself. His personality and demeanor differed from the day at Lane's office. She realized why he kept his face averted from the cameras in the surveillance video.

Katie aimed her weapon at him. "Sorry, but I'm not here to play your game. Show me your hands."

Cisco growled, waiting for the command to attack. He gave three rapid barks.

Instinctively, Katie took a step backward, steadying her hands.

"I would be happy to," he said and showed her a small black device that she knew was a detonator. "I don't think you're going to do that; in fact, I know you won't. Otherwise, your friends are dead. Dead. Dead. *Dead!*"

"Where's Cecelia?"

"Somewhere safe."

"Where!"

"She's close," he whispered. "And no, don't worry, she's still alive and above ground." He still laughed. "Lower your weapon. Otherwise, we go boom."

"Why are you doing this?"

He cackled loudly, reminding Katie of Holden. "Because I can."

"Who's pulling your strings?"

"Oh, you really haven't figured it out. No one, my pretty little detective. No one. I wouldn't trust this to anyone—until you, that is. But I think I might've made a mistake." He took a step toward her and whispered again. "They're watching and listening, you know."

Katie's mind raced as she tried to figure out how to defuse the situation. "No one is watching and they won't charge in here," she said, hoping that everyone understood. "So, who's watching you?"

"No one. Because that's how I like it."

"Terrance Lane?"

"He hasn't a clue. He's just the conduit, the means for me to get what I want. *What I need!*" He struggled then got control of his emotions after his outburst. "He's my friend. My only friend, in fact. Everyone needs at least one friend, don't you think?"

Katie didn't flinch. She felt Cisco tense beside her, wanting to take the man down.

"You're not going to let that dog loose."

"No. He's worth more than you."

"Ha!"

Katie realized that her assessment of the killer wasn't far off. Hyde was deranged and paranoid, but had somehow managed to be a proficient killing machine, staying a step ahead of the police. "Why kill those innocent girls?" She wanted to keep him talking—mostly about himself—in order to buy time.

"Innocent? No one is innocent. Haven't you been paying attention?"

Katie watched his face change expressions rapidly, as though he was several different people depending upon what he was saying. "That's all I do."

"Well, my dear, you know nothing then. Pity... I had such high hopes for you and I working together... I've studied you and read all about your previous cases."

"You must've experienced a catastrophic loss..." she pushed.

"You know nothing," he hissed.

"Oh, but I do. You're weak and you prey upon the innocent," she said, watching his body language change from tough and assured to curious and ready to pounce. That was when he would make his mistake. "And you're so insecure that you take their eyes away so they can't see what a coward you are. You're scared of that. Terrified."

"You're not at all like the articles written about your solved cases."

"Sorry to disappoint you." She clenched her jaw, standing her ground.

"You're just as useless as the others."

"Who?"

"The others!"

"Who is Holden to you?"

"An opportunity. It was perfect. He was easily pliable in my hands—took the fall to be famous. The things that some people do for fame... predictable and pathetic. It was a foolproof plan to replicate the crime scenes—put him back in the spotlight and to keep the police unbalanced. Not to mention, my skills were a little rusty at first, but I improved." He laughed again.

"You seem to use others because you can't do things for yourself." She watched him. "That's sad, in my book."

"It wasn't sad when those girls were out joyriding after drinking in a bar deciding it was okay to drive. That's when..."

He stopped himself. "You think you're clever. Perhaps, I may have misjudged you—a little. Maybe I should have killed you when I could have... on so many occasions."

The thought made her shiver that he had been watching her so closely. "Why the fabric at the cabin? Why the note to Winslow?"

He laughed. "Because I can! I'm brilliant. And you have to admit, it kept you chasing your tail. I was watching your crime scenes and tailing you and the others the whole time. There's nothing so real... so intoxicating as natural fabrics."

"It's sad that you spent so much time with all your clues, because in the end you're still a coward."

"It's amazing the government trains people like me—that's how I know they're watching. You see they're *always* watching." He laughed again. "They trained, and actually trusted me, to perform explosions. *Boom!* And of course other diabolical duties involving killing. Too many to have a favorite."

"What happened that night?" she said, trying to get him back to the trauma that had triggered everything for him.

His face turned sour and he began to play with the trigger. "I'm bored. You need to go now."

"Everyone needs to go," she said. She hoped that McGaven and John cleared away from the building, calling in backup for mop-up duty, whatever happened, and Evan was on his way out to safety. She knew that Sean Hyde would blow up the building —it was just a matter of when.

"I know what you're doing. Always looking out for others. I commend you—not."

"What happened? Did your family die?"

"What do you know?" He moved toward the next office. "Well, I have a surprise for you." He quickly opened the door where there was a body lying on its side.

Katie instantly recognized the woman. It was Cecelia. Katie instinctively lunged toward Hyde.

"Nope," he said, showing her the device.

Katie knew that she couldn't take it from him. She had to wait for her opportunity and pray for the best. All of her military and police training came into play and she hoped it would be enough.

He pulled at Cecelia and she became conscious enough to be at least partially aware of what was going on. "Get up," he said to her, pulling the frightened woman to her feet. Her eyes were wide with terror, face red, and eyes bloodshot.

"Let her go. She had nothing to do with your family," said Katie keeping her voice level.

"Everybody had something to do with me losing my wife, my four-year-old daughter, and my unborn son. *Everybody*. They died a horrible death as the innocent victims in the head-on car accident. Their bodies were barely recognizable, even their eyes were gone. Gone!"

Losing your entire family hit home with Katie, but she kept her eye on the broken but extremely deadly adversary in front of her. It made more sense why he removed the eyes of his victims and then covered the gaping holes as a sign of respect that he didn't feel his own family received.

"Oh no, Detective. I'm tired. I've performed my last funeral. It's too much work. Searching for the perfect women without family close, cleaning them with perfectly mixed natural fluids, preparing them. Coordinating the sites and erasing the tracks. Playing the police games. So daunting. So my time is done here." He shoved Cecelia against the railing where it partially gave way, pushing her off the landing, sending the woman into a panic as she clung to the available rungs.

"*No!*" Katie couldn't get to the screaming woman, who was barely hanging on.

"Too late. Too slow."

Katie saw her moment and lunged at Hyde. She took him

down and was able to grab the trigger device. Cisco took hold of his forearm with perfect timing.

Hyde wouldn't let Katie go so easily even with the dog latched onto his arm.

He looked at her with a curious expression—almost child-like. "Where's Chad? Don't you know?"

Her voice stuck in her throat as she gasped and hesitated.

He lunged at Katie, grabbing her neck and pressing hard. He pinned her by climbing on top of her.

Cisco clamped down harder, shaking his arm furiously, but it didn't seem to slow Hyde down or make him lose strength.

Katie could feel his fingers pressing against her larynx as everything spun in her vision. She fought with everything she had, trying to loosen his grip. Her breath stalled as she battled to stay conscious. It was as if everything slowed down into an almost dreamlike state.

Two gunshots exploded, making her ears ring.

Katie found herself still on her back, covered in blood. She looked up and saw Evan at the end of the hallway, in a shooter stance, with Mac next to him in a down position.

"No," she barely whispered. *"No!"* She pushed Hyde, who had part of his cranium blown apart, off her. "Where is he?" she yelled shaking the dead man. She wanted to know what he meant by his comment about Chad. "No!"

"Katie!" said Evan.

She looked down in her hand. The trigger wasn't a hand-held detonator as she had thought—it was a preset timer counting down from...

Twenty seconds...

Nineteen...

Eighteen...

"Get out! It's a timer!" she yelled. "The building is going to blow. Get out! There's no time to disarm!" She began to cry, not for herself but for Chad. She needed to save Cecelia but she couldn't save him... she couldn't save the love of her life. She looked at the woman who had been miraculously still holding on.

Seventeen...

Sixteen...

Fifteen...

Evan was at her side, helping her up.

"No! Go!" she pleaded. "Go now!"

Evan pushed her and the dogs toward the ladder leading to the roof. He had made a quick decision and climbed up, pushing the top hatch open to help them through.

Fourteen...

Thirteen...

Katie directed the dogs as they made their way up to Evan. Mac was up and she unhooked Cisco as she pushed him up.

Twelve...

Eleven...

"C'mon, Katie!" He held his hand toward her. "C'mon!"

Ten...

"Go! Get them to safety!" she begged. "Please. Go! I have to get Cecelia."

"There's no time," he said as she turned away from him. She couldn't bear seeing his face and worried expression looking down at her. It was probably the last time she would see him.

She ran.

Nine...

Eight...

Seven...

Katie dropped to her knees next to Cecelia, grabbing her wrists. "C'mon."

Six...

Five...

Katie managed to pull the woman up and dragged her toward the farthest corner of the floor, knowing what was going to happen. She prayed that they would somehow be safe. But she realized in the fleeting seconds that her course had already been set in motion.

Four...
Three...
Two...
But she knew.
One second...

FORTY-FIVE

Thursday 2355 hours

In Katie's mind, she still saw Evan's handsome face looking down at her as the explosion violently shook the building like several freight trains barreling down, deafening, and then it ripped through the middle of the building from below at the north area near the stairs.

Massive debris flew. Windows blew out with a horrific force. Part of the railing fell inward. Walls crumbled and burst. The floor shook and the building swayed, feeling like a roller coaster and a large ocean wave rolled into one.

Katie had pushed herself and Cecelia toward a southern corner, shielding their faces and making their bodies as small as possible, hoping they wouldn't be smashed or eviscerated from rebar in the walls.

The only thing she could think about was Chad... and where he was... was he alive... if he suffered... did he think of her... and was he thinking of her now... as the building began to collapse.

What seemed like an eternity was really less than a minute until the unsettling shaking stopped. A thick powdery mixture swirled through the air in thick clouds. When Katie thought it was safe, she looked up, coughing from the heavy cloud of building dust. Her ears rang with a strange unrelenting pitch. She felt blood trickle down from her nose. Covered in thick dust, she couldn't see anything as she slowly stood up. She was alive, but wasn't sure of the condition of the building or if they could get out without being buried alive.

Cecelia also stood up dazed. She had managed to survive too, thanks to Katie's quick thinking.

Looking up, Katie saw the ceiling opening. It was still intact, along with most of the roof. Half the building appeared to still be undamaged. Her heart ached thinking about Evan and the dogs.

Cisco...

Katie coughed. Her balance was off as she tried to steady herself—staggering steps while the room spun dizzyingly all around her.

That's when she heard Evan's voice. "Katie! Katie!" followed by several excited barks.

They were alive and safe. Katie closed her eyes and said a thankful prayer.

"I'm... I'm here..." she said as her voice was barely above a soft whisper. "We're here!"

The brownish white dust began to settle like a soft first snow.

Katie looked at the opening and saw Evan.

"C'mon, you can't go down. Both of you have to come up here."

Katie steered Cecelia to the ladder and guided her up to Evan.

Then it was her turn.

Evan reached his hand to her.

Katie managed to climb up and was greeted by both dogs.

Happy whines and licks. The fresh cool night air was a relief giving her energy and hope.

Evan steadied Cecelia and had her sit down.

"You okay?" he said, hugging her tightly.

"Yes," she said. It felt good to be in his arms.

Katie then dropped to her knees to inspect Cisco. "You okay?"

"They're fine. We just rode it out like a wild California earthquake. But I don't really know how we're going to get down." She had lost the rope that she had attached to her vest.

Katie heard excited voices. Her earpiece was miraculously working again.

"Katie! Evan! Can you hear me?" said McGaven. Panic was clear in his voice.

"Yes," she said. "Can you hear me?"

"Yes! You guys okay?"

"Yes. We're on the roof. All five of us... Did you hear everything with Hyde?"

"Affirmative. But we need to get you guys down to safety. The building doesn't look stable. Hold tight. SWAT is en route along with the fire department. ETA six minutes."

"Copy that," she said. Katie walked toward the wreckage, trying to get her thoughts straight. "Why? Why all this just because he had a traumatic loss?" she said, thinking about what Hyde had told her. She turned to Evan.

"Sometimes people break into pieces, while others hold strong." He looked at her, standing close.

"I think he knew something about where Chad is. It wasn't just a taunt or a way to make himself seem important... but what if he kidnapped him and now there's no one to..." Katie couldn't finish her sentence.

"We don't know that for sure. We're going to keep searching and we *are* going to get some answers. Maybe that arson at the Walton house might have some answers?"

Katie nodded and tried to stay hopeful. She held tight to her emotions and tried not to let the tears fall.

There was suddenly a strange sound—a groaning creaking noise. Katie turned to Evan as the roof beneath their feet began to move in a wavelike motion as if a snake was slithering underneath them.

"Evan," she said as she grabbed Cisco's harness, holding tight. Evan did the same with Mac and held to Cecelia.

The roof slowly moved and began to slant downward from the north side. It was a strange and sickening motion, accompanied by scraping and ear-piercing screeching noises. The building was continuing its breakdown and was rapidly going to collapse into itself. The warehouse wasn't done with its own demolition and was going to take everything... and everyone with it.

The five of them slowly slid as Katie and Evan tried to grab anything to keep from falling into the abyss.

Sounds of the interior of the building slamming hard to the first floor below came up to them. Crashing. Small explosions of the fabric of the building collapsing and dropping an entire story.

Evan had more difficulties with Cecelia, trying to keep her from falling as she faded in and out of fainting spells. He was taxed to the limit. It was clear to see his muscles contracting with intensity.

Katie managed to grab part of an air-conditioning accumulator. She held strong to Cisco and managed to hook him back into her belt. The cool night air pushed past her making her shiver though perspiration saturated her clothes.

Evan grabbed a vent and scrambled to hold Mac, Cecelia, and himself while bracing the weight of all of them.

"Hold on!" yelled Katie. She was having trouble keeping her own grip but held on.

They managed to scratch and scuffle with their K9 partners until there was a familiar sound approaching.

Within minutes a ladder truck with the extension came up, with SWAT Sergeant Ryan West at the helm, his strong features and serious expression greeting them. It was the best sight to see and Katie gave a momentary sigh of relief.

The sergeant was able to get to Cecelia first and then threw a rope to Evan and Mac. After a few daring maneuvers, they were on their way down to the ground much to Katie's relief. Safe. Cecelia was immediately taken to a nearby ambulance.

"Okay, Detective Scott, it's your turn," said Sergeant West. "Slow now."

Katie didn't want to, but she slowly had to let go of Cisco.

"I've got him," he said, readying himself to grab the dog.

Katie unhooked Cisco's leash from her vest and the dog slid toward the sergeant, but missed the mark. The dog whined and let out a startled bark with paws flailing. The SWAT sergeant lunged and grabbed the leash before the dog went completely over the side. Cisco dangled for a moment until the SWAT officer grabbed him around the torso, pulling him to safety.

"You got him?" Katie said. She could barely breathe as she watched the scene unfold, imagining the worst-case scenario.

"Got him," he said as he handed the dog down to waiting SWAT and firefighters. "Okay, your turn." He looked to her with a reassuring look.

Katie could barely feel her hands—they were numb. Her arms and legs trembled with weakness from the strain, but she closed her eyes and let go. She slid smoothly toward the edge where the sergeant caught her, hooking her around the waist with his arms.

"You're okay," he said, trying to keep her calm. He whispered in her ear, "You're going to be fine."

She nodded.

As Katie made her way down, she felt strange.

Evan, McGaven, and John were all waiting. She could also see bomb squad technicians and a dozen police officers moving about. She saw her uncle moving quickly through the masses—relief overwhelmed her. She saw Evan had Cisco and Mac. It seemed like everyone was there. Everyone except...

Katie was relieved when her feet touched the ground and everyone she cared about was waiting. It was the most comforting feeling in the world. It was like being home. She felt light and suddenly nothing in her body hurt anymore. She wasn't tired. Her hands... Her legs... She looked down at her fingertips and saw there was blood streaming downward from her arms and chest. Katie walked toward her uncle and the rest of the group. She suddenly felt weak, lightheaded, and then collapsed on the ground.

FORTY-SIX

Friday 1145 hours

"How are you feeling?" said a soft familiar comforting voice.

Katie was still sedated after recovering from the serious lacerations she received across her torso and left arm from the flying building fragments. She had been taken to the hospital after her collapse due to loss of blood. She had a difficult time becoming fully awake, but she felt Chad's arms around her and that comforted her. His warmth. His breath against her neck. It was right where she wanted to be.

"I'm glad you're okay," he whispered, kissing her forehead and cheek.

Katie could smell the scent of his subtle soap after a shower. "I love you," she said softly.

"Love you more."

Katie abruptly awoke to find herself in a hospital room. Alone. She tried to sit up but the pain stopped her. Chad wasn't there—again. The loss of the past month flooded back. Suddenly emotions rose to the surface threatening to overflow.

Chad...

"There she is," said McGaven as he cheerfully entered her room with Denise.

John and Evan stayed at the doorway making sure she was okay before entering.

"Hey," she said. "Thank you all for coming, but I'm still really out of it. They gave me some serious painkillers."

"Of course we'd be here. Where else would we be?" McGaven carried flowers and a teddy bear, setting them down. "Nick is at your house with Cisco, otherwise he'd be here too, but you'll see him soon. The doc says that you aren't going to be doing anything for two weeks after you get out of here. And we're all going to take turns making sure you obey doctor's orders."

"Two weeks? No way," she said.

"Yes way," said Sheriff Scott as he entered the room.

Everyone chatted for a few minutes, but then left the sheriff alone with his niece. He sat down next to the bed holding her hand.

"Uncle Wayne," she said. "Has there been any news on Chad?"

He sighed. "I'm sorry. Not yet."

"Oh."

"What's the matter?"

"Nothing. It's just Sean Hyde said some things about Chad. And I just thought maybe... well... anyway..."

"You okay, Katie?" he said watching her closely. "I know this has been excruciatingly unfair and tragic for you, but it's not over. Not by a long shot."

"What do you mean?" She watched her uncle's expression that was a mixture of deep sorrow and concern knitted together. He hesitated before answering.

"We're going to get to the bottom of everything. We don't know for sure that Hyde was behind Chad's disappearance, but we're not going to stop until we do know. Chad's case is open but we're not going to let it go cold. Understand? I give you my word," he said.

Katie slowly nodded as she felt the extreme emotions begin to well up.

"We will hire experts for the videos and anything else. Thanks to you. We found some of those broom grassy fibers in Hyde's residence. We'll rework every piece of evidence no matter how long it takes. Understand? We're moving forward and we will find him. I promise you, Katie."

Katie's heart was broken. "Did they visit Terrance Lane?"

"Oh yes, and he wasn't as innocent as Hyde made him out to be. He was involved. Another pawn in this mess. He helped to fill in some of the blanks. The DA is going to charge him with conspiracy and accessory to murder. And we're just getting started... we're going to turn over every rock to find out everything."

"Really? There goes his political career."

"McGaven and Hamilton are piecing the rest together, so we'll know more soon. Most of your profile and theories are true."

"But..."

"No, you're going to take two weeks of actual rest. You did all the heavy lifting and now the details are in good hands and are being taken care of. You helped to get a serial killer off the streets so that he wouldn't begin his crime spree again. Now it's time for you to rest. Understand?"

Katie sighed. Her chest hurt and she wasn't sure what she was going to do for two weeks. "Okay. What about Holden?"

"Simon Holden?"

"Yes."

"All those cases are being looked at thoroughly. Even if he didn't orchestrate them, he was still an accomplice. It still holds a life sentence. It's just a change of paperwork, that's all. No one is going to get away with anything."

She closed her eyes and felt extremely tired. "I'm sorry, but whatever they gave me it's making me very tired. I can barely keep my eyes open."

"Don't ever scare me like that again," he said, leaning forward and kissing her forehead.

"I don't plan on being in any building that blows up anytime soon—that's three now. Maybe it's a record..." Her voice was fading.

The sheriff shook his head. "Katie, what am I going to do with you?"

"Give me a raise." She sighed closing her eyes.

He laughed. "You just rest. I'll be back later with some of your favorite food."

"Sounds good..." Her voice faded.

The sheriff squeezed her hand and kissed her forehead again. He hesitated as he watched Katie fall asleep before he left.

Katie drifted off to sleep. This time she didn't dream of murdered victims, but sitting by a cozy fire with Chad.

FORTY-SEVEN

They say love is forever in your heart. They say that love can conquer all, it can mend anything, and it can connect people on many levels. These are all true. But what they don't tell you is that it can come in many different forms and you can find love wherever you look for it. Sometimes love comes when seeing something new or discovering a new challenge. And sometimes it's from watching something so innocent and free that it brings joy to your life unconditionally.

Two weeks later

Katie stood along the fence line, watching several military working dogs help new handlers with their training. They heeled and sat on command. They worked the dogs through an agility course, building bonds and confidence. Watching the K9 dance between dog and handler was a wonderful thing to see.

Katie's external wounds were healing, but her internal ones would take much longer to mend. The weather was sunny and warm, making it a perfect day to go on a field trip and she was happy to oblige. She felt better already and her anxiety ceased.

As she watched the amazing dogs act as a training aid to better prepare these novice handlers to begin their journey of becoming a military working dog handler and bonding with their new dogs, it made her happy and reminded her of what it was like to love unconditionally. The trainers were hardworking men and women with a strong dedication and purpose. Most people weren't even aware of the great work they did. But Katie knew firsthand, and it mattered to her.

There were mostly German shepherds and Belgian Malinois dogs trained extensively for protection, explosives, and drug-detection work. These incredible working breeds were eager and driven to go to work. The handler had to be the best at their skills because they would soon be in combat situations, military bases, border patrol, and wherever they were needed to help keep soldiers and civilians safe. These specialized K9 units were an integral part of the military branches keeping the rest of the world safe.

Katie remembered when she had trained long hours and honed her skills—thanks to Evan. Then she had found and partnered with Cisco—everything had changed. She couldn't imagine now what it would be like without him. She smiled fondly, remembering the day she first worked with him. They had been through so much together and he still was at her side for her future. There wasn't a day that went by that she didn't have him with her.

"I like that black shepherd. What do you think?" said Evan smiling and watching the training.

"I noticed him earlier. His odor-detection skills are amazing. Fantastic alerts."

"I'm partial to that sable shepherd too though." He laughed. "Reminds me of Mac in the beginning."

Turning to Evan, she said, "Thank you for bringing me here today. I really needed this. I actually feel at peace here."

"I'm glad you wanted to come. I thought that you might be

getting a little stir-crazy being at home and not working a homicide case—cold or otherwise." He smiled at her. When he did this his entire face smiled, even his eyes crinkled around the edges.

Katie returned his smile and then continued to watch the training. There were six new handlers. "That's actually an understatement," she said, referring to not working cases.

"It's nice to see you smile."

"It's hard not to," she said, observing the training. "And I never officially thanked you for saving my life."

"No thanks necessary." He watched the dogs. "Not only have I seen you turn into a great military working dog handler, but I've witnessed what an amazing detective you are, well, even though you almost got me killed more than once."

"You've been a really good friend and the best dog trainer I could hope for," she said, looking at him. "Thank you for everything you do and have done... and for being my friend."

"It's been my pleasure, Detective Scott. It's definitely never a dull moment."

A LETTER FROM JENNIFER CHASE

I want to say a huge thank you for choosing to read *Her Dying Kiss* (Book 10). If you did enjoy it, and want to keep up to date with all my latest releases, just sign up at the following link. Your email address will never be shared and you can unsubscribe at any time.

www.bookouture.com/jennifer-chase

This has continued to be a special project and series for me. Forensics, K9 training, and criminal profiling has been something that I've studied considerably and to be able to incorporate into a crime fiction novel has been a thrilling experience for me. I have wanted to write this series for a while and it has been a truly wonderful experience to continue to bring it to life.

One of my favorite activities, outside of writing, has been dog training. I'm a dog lover, if you couldn't tell by reading this book, and I loved creating the supporting canine character of Cisco to partner with my cold-case police detective. I hope you enjoyed it as well.

I hope you loved *Her Dying Kiss* (Book 10), and if you did I would be very grateful if you could write a review. I'd love to hear what you think, and it makes such a difference helping new readers to discover one of my books for the first time.

I love hearing from my readers—you can get in touch on my Facebook page, through Twitter, Goodreads, Instagram, or my website.

Thank you,

Jennifer Chase

www.authorjenniferchase.com

 facebook.com/AuthorJenniferChase
twitter.com/JChaseNovelist
instagram.com/jenchaseauthor

ACKNOWLEDGMENTS

My sincere thank you goes out to all my law enforcement, police detective, deputy, police K9 team, forensic unit, forensic anthropologist, and first-responder friends—there's too many to list. Your friendships have meant so much to me over the years. It has opened a whole new writing world filled with inspiration for future stories for Detective Katie Scott and K9 Cisco. I wouldn't be able to bring my crime fiction stories to life if it wasn't for all of you. Thank you for your service and dedication to keeping the rest of us safe.

I would like to express a very special thank you to A.N.R. for your military service and for giving me a firsthand appreciation and insight into the world of military working dog training. Without your great friendship, patience, and military K9 training expertise, this book would never have been written.

Writing this series continues to be a truly amazing experience for me. I would like to thank my publisher Bookouture for the incredible opportunity, and the fantastic staff for continuing to help me to bring this book and the entire Detective Katie Scott series to life.

Thank you, Kim, Sarah, and Noelle for your relentless promotion for us authors. A thank you to my brilliant editor Kelsie and the amazing editorial team—your unwavering support has helped me to work harder to write more endless adventures for Detective Katie Scott and K9 Cisco.

Printed in Great Britain
by Amazon

35411116R00199